Kokopelli and the Virgin

PATI NAGLE

Kokopelli and the Virgin

PATI NAGLE

Evennight Books/Book View Café

Cedar Crest, New Mexico

Kokopelli and the Virgin

Copyright © 2014 by Pati Nagle

All rights reserved, including the right to reproduce this book, or portion thereof, in any form.

This is a work of fiction. Any references to historical events, real people, or real locales are used fictitiously. Other names, characters, places, and incidents are the product of the author's imagination, and any resemblance to actual events or locales or persons, living or dead, is entirely coincidental.

Published by Evennight Books, Cedar Crest, New Mexico, USA, an affiliate of Book View Café Publishing Cooperative

Publication team: Pari Noskin, Phyllis Irene Radford, Chris Krohn

Cover art: jenX

Kokopelli graphic based on a photo of a petroglyph at Petroglyph National Monument, Albuquerque, New Mexico

ISBN: 978-1-61138-461-1

Book View Café Publishing Cooperative
P.O. Box 1624, Cedar Crest, NM 87008-1624

USA
http://bookviewcafe.com

for Hunter

Acknowledgments

Many thanks to those who helped me bring this book to publication, including Pari Noskin, Phyllis Irene Radford, Hunter Raincaller, Scott Silverii, the good people at Petroglyph National Monument in Albuquerque, my colleagues at Book View Café, and my ever-patient and loyal partner and first reader, Chris Krohn.

Rosa strode up the dusty footpath toward the mesa of black volcanic rock. A dry breeze stirred her hair and brought her the smells of chamisa and baking soil. It also carried the sound of traffic from the new four-lane extension that now cut through the cliffs.

A pang of sadness for the lost quiet of the landscape made Rosa's forehead tighten, but she shook it off. She had come to visit the petroglyphs of the Piedras Marcadas Trail, to seek peace and connection with the land, if she could still find it.

The housing developments that sprawled all over Albuquerque's west side were encroaching on the cliffs, more every year. When Rosa was a kid and her parents had brought the family up here to look at the ancient rock pictures made by prehistoric Indians, the city had always seemed far away. Now it was right here.

She paused on the trail below the first cluster of mask face petroglyphs and looked back across the city. Albuquerque sprawled in the Rio Grande Valley between the west-side escarpment where she stood and the Sandia Mountains that loomed to the east. In the bottom of the shallow bowl, the green swath of the cottonwood *bosque* divided the city, marking the course of the Rio Grande.

Rosa couldn't see the river from here — it was hidden by the trees — but there wouldn't be much to see anyway. It was August, and the growing needs of the city, combined with all the farms along the river, had pretty much sucked it dry. The monsoon rains hadn't come this year, and two fires had already broken out in the *bosque*. A dry year. A bad year.

Turning back to the cliffs and the pictures laboriously hammered into their flat surfaces of sharp-edged basalt hundreds of years ago, Rosa drew a deep breath. The petroglyphs were sacred to the Pueblo people of New Mexico, the descendants of those patient ancients who had made the pictures.

Sacred pictures. Rosa had noticed that they tended to be clustered around the dry washes that would run with water after a storm. Water was sacred here in the desert.

She walked a little farther and paused to look up at another mask: round face, two eyes and mouth, and a feather sticking straight out of the side of the head. It was a common image here, along with the hands, turtles, lizards and lightning. Rosa wondered if the feather-head was a god.

She smiled, remembering crawling all over these rocks with Miguel and Gloria when her family used to come up here for picnics. The petroglyphs weren't their heritage, exactly—they being chicano rather than Indian—but as a native New Mexican, Rosa felt she had some claim to the history of the rocks.

Part of a national monument, this land was supposed to be protected. Rosa looked back at the houses within view, neighborhoods for whom the petroglyphs were back-yard curiosities and targets for the destructive impulses of countless kids. Not much protection from progress.

Some of the petroglyphs were already scarred with bullet holes. Some of the rocks bore clumsy scratched-in modern pictures, people's initials or names, stupid thoughtless desecrations. The real pictures, the old ones, had been made as acts of devotion. They deserved respect.

Frowning a little, she turned her back on the city and strode ahead on the trail that followed the foot of the cliff. She had meant to be peaceful on this walk, and she'd let herself get upset before she'd even started. She paused, closed her eyes, took a deep breath, and let it out slowly as Cruz had taught her, exhaling all the dark thoughts, drawing in peace with a fresh breath.

Balance was what she needed. Always a challenge, when one had a foot each in two different worlds. Cruzita Cordova—her teacher, her *maestra*—liked to say that the path of the *curandera* was one of constant change. As an apprentice to that healing art, Rosa was learning to view the world as a living spirit, so different from the conventional way of seeing it.

She heard a high-pitched sound, a falling note, off in the distance. It sounded like a flute, but she figured it was some bird. Listening, she waited for it to come again, but only the memory echoed in her mind.

The birds are mourning, too, she thought. With a sad smile, she started forward again, making her way to the far end of the cleft between arms of the mesa, to a high tumble of large boulders that bore a wealth of pictures. Many visitors didn't bother to walk this far, but Rosa knew that the pictures got better and better as you continued.

She paused to gaze at each cluster of petroglyphs, pondering why the ancient artists had chosen these particular images. A macaw with antlers, one of her favorites from childhood. Many hands, many masks, many animals and birds. Warriors bedecked with feathers and tall headdresses. Stalks of corn that could also be spears.

At the back of the little valley the city sounds faded to a distant thrum, easily ignored. Rosa listened to the breeze in the sagebrush, the cries of small birds and the buzz of insects. The sun was warm, making her drowsy. She stopped in front of a pair of Kokopelli images above a spiral.

The little humpbacked flute players had always delighted her. There was a third Kokopelli somewhere around here—a secret one. You couldn't see it from the trail, you had to find it. Rosa peered at the rocks up the hillside, trying to remember.

She didn't see the third Kokopelli, but she did find another childhood favorite—a hand, all white against the black of the rock, the result of infinite patience hammering away with some small tool. She could imagine the maker laying his or her own hand against the rock and carefully pounding out the outline, tracing each finger, then spending hours or days, maybe, filling it in.

Rosa climbed up the short distance to the rock and held her own palm over the hand as she had done a hundred times before, not touching it because that was bad for the picture, but holding it just above. Her fingers extended beyond the petroglyph's fingers now. As a child her whole hand had nearly fit inside the palm.

"Oh, better not move now, better not take your hand away or the world will fall!"

She turned to see who had spoken, heart pounding with sudden fear. She hadn't heard anyone approaching, but there was a little old Indian man standing on the trail a couple of steps away.

Black eyes gleamed in his weathered, gnome-like face beneath a cap of silver hair. He wore dusty old baggy trousers and a loose-fitting shirt of a faded dark red. A sash gathered in the shirt at his waist, with beads and a couple of feathers dangling from the ends. At first Rosa thought he had on a knapsack, then she realized he was bent with age.

She relaxed a little. "I didn't hear you coming."

"Didn't hear? Can't hear? Have to play louder, then, huh."

He grinned and pulled a wooden flute from his belt, blew a few notes through it, then grinned again. Rosa smiled indulgently.

"Pretty."

"Pretty," he repeated. "Huh."

He played some more and started dancing, a little shuffling dance back and forth across the trail. Rosa didn't want to offend him so she waited. He was some old shaman, maybe. He could be here for the same reason she was — to visit the petroglyphs.

He stopped dancing suddenly and pointed his flute at her. "You the only one awake around here. You got to put up your hand or the world will fall!"

"M-me? I'm sorry, *Abuelo*, I don't know what you mean."

He wasn't smiling any more, and a tiny thread of fear crept back into Rosa's heart. The old man jabbed his flute toward her with each word.

"You got to pay attention! You got to fight the land-eaters! You got to kill the serpent before it swallows the river!"

Still confused, Rosa shook her head a little. "I can't fight the land-eaters, *Abuelo*. They've already won."

She glanced at the petroglyphs nearby, the hand and an upside-down person and some giant bird tracks. The old man let out a huff and stomped his foot.

"Not these old rocks, stupid girl! These old rocks already told their story. You got to pay attention or there be no corn for your babies, no gourds to make rattles. Land-eaters gonna turn everything to dust!"

Rosa stared at him, breathing fast, trying not to show her alarm. She didn't have any babies. What was he talking about?

"You learning medicine. Earth mother needs medicine, big, strong medicine! You got to put up your hand."

Rosa's eyes narrowed. He was freaking her out, now. Learning medicine—he must mean her studying with Cruz, but how could he know about that? Who was this old man, anyway, and why had he followed her here?

"Find the dragonfly," he said, thrusting his chin out aggressively.

There was a dragonfly petroglyph nearby, she knew. Only one on this trail, maybe the only one in the whole park. She glanced up at the rocks above her, looking for it, but she didn't think it was in this cluster. Maybe it was a little farther along the trail. She looked back down, and the old man was gone.

Rosa stood still, peering along the trail that ran back the way she'd come to her left, forward along the cliff to her right. Both sides led toward the city from the point where she was standing. Both were empty. The old man had disappeared.

Maybe he'd stepped behind a boulder. Maybe he'd decided to sit in the shade a little while. There were thousands of places to hide among the tumbled rocks. It wasn't that unusual that she'd lost track of him.

Rosa listened, straining to hear the shuffling of his moccasins, but heard nothing. Nothing but the echo of a distant flute on the wind, and that must be in her head.

"Crazy old man," she muttered, starting to climb back down to the trail.

She wasn't going to let him spoil her visit. She had a nervous thought that she might find him waiting when she got back to the parking lot, but she dismissed it. She'd deal with that if she had to, but right now she wanted to finish what she'd come for.

As she reached the ground she saw a petroglyph on her left. The third Kokopelli. It was on the back of a rock—you couldn't see it from the trail. Only if you stood right here.

A tingle went down her arms, chill despite the warm summer sun. Closing her eyes for a moment, she took a deep breath and let it out. *Center your thoughts*, Cruz's voice told her. *Be still inside, and the world can storm around you all it wants.*

Opening her eyes, Rosa started forward again, following the trail around the next arm of the mesa, peering at the pictures on the rocks. There was the dragonfly, on a rock a few steps above the trail, along with a critter with a zig-zag tongue that might be a frog trying to eat it.

Rosa left the trail to stand before the dragonfly. No other picture-rocks close by, and only an empty mesa above. She frowned, wondering what the old man had meant.

She tried to remember if she'd ever seen a dragonfly on pottery. The Pueblo potters were always quick to explain the designs if you showed interest in a pot. The parallel lines that meant rain, the stair-step clouds, the colors of earth and storm. Was there a dragonfly clan at one of the pueblos? She didn't think so.

She shook her head. Trying too hard to find a hidden meaning in something that might not mean anything at all. She gazed at the dragonfly petroglyph, then let her eyes drift. A deep, mechanical grunt drew her attention and she turned around. From here she could see the construction zone where Paseo del Norte was being extended westward. The grunt came from a backhoe digging a utility trench. Working on a Saturday.

Land-eaters. Rosa frowned.

The old man had said he wasn't talking about the petroglyphs, though. Land-eaters, but not these land-eaters.

Maybe he hadn't been talking about anything at all.

Giving up, she turned back and followed the short-cut trail that led straight back to the parking lot instead of meandering along the foot of the cliffs. Suddenly she was back in the metropolitan sprawl of the city, no longer in the wind-blown silence of the cliffs.

Albuquerque had grown a lot in the twenty-five years of her lifetime. The housing developments just kept on marching up the west side, and now they were about to spill through the cliffs on that new extension and climb across the mesas.

Houses squeezed close together, without the lazy space around them for yards and weeds and maybe a horse to graze like in Rosa's neighborhood in the North Valley. These houses were all identical, crammed together with token patches of yard in the front and back. Easy to take care of. Half of them had gravel instead of plants.

That was supposed to be good. Plants used water, especially

the non-native bluegrass lawns that a lot of people who had moved here from the east liked. But surrounding yourself with just rocks—Rosa couldn't imagine living that way. She needed life around her, growing things. They didn't have to be water-guzzlers.

There were lots of pretty plants that were native to New Mexico. She had a desert willow in front of her little house, with its long dangling leaves and orchid-like flowers. Blanket-flowers and coneflowers and sunflowers all over the yard. And her little herb garden out back.

A squeal of laughter drew her gaze to where a couple of kids were romping around up in the rocks. Rosa smiled, remembering when she'd done the same.

Not far from them an Anglo guy was picking his way among the rocks, his ball cap on backwards, a knapsack on his back. He climbed up from the trail now and then to get closer to a petroglyph with his camera. Taking pictures, maybe for a book. He'd have to come back at different times of day, or just spend the whole day here. The sun shone on different petroglyphs at different times.

Rosa watched him work his way up to a pair of masks halfway up the cliff. He'd find another mask, a better one, on the side of the same rock, if he looked. She walked on, quickening her stride as she realized the sun was starting down toward the cliffs.

Cruz had asked her over for dinner tonight. She'd get a lesson afterward, as usual. Nearly every Saturday, unless one of them had another commitment, they had dinner either at her place or at Cruz's. Rosa always looked forward to it.

A high cry sounded on the wind, a falling note, some mournful bird. Rosa looked over her shoulder but didn't see it. She gazed back at the black cliffs, knowing they'd still be here but that they were losing a little of their magic every year. That made her sad, but she had no power to change it. At least she could honor the magic and beauty that remained.

"You're early, *hija*. Come on in."

Rosa smiled as she stepped through Cruz's blue-painted front door. The old adobe house smelled of sweet herbs and something savory simmering on the stove. Sunlight spilled in through the glass-paned doors at the back, filtered by cream-colored curtains covered in green vines that made Rosa feel like she was deep in some jungle.

"These are for you, *maestra*."

She handed Cruz a bunch of flowers she'd cut from her own garden not half an hour ago. Bright sunflowers, purple coneflowers, galliardias that looked like an open half of a peach, and a stalk of brilliant blue larkspur.

Cruz smiled, the sun-browned skin at the corners of her eyes crinkling. "Thank you, *hija*, they're beautiful. Let's put them in water before they droop. Come on in the kitchen."

Rosa followed her teacher into the small, cheery and pleasantly cluttered kitchen. The walls were sunny yellow with vines of red and blue flowers twining along their top edges. Rosa had helped paint them, a couple of years ago. Aloe vera plants rioted in the window over the sink, and a dozen or more baskets hung from a big iron ring suspended in one corner. Bunches of drying herbs hung between the baskets, and a set of shelves behind them held jars of more herbs.

Cruz, who was half a foot shorter than Rosa, stretched a wiry arm to take down a blue glass vase from a cupboard. She poured in some water, then slid Rosa's flowers into it and turned to Rosa with one of her quick, flashing smiles.

"Why don't you arrange them and I'll make the salad? You always make flowers look their best."

Rosa played with the flowers, pulling off a few extra leaves and shuffling the blooms in the vase. Cruz took a quick peek into a covered skillet on the old gas stove, letting out a puff of steam that made Rosa's mouth water.

"*Paella*," Cruz said, taking down a wooden salad bowl. "It's almost done."

Rosa watched her teacher make a salad. Cruz could make any activity a dance and a meditation at the same time. Her purple broomstick skirt and her long, black braid both swayed as she walked back and forth from the cutting board to the refrigerator to the sink. Her hands, brown and sure, wielded the sharp knife with a speed that reminded Rosa of a flamenca's flashing fan.

"Go out in the garden and pick us a couple of tomatoes, OK, *hija*? I forgot to get them."

Rosa went out the kitchen's back door and down the old wooden steps into the yard. Cruz had a patch of lawn under a tall pecan tree with a picnic table beneath it, but most of the garden was given over to herbs and a few vegetables. Rosa went to the tomato plants basking in the afternoon sunshine against the west wall of the house, and picked a couple of plump red ones.

She stood in the lacy shade of the pecan and gazed around the yard for a minute, soaking in the peace and vibrancy of it before going back inside. Her own garden wasn't nearly as rich, but she'd only been working on it for a few years. Cruz had inherited it from her mother, and had taken over the garden even before her mama's death.

A tiny trickle of water sounded from a little fountain mounted on the back wall of the house, underneath a ramada that shaded the deck where a patio table and chairs stood. The sound of the water made it seem cooler. She took the tomatoes back in and finished the salad, then filled tall glasses with iced tea.

"How is it out back?"

"Nice. Not too warm."

"Take those out there, then. I'll bring the paella out in a minute."

Rosa loaded a tray and carried it out to the patio table. A rolled bamboo screen hung from the west end of the ramada. She lowered it halfway to shade the table from the setting sun, then arranged the place settings and went back to the kitchen to fetch the flowers. Cruz was just picking up the heavy skillet with oven-mitted hands, and Rosa held the door for her as she carried it out. The patio table was metal, so Cruz set the skillet right down on it and lifted the lid.

"Need a spoon," she said.

"I'll get it."

Rosa set the flowers on the table and hurried back into the kitchen for a serving spoon. When she got back Cruz was sitting, sipping her tea.

"This is nice," Cruz said, taking the spoon from Rosa and dishing up steaming paella.

Rosa accepted a plate piled with saffron-hued rice, chunks of tender chicken and big, pink shrimp, all smelling of savory herbs and garlic. Cruz was a good cook, something else Rosa was working to learn. Rosa's mother had taught her basic cooking, but Mama rarely ventured away from her own traditions.

Cruz had spent some time in Spain, and she alternated Spanish cooking with New Mexican and sometimes combined them, building layer upon layer of flavors with herbs, special oils, spices and unusual vegetables. Rosa's Mama was a good cook too, but she had never cooked a shallot in her life.

Cruz took Rosa's hands and said a short prayer over the meal, then they both dug in. Rosa ate a shrimp, closing her eyes while she savored its hot tenderness and tried to identify all the flavors of the seasoning.

"Lemon thyme?" she asked, looking at Cruz. "And something else ..."

"Bay leaf. Good, you can taste them through the garlic. I was afraid I'd put too much."

"No such thing."

The rice was still steaming hot, so Rosa dished up some salad to eat while she let the paella cool. She passed the bowl to Cruz.

"So, what did you do today?" Cruz asked.

"Went up to Petroglyph Park. I met this funny old man there. He told me I had to stop the land-eaters."

"What?"

Rosa described the old Indian man and the things he had said to her. Cruz listened intently and, when Rosa was finished, leaned back in her chair.

"*Hija*, that sounds like a summoning to me."

"But he didn't make any sense. He was just a crazy old shaman or something."

"Don't you belittle a shaman, girl! They have power and a lot of wisdom. Our tradition isn't the only one with truth in it."

Abashed, Rosa reached for her tea and drank a long, cool swallow. She'd expected Cruz to agree with her, not to take the old guy seriously.

"He was dancing around, playing the flute," Rosa said, a little defensively.

"A flute?"

"Uh-huh."

"And you said he was a hunchback?"

"He was pretty bent over, yeah."

"Ever hear of Kokopelli?"

Rosa almost choked on her tea. She put down her glass, sharp enough that the ice rattled and resettled itself.

She'd been standing by the Kokopelli petroglyphs when she'd seen the old man. Why hadn't she thought of it?

Because it was crazy, that's why. She looked at Cruz.

"T-that's just a myth, isn't it?"

Cruz shrugged and stabbed a piece of chicken with her fork. "Lot of myths have truth behind them. I've seen some pretty strange things. You believe in *La Guadalupana*?"

"Of course I do."

"Don't think she's a myth?"

"She appeared to Juan Diego. She made miracles."

Cruz's fork flashed in a ray of setting sunlight as she pushed aside a chunk of carrot to get at a shrimp. "Rosebushes blooming in winter, pictures inside a cape. Sounds like myths to me."

"The Holy Virgin is not a myth!"

Cruz looked up with a slow smile. "But have you seen her yourself?"

Rosa sat blinking angrily. "No."

"OK. So things that sound like myths can be real, maybe. Kokopelli—or maybe I should say *Lahlanhoya*—is as real to the Indians as *La Guadalupana* is to us."

"Well, why doesn't he go talk to some Indians, then?"

"Good question. I think that's your lesson for tonight, Rosa. Think about this old man and what he said to you. Try to understand what it means."

"I tried to figure it out already. Didn't get anywhere."

"Try some more. It won't kill you. We need more tea."

Cruz stood up and went in the house, leaving Rosa to stew in her thoughts. She glared at the sunlight slanting in beneath the bamboo to spill across the table, lighting up her dinner into brilliant colors—green, yellow, pink.

Cruz came back with the pitcher of iced tea and offered to fill Rosa's glass. Rosa nodded, and watched the ice dance around as the amber liquid poured over it.

She ate the rest of her dinner slowly, thinking over what the old man had said. He wanted her to stop the land-eaters. Was that the backhoes, or did he mean the whole project, or the developers behind it? He didn't care about the petroglyphs, though. He seemed to think the land-eaters were going to lay waste to everything, which didn't make a lot of sense to Rosa.

The sun sank over the escarpment in a haze of peach and orange. Cruz rolled up the bamboo screen when the sun had set, and she and Rosa sat watching the few scraps of cloud in the sky light up a bright, pale yellow, then go orange, then ruddy. A train went by, blowing its crossing call. A low-rider rolled down the next street over, the amplified boom of its speakers pounding out a rhythmic thump that faded as it drove away, heading for downtown or some other cruise. Cicadas set up their buzzing, monotonous but soothing.

Cruz gathered the dinner plates and took them inside, waving Rosa back to her seat as she moved to help. A few minutes later the smell of brewing coffee drifted out from the kitchen.

Rosa sighed and closed her eyes, trying to concentrate on what the old man had said to her. Land-eaters. No corn, no gourds. A serpent swallowing the river. Dragonfly.

"Oh!"

She sat up, opening her eyes, blinking. She looked up at the escarpment, where the sky was now fading, where the petroglyphs lay silently awaiting the night. From there she let her gaze drift down to the *bosque*. Cruz's house was just east of the river, half a mile or so. Not right in the *bosque*, but close. The bushy green tops of cottonwood trees marked the course of the river. From here it looked more like the forest it was.

Cruz came back with a tray loaded with coffee, cups, and a small flan on a plate. She divided the caramelized custard into two bowls and handed one to Rosa, then poured the coffee.

"Mmm." Rosa let a bite of flan slide down her throat. "Wonderful. Will you share the recipe?"

"It's in the *Cocinas* cookbook I gave you."

"Mama never made flan. I think she doesn't like it."

"More for you and me."

Rosa laughed, then ate another bite, licking the caramel juice off her spoon. She glanced sideways at Cruz, who was watching the western sky darken. Venus was out, glowing bright above the horizon.

"I think I figured it out."

Cruz turned her head, looking interested. Rosa ate another bite of flan, then set down her bowl and took a sip of coffee.

"Water. I think he meant the land-eaters were going to use too much water."

"Hmph. What else is new."

"I know, but that's all I can come up with."

They were silent for a while, finishing their dessert and coffee. The horizon darkened to a glowing blue, a color Rosa loved. She gazed at it, drinking it in, watching Venus descend toward the volcano cliffs.

"Water, huh? You may be right." Cruz refilled their coffee cups. "Wonder why it was so important to send that message now."

Rosa reached for the cream. "And why he came to me."

"Yeah, that's a good question. Keep working on it."

"I am, *maestra*."

"*Bueno*."

Sean stood near the new gazebo on Santa Fe's plaza, watching the Indian vendors set up on the *portal* of the Palace of the Governors. This section of the street was blocked off and only the vendors' vehicles were allowed to unload at the curb before parking elsewhere. Every one of those vendors had a permit entitling them to a few feet of precious space to lay out their goods on a blanket under the wide, high roof. Hundreds of tourists passed beneath that *portal* every day of the year, eager to find a souvenir of their visit to the City Different.

There were a few tourists drifting around the plaza already, though it was still early for a Sunday morning. Some were shopping at the folding tables set up by non-Indian vendors along the plaza side of Palace Avenue. Despite their casual appearance, those spots were valuable too, and required city-issued permits. It was all very organized, very methodical. Very unlike Sean's childhood memories of the plaza and the *portal*, of sleepy, dusty afternoons before Santa Fe had become trendy.

Aspenized. Lot of folks used that word. Sean remembered his parents talking about the changes Aspen had gone through in the middle of the 20th century, and how a couple of decades later the same thing had happened to Santa Fe. He just barely remembered Santa Fe before the change was complete, when you might still see a "For Rent" sign in a shop window near the plaza.

A blue pickup truck with a camper shell pulled up to the curb and Sean ambled across the street to it. Ruby Madalena hopped out of the driver's seat and shot him a quick smile before going to the back of the truck. She was built like what Sean thought of as the classic Pueblo woman: sturdy, short, with a moon-shaped face. She wore a red t-shirt and blue jeans, and had her black hair swept back tightly into a ponytail.

Sean tagged along after her and accepted the ice chest and stack of blankets she handed him. Her brother, Angel, also in t-shirt, jeans, and ponytail, picked up a milk crate full of what looked like crumpled newspaper and glanced at Sean with a quiet smile. They carried their burdens to the *portal*, to Ruby's space near the main entrance of the Palace. The Madalenas were lucky to have such a good space. Their father had used it for thirty years, and handed it down to them.

Ruby's neighbor to the right, sitting with his back against the wall and his shining silver jewelry with big chunks of turquoise arrayed on a blanket in front of him, glanced up and nodded, then went back to sipping coffee from an insulated mug. Sean put the ice chest down by the back wall of the *portal* and laid the blankets on top of it, then returned to the truck. Ruby handed him another newspaper-stuffed milk crate, and carried a third herself. There were three more crates in the truck, which they unloaded before Ruby shut the back doors with a slam.

On the *portal*, Angel had spread out a cream-colored blanket and was kneeling on it, carefully taking wads of newspaper out of a crate and unwrapping the paper from beautiful pots that Ruby had made. They were shades of soft orange-red, the color of earth, painted with white and black.

"I'll do that," Ruby said. "You go ahead and have your lesson."

She took a wrapped bowl out of Angel's hands and shooed him away from the blanket, then sat down on the ice chest. Angel leaned over to kiss her plump cheek. She pretended to frown.

"Go on, go on. I'll see you later."

Sean caught Ruby's eye and waved a farewell. She gave him another brisk smile and continued unwrapping her pottery.

Sean followed Angel back to the truck. Angel was slimmer and taller than his sister, and often went for hours without saying a word. Where Ruby was as practical as earth, Angel seemed to walk in the clouds.

They climbed in the truck and Angel drove toward Sean's house on the west side of town. Sean had left his own car there and walked to the plaza, as he did every Sunday. It had become his habit shortly after moving to Santa Fe, at first just to get a little exercise and as an excuse to have breakfast out. After he'd met Angel it became more of a spiritual ritual, almost a pilgrimage.

Sean laughed at himself at the thought. Angel wasn't a big spiritual leader or anything. He wasn't a shaman. He was a musician, and he was teaching Sean to play the flute.

It was just that the *way* Angel taught the flute, like the way he did pretty much everything, fascinated Sean and made him want to emulate him. Angel walked through life in what seemed like perfect balance, and Sean wanted to capture that balance, or even just an echo of it, for himself.

That wasn't to say that Sean was one of those nutjob spiritual seekers looking for a guru and to soak up the Santa Fe vibe. He'd moved here for a job, a good programming job at Analysis Visions. He'd been lucky to land that job, and delighted that it allowed him to return to New Mexico. Four years of Silicon Valley had been enough. He'd missed the mountains and the desert sky, the piñon and the multicolored cliffs of northern New Mexico where he was born. This was his home.

His mother still lived at her studio in Dixon, a tiny village half an hour's drive north of Santa Fe. She still painted old broken-down tractors and junked-out cars and occasionally, if she needed some extra money, western tropes like cow skulls hanging on barbed wire fences. Her paintings sold steadily in galleries in Taos and Santa Fe. She was a little nuts and she made a decent living, and Sean was glad to be within reach, because she was getting a bit old to be alone.

Angel turned the truck into Sean's driveway and shut off the engine. For a moment he sat still, listening to the engine ticking as it cooled down, then he turned his head and smiled at Sean. Sean smiled back and got out, fishing in his pocket for his keys. Angel retrieved a long buckskin bundle from behind the seat and followed him to the house.

It was a small place, an older house, frame-built and stuccoed dirt brown like most of the others in the neighborhood. Sean had made a sizable down-payment on it with money he'd saved from his high-income Valley job, which had brought the mortgage payments down to a reasonable level. Houses in Santa Fe were expensive. Everything in Santa Fe was expensive.

Sean opened the door and welcomed Angel in with a gesture. Angel headed for the living room, where sunlight spilled down from a high window across the brick floor and onto two wooden dining room chairs that Sean had moved there that morning. The sofa and armchair were too soft to sit in if you were playing the flute. You couldn't breathe properly.

Sean went to the kitchen and filled two glasses with water, then carried them out to the living room. Angel was sitting in one of the straight-backed chairs, unwrapping the buckskin from around his flutes. His movements were slow and deliberate, and he ran his hands over the flutes before selecting one to play, almost as if he was greeting them. Sean didn't know what was really in Angel's head, but imagined it was something like that. Angel took music seriously.

Sean set a glass of water on the floor by each chair and took his own flute down from its place of honor on the mantel over the kiva fireplace. He'd bought the flute from Angel, who'd made it himself.

Sean could still remember talking with him on the Palace *portal*, discussing the three flutes that lay on Ruby's blanket next to the pots. Angel didn't often sell flutes, Sean had learned later. He'd just been lucky to walk by on a day when the Madalenas needed extra money. He remembered Angel's concerned expression as he'd asked if Sean intended to play the flute or just hang it on the wall. From that moment Sean had been hooked.

He sat in the second chair and waited, holding his flute loosely as his hands rested on his lap. He was conscious of the hum of the swamp cooler in the background and considered turning it off, debating whether the silence would be worth the heat. Before he could move, Angel set his other flutes aside and raised the one he'd chosen to his lips. Sean held still, watching. Angel closed his eyes and breathed in and out a couple of times before playing.

The first note was long and low, the bottom note, the ground the music walked on, as Angel liked to say. Sean raised his own flute and played the same note for as long as a breath lasted. Angel listened, eyes still closed, face set in a slight frown of concentration. When Sean's note ended, Angel played again.

They went back and forth for a while, just playing long notes, then suddenly Angel leapt into a melody. Sean listened intently, then tried an answer.

It was all improvisational, and Sean was just beginning to get the hang of it. He'd taken music classes in grade school, but western music wasn't much like Angel's music. There were modes, but they weren't the same modes. What sounded deceptively simple in Angel's music took a lot of effort and focus. Sean's answers to Angel's calls were still a little hesitant, and when he stumbled over a descending phrase, playing a note that didn't belong in the mode, it broke the conversation. Angel lowered his flute and opened his eyes.

"Sorry," Sean said.

Angel smiled, and reached for his water glass. "It's OK. You know what happened?"

"Yeah."

Angel took a long sip, then another, then put the glass down. "Try that again."

Sean played the phrase again, this time without the bad note. Angel nodded and played a quick little flurry of notes, shifting the mood and also the mode. Sean echoed the last few notes, and they were off again.

They played for an hour, then took a break while Sean made lunch. Angel stood by the sliding glass doors that led from the living room to Sean's neglected back yard, looking out at the dappled sunlight beneath the elm trees.

There'd been lawns front and back when Sean bought the house, but lawns took a lot of maintenance, not to mention the water they used. Santa Fe had suffered bad droughts lately, so Sean had decided to let the lawns go. He was thinking about putting in some xeriscaping, but hadn't had time yet to do any serious planning. The grass was still struggling to survive, though it had gotten patchy. A couple of scrawny rose bushes in the back yard had put out some feeble leaves, but no flowers. He really ought to give them some water.

Sean carried the sandwiches he'd made to the dining table along with a couple of sodas and a bag of tortilla chips. He sat down and opened his ginger ale. The sound attracted Angel's attention, and he came over and joined Sean at the table.

"Thank you," he said, smiling as he picked up his sandwich.

He always said thanks, even though it was understood between them that lunch was part of his payment for the music lesson. Angel never took anything for granted, not the smallest thing.

"You're welcome. Thanks for the lesson. I think I understand that new mode better."

Angel nodded and swallowed a bite of sandwich. "Ready for another one?"

"Maybe not quite yet."

They ate in comfortable silence. Angel wasn't big on small talk. Sean had learned that if he asked some innocuous question, like how Angel's mom was doing, he'd get a detailed and thought-out answer.

Sometimes, though, he couldn't help making a conversation-starting comment. He'd been brought up in the western social tradition, which disapproved of silence.

"Wish it would rain."

Angel glanced toward the window, then nodded. Sean pulled a couple of chips out of the bag and crunched one.

"You ever play to call the rain?"

Angel sat gazing at the table, slowly chewing. He looked as if he hadn't heard, but Sean knew he was just thinking. It had been kind of a nosy question. Sean usually avoided asking things like that, because he respected Angel's privacy. He knew that a lot of Angel's music was actually a form of prayer, and felt privileged to be allowed to share it.

Angel put down what was left of his sandwich and took a drink of soda. "We pray every morning for rain."

Kind of an answer. Sean nodded, accepting that it might be all he would get.

"I could play a chant for you, if you like."

"A rain chant?"

Angel nodded. "I've made a couple."

Sean felt a tingle of anticipation. Angel very rarely shared details about the intentions behind his music. When he did they were illuminating, little glimpses into the music's spirit.

"I'd like that."

They finished their lunch and cleared the table, then returned to the living room with fresh glasses of water. The sun had shifted away from the chairs. They had about an hour left before Angel would have to head back to the plaza to mind Ruby's space while she ran some errands. Sean had kept him company once or twice, but the other vendors didn't really like having an Anglo sitting on the *portal*.

Angel took a drink of water, then picked out a different flute from his bundle. He held it on his lap for a minute, eyes closed. Sean was sure he was doing some kind of blessing. At last he opened his eyes and raised the flute.

"Rain chant."

He played a slow melody, full of long notes. It evoked the quiet before a rainfall—the waiting space beneath a gray cloud ceiling. There was an ache of longing in the tune. When it ended and Angel lowered the flute, Sean realized he'd been holding his breath.

"Beautiful," he said.

Angel smiled. "Would you like to learn it?"

"May I?"

"Will you pray for rain when you play it?"

"Absolutely!"

That was a no-brainer. Anyone who grew up in New Mexico knew that rain was precious. If Angel taught him a prayer, he'd treat it as a prayer.

Angel gave a nod and leaned forward as he did when he wanted Sean to listen closely. He played the beginning of the chant, the first phrase, then stopped. Sean tried to play it back to him, but didn't get it quite right. Angel shook his head and played the phrase over again. They repeated it back and forth a few times until Sean had it, then went on to the next part.

This would all be easier if the music was written down, but Angel didn't know western musical notation, and Sean knew better than to ask him to wait while he transcribed. He'd done that once, in an early lesson, and Angel hadn't liked it at all. Angel had said it was wrong to try to tie the music down onto a piece of paper.

Instead, they worked their way through the chant a little at a time while Sean memorized it, building on the beginning, adding a bit more to it at each step. It sounded simple but was not; there were perhaps five notes in the whole tune, but the patterns never repeated exactly the same way. Despite sounding as though it might be improvisational, the chant had an exact structure and

Angel insisted on Sean's playing it without deviation. By the time he had learned the whole chant and played it through to Angel's satisfaction, Sean was sweating with the effort.

"That's a good start," Angel said, putting away his flute. "Practice."

"I will. Thanks."

Sean walked with him to the front door and handed him three folded twenties. He'd had to talk Angel into taking that much—it was more than double what Angel had initially asked for—but it worked out to about the same as Sean's hourly wage, and he figured Angel's time was at least as valuable as his own.

Angel accepted the money with a slight bow. "Thank you."

"Thank *you*. See you next week."

Sean watched him walk to the truck. Angel's ponytail hung halfway down his back, longer than Ruby's. Sean often wondered what Angel looked like when he played for his own people—he must dress in traditional clothing, and maybe have his hair loose. Would he play chants in a kiva ceremony? Sean didn't know. He suspected his imaginings were a bit romanticized.

He watched Angel drive away, then went back into the house and played the rain chant two more times through. He wanted to make sure he didn't forget it before next Sunday. He knew he was missing some of the nuances, but Angel would correct him. As long as he had the basic tune down he'd be OK.

He sat thinking, gazing at the white patch of sunlight on the brick floor. After a while he played the chant once more, but he felt like something was missing. Maybe the thing to do was play it outside. He liked playing the flute up in the woods. Angel had taught him some songs before, but this was the first chant he'd learned. He felt it belonged outdoors, where the rain gods or whoever would hear it.

He got up, left his flute on his chair, and carried the water glasses to the kitchen, checking the clock while he was there. Three-thirty. He had time for a short hike.

He filled a water bottle and put his cell phone in his pocket, then took his flute out to the car. He'd go up Canyon Road to the watershed. You couldn't get up to the actual reservoir—that had been closed to the public for decades—but there was a nice meadow by the watershed of the Santa Fe River, and some walking trails. It was a watery place even though it was usually dry. Appropriate for a rain chant, he figured.

He drove east, trying to hold onto the sense of peace left from spending time with Angel while he fought his way through the traffic. In a couple of weeks it would get worse, with Indian Market drawing huge hordes of visitors.

August was peak tourist season in Santa Fe, though these days the tourists never really went away. Every day of the year they were there, wandering around the plaza, stepping out into streets without looking. A couple had been hit and killed in recent years, leading to the permanent closure of some streets near the plaza.

Canyon Road was crowded with them, as always. They walked along the narrow street, some dressed in colorful Guatemalan clothing they'd bought in town without realizing it didn't come from Santa Fe. They went in and out of galleries, taking pictures of anything and everything, looking tickled just to be here. Sean kept a sharp watch as he drove slowly up the road. You never knew when one might step right out in front of your car.

Once he'd wound his way past the last of the galleries and shops, he could drive a little faster. The road climbed toward the foothills of the Sangre de Cristos as the galleries gave way to houses behind adobe walls that towered over the narrow sidewalks. Incredibly expensive real estate in this part of town. Really rich people, many of them also famous, lived behind those anonymous, irregular walls.

Finally the houses gave way to mostly woods. Sean reached the Audubon Center and parked by the top of a trail that led out to the meadow of the watershed. He inhaled deeply as he walked among the pines, glad to be out of the city and up in the feet of the mountains.

The air smelled hot and dusty with a sharp bite of evergreen sap. Rain was needed, badly needed. Usually it started raining in July, but so far this summer, nothing.

Sean reached a tall ponderosa where he liked to sit looking over the dry, cobbled bed of the Santa Fe River. He remembered the first time his parents had brought him up here. There had been water in the river then. He'd made a mess of himself playing in it.

It had been a long time since water had been allowed to flow in the Santa Fe River. It was all hoarded in the reservoir upstream, now, and they were years into a devastating drought. The dry riverbed made him sad.

He sat beneath the old pine and tried to relax. He could hear the whisper of the breeze in a cottonwood tree farther up the river. There were a few other deciduous trees up here, but not as many as there once had been. Mostly it was pine and juniper and piñon, and the million different shrubs that could handle drought.

Sean closed his eyes and just held his flute for a while, letting go of the trip up here, letting go of thoughts about tourists and worry about water. He took deep breaths and let them out slowly, listening to the woods around him. Birds chittered in the trees. He heard a scrub jay scolding not far away, and the falling call of a chickadee. He let these sounds fill his awareness along with the smell of the evergreens, the heat in the air. When he felt he'd attained a peaceful balance, he raised his flute to his lips.

He faltered the beginning of the chant and stopped. Frowning slightly in concentration, he started over. The phrases didn't flow as smoothly as they did when Angel played them. He was still struggling to remember the tune, but he got all the way through it. He sat quiet for a while, then played the rain chant through again, more confidently this time.

He lowered his flute, satisfied. Listened to the woods again. The birds had gone quiet. He waited for them to come back, but didn't hear them for a long while. Maybe someone else had come up one of the trails without his noticing. He opened his eyes.

A woman stood downhill from him, light shining in a dazzling radiance all around her. Sean blinked, thinking at first that the sun was behind her, but it couldn't be. He was looking north, not west, and she was standing below him.

Standing on water, he realized. She was standing in the middle of the river bed, and the river was flowing beneath her.

Fear tensed all the muscles in his body. She was standing *on* the water, not in it, with the light all around her. The water flowed noiselessly, smoothly, not like the chuckling mountain stream it should be.

Sean's breathing quickened. He stared at the woman, trying to see past the brilliance to her face. It was serene and sad, with a fold of blue cloth draped over her brow like a hood.

He'd seen that. Cold tingled down his spine. He knew who she was, but he couldn't believe it. He must be hallucinating. Blue cloak—he could see now that it had gold stars scattered over it—and underneath it a long pink gown covered with scrolling designs in gold. Her hands were folded before her as if in prayer, and she looked up at Sean with brown eyes filled with woe.

"My children will die," she said.

Sean's mouth dropped open, but he couldn't say anything. What did she mean, saying that to him? What on earth could he do about it?

She continued to gaze at him, but the light around her was fading, and so was she. Puffs of light blossomed around her like little firework flowers, fading as quickly as they bloomed. Sean stared, transfixed, while she disappeared completely. Soon all that was left were the dappled ripples of light on the water, and then the water faded as well, seeping into the ground, leaving the dry rocky riverbed.

Sean took a couple of ragged breaths. He was clutching his flute so hard he was afraid he might break it. He made his hands relax and let go. His palms were sweaty and he rubbed them on his jeans.

"Holy—"

He stopped himself before he uttered something obscene. He was positive it wasn't right to cuss when you'd just had a visit from the Virgin of Guadalupe.

"I'm not even religious!"

Sean slapped the steering wheel in frustration as he drove back down into town. He couldn't figure out why *La Guadalupana* had appeared to him, what she wanted from him, or if he'd just imagined the whole thing. He thought he'd better get some advice.

He made his way toward the plaza, parked near Palace Avenue and strode up the street to the Palace of the Governors. Most of the vendors on the *portal* had packed up and left by now, including the Madalenas. Sean stood frowning at their empty space for a minute, then turned back.

He could ask someone at the cathedral, maybe. Basilica, rather—it had been upgraded in status. Services would be over for the day, but there might be someone around that he could talk to.

He crossed the street to what he still thought of as St. Francis Cathedral, the huge stone church built by Bishop Lamy in the 19th century. Willa Cather had shone a homey light on Lamy's adventures in Santa Fe, but the bishop had been a wily and ruthless politician, and St. Francis was a testament to his ambition. At a time when most of the buildings in town were still made of mud-brick adobe, Lamy had caused this massive stone edifice to be built. It had huge front doors carved with scenes from Lamy's life, and a gigantic rose window above them, imported from France. More stained glass all through the cathedral. Sean had been inside it lots of times, and was always impressed.

La Conquistadora resided there for a few days each year. Soon, at Fiesta time, the little statue of the Virgin Mary would be paraded through the streets of Santa Fe and take up residence in her own special chapel in the custom that was at the foundation of Santa Fe's centuries-old Fiesta.

Sean walked past the front of the cathedral to the south side, noticing a new statue in the courtyard. It was *La Conquistadora* in marble, a little larger than the original yard-high wooden figure that dated back to the second Spanish colonization. Unlike *La Guadalupana*, who gazed downward with hands folded in prayer, *La Conquistadora* stood erect and gazed forward, commanding. Her hands were held out before her, a rosary draped around her wrists, her cloak spreading stiff and fan-like from her shoulders.

Sean walked on past to the side door that entered the south wing of the cathedral. It was not *La Conquistadora* who concerned him now.

The door was unlocked, and Sean stepped in, feeling the heavy hush of the church descend around him. An old Hispanic woman sat bent over her rosary in the chapel's front pew, praying alone and in silence. Sean quietly walked past, along the aisle, looking for someone from the cathedral to talk to. A bank of flickering votive candles cast colored shadows, mostly red, at the feet of a statue of the Virgin. Sean paused to look at her.

Not *La Conquistadora* or *La Guadalupana*. Just generic Mary.

"Can I help you?" said a man's voice quietly.

Sean glanced up and saw a middle-aged Anglo man standing nearby, his hair blond going to silver, white collar proclaiming him a priest. He wore a black jacket and slacks rather than robes. Casual dress for after hours?

Sean smiled, reminding himself to be respectful. "Yes, I was hoping to talk with someone about something I saw today."

The priest raised an eyebrow, glanced toward the woman praying, then gestured for Sean to follow him. He went through a door on the right and down a narrow hallway lined with doors, one of which stood open to a small office. The priest stepped inside, then turned to Sean and offered to shake hands.

"I'm Father Mahan."

"Sean Carpenter."

The priest smiled. "Good Irish name, Sean."

"Actually, my mom just liked the way it sounded."

Father Mahan's brow rose again, but he made no comment. He gestured to the guest chair in front of a mahogany desk.

"Have a seat, Mr. Carpenter. Unless what you want to

discuss should be said in confession?"

Sean shook his head and sat down. "I'm not Catholic."

"I see."

The priest settled himself in the executive chair behind the desk. The room was tidy and not overtly religious except for a small cross hanging on one wall. A few papers were scattered on the desk, where Father Mahan had apparently been working. He tidied them into a stack and set them aside, then folded his hands on the desk.

"Well, how can I help you?"

Sean thought for a minute, trying to find a way to say what he'd seen without sounding like a nut case. He couldn't think of one, so he gave up and plunged in.

"I think I saw the Virgin of Guadalupe this afternoon."

Father Mahan's brow creased in a slight frown, but he didn't say anything, just waited for Sean to continue. Sean cleared his throat and described his visit to the watershed, explaining that he'd gone up there to play his flute in the woods. He didn't mention Angel or the rain chant, because he was *sure* that would make Father Mahan think he was a kook.

The priest listened patiently, though the frown increased as Sean went on. When he'd finished describing the virgin and how she'd faded away again, Mahan took a long breath.

"How do you know this was the Holy Virgin?"

"Um, blue mantle with stars on it, pink robe, light radiating from her in all directions? It's true she wasn't standing on a crescent, but she *was* standing on the water."

"Forgive me, but why should she appear to you?"

"I was hoping you could help me figure that out."

The priest sighed. "Well, I would recommend that you seek guidance in prayer."

"That's it? Pray for guidance?"

"What exactly do you want, Mr. Carpenter? Are you claiming this is a miracle?"

Sean kept a rein on his growing frustration. "I don't know. You tell me."

"She didn't do anything other than appear on the water?"

"And said 'My children will die.'"

"And nobody else saw this?"

"I was alone."

Mahan raised his folded hands to rest his chin on them. "I don't think it qualifies as a miracle, then. Perhaps it was just an answer to some prayer of yours, or perhaps...I don't mean to offend you, Mr. Carpenter, but sometimes a vision like this can be the result of fatigue, or — other factors."

Sean leaned back in his chair. "I was stone-cold straight. I haven't had so much as a beer in the last twenty-four hours."

"All right."

"I'm not a nut. I'm just trying to understand something that doesn't make a lot of sense."

Mahan looked as if he agreed with the last part, at least. He gazed at Sean with sympathetic concern.

"I can pray with you, if that would help."

Sean bit back an impatient answer. "Thanks, but I think I can handle it."

The ironic thing was that he *had* been praying, in a way, when the Virgin had come to him. Praying for rain, with an Indian chant. Maybe Angel had more power than either of them realized. Sean sighed and stood up.

"Well, thank you for your time, Father Mahan."

The priest stood and followed him to the door. "I'm sorry I couldn't be more help. If this happens again, do come back and let me know."

"OK." Sean hoped very much that it wouldn't happen again.

"I'll ask my colleagues about it, also."

"Please don't make a big deal out of it. Maybe I just imagined it."

Father Mahan tilted his head, gazing at Sean as if trying to figure him out. Nut-case, or honest programmer with a vision of the Virgin? Who could tell?

Mahan walked with Sean back down the hallway and out through the chapel, seeing him to the door. Escorting him off the premises, Sean thought wryly. Maybe Mahan had reserved judgment, but he wasn't taking any chances.

Sean thanked him again and walked briskly away, going back around the front of the cathedral on the way to his car. When he reached Palace Avenue he paused, wondering if he might find help in a book. There had to be dozens of books about

La Guadalupana. She was the patroness of the New World, she was everywhere.

The library was closed on Sunday, but the Palace of the Governors had a gift shop that sold books, and there were a couple of other bookstores near the plaza. Sean headed that way and found the gift shop still open, though mostly empty. A couple of people were browsing the jewelry cases and the shelves of high-priced pottery and *katsinam.*

Sean made a beeline for the book section. It was small, but he found a shelf of stuff about Hispanic culture that included three books about *La Guadalupana.* One was a coffee-table book, heavy on the pictures. Another was very scholarly and had mostly to do with analyzing religious practices in New Mexico from Spanish Colonial times to the present. The third looked a little fluffy but included a chapter on the history of *La Guadalupana's* first appearance in Mexico, and another on how she'd grown into the cult figure she was today. Sean carried it to the counter and handed it to the wearily cheerful clerk along with his credit card.

With the book tucked under his arm, he headed back to his car. At the corner of the side street where he'd parked he paused to look up at the mountains.

The air was just beginning to get that golden tint that signaled the day was ending, though the sun wouldn't set for another hour or so. The tops of the mountains would turn pink then, the display that gave the Sangre de Cristos their colorful name. Not so vivid a pink just now, when there was no snow on the peaks. Sean frowned, remembering childhood summers when the snow had lasted all year.

No snowpack meant less water in the rivers and streams, in the reservoir and the old *acequias.* The Santa Fe River was dry most of the year nowadays.

My children will die. What had she meant by that? Was she talking about the low reservoir? Did she come in answer to his rain prayer?

More questions than answers. Shaking his head, Sean turned up the street to his car.

Monday morning at the bank was always busy. Rosa's desk behind the teller line was buried in night-drop deposits from the weekend, mostly large commercial deposits. She kept an eye on the tellers while she worked her way through the stack of bank bags. A couple of accounts still used the old-fashioned kind that locked, and she kept the keys on a big ring in her desk.

The lobby was fairly quiet. The drive-up tellers were busier, as usual. Their window was off to the side, screened from the lobby but still in view from Rosa's desk. She had started out working drive-up, and eventually moved up to head teller. Had she really been working here five years? It didn't seem that long.

The cold cash and numbers she worked with all day long couldn't be more different than her studies in *curanderismo*. In the banking world, everything must be precise. In *curanderismo*, all was intuitive. Rosa thought about the contrasts a lot. Her job brought her money to live, to pay rent on her little house, to buy a few nice things for herself, but it did not feed her soul. Someday she hoped to live as Cruz did, to spend her days in healing, and earn her living through the gentler art.

She finished the last deposit and slid the receipt into the bank bag, then locked the cash in her desk and carried the stack of empty bank bags to a side counter where the tellers could get them as customers came in to pick them up. She still kept a teller's cash drawer and occasionally stepped onto the teller line at rush times, like on end-of-the-month paydays.

A couple of customers were waiting in line in the lobby. Drive-up was quiet for the moment. Rosa stepped over and spoke to the nearer of the two tellers, a black-haired Anglo girl just out of high school who'd hired on at the beginning of summer. She was fast and accurate, but her multiple tattoos had consigned her to the drive-up, even though her clothes—which were almost always black—covered most of them. Banking was still conservative.

"Sandy, could you keep an eye on the lobby and help out if they need it? I'm going to get some coffee."

"Oh, get me some, please?" Sandy said, holding out a mug with a picture of a black widow spider on it.

"OK. Be right back."

Rosa picked up her own mug from her desk and checked to make sure she had her keys before leaving the teller line. She crossed the lobby to the break room, where she found the coffee pot nearly boiled dry so she rinsed it out and started a fresh pot, then stood musing about Kokopelli while she waited.

If that was really who the old man was. Or Leyha—she couldn't remember the name Cruz had said. She knew "Kokopelli" had been made up by some white guy in the nineteenth century. The hunchbacked flute player appeared in a lot of different Indian cultures all across the west. They probably each had their own name for him.

The coffee machine gurgled. Rosa glanced at the pot and saw there was enough in it to pour. She put her mug on the hot plate to catch the stream and filled Sandy's mug from the pot, then topped off her own mug and returned the pot to the machine. A drip of coffee hissed on the plate as she made the switch.

She didn't like the artificial creamer the coffee service provided, so she kept a pint of half-and-half in the fridge. She poured a little into her mug, then carefully carried the two mugs back to the lobby.

Arturo Gonzales, the branch manager, was there chatting with a tall Anglo guy in a dark, tailored suit. Rosa thought the man looked familiar, but couldn't place him. He had brown hair tinged with gray at the temples and a golf course tan. Business owner, maybe.

He caught her eye as she walked past and gave her a grin that bordered on a leer. She smiled briefly back and continued across the lobby to the teller line. *He* wouldn't be picking up his empty deposit bag. That sort of task was left to underlings.

She gave Sandy her coffee and returned to her desk, glancing up at the lobby before she sat down. Arturo was leading the businessman into his office. A third figure followed them, and Rosa stood frozen as she stared at him.

It was a man, she knew, because his chest was bare. He wore

a black kilt-like skirt and moccasins. His body was painted all over in broad black and white horizontal stripes, including his head, which had two points like a jester's cap that stood up straight and were tipped with tufts of corn husks. He carried a yucca whip in one hand. Rosa took shallow, frightened breaths through her nose as she watched the figure disappear into Arturo's office.

Hadn't anyone else seen him? Where were the security guards? Why didn't the customers freak out? Why weren't the account executives at the desks in the lobby protesting this guy who came in dressed as a kachina?

"You OK? You look like you've seen a ghost," said Frank Archuleta, one of the tellers.

Rosa became aware that she was standing behind her desk, still holding her coffee mug. She set it down carefully. "Fine. Just distracted for a minute. Did you see that guy who just went into Arturo's office?"

"Kyle Robbins?"

The name clicked into place with the businessman's face in Rosa's memory. Kyle Robbins was a big-time developer, a big wheeler-dealer. He'd put up a lot of those new neighborhoods on the west side.

"I thought he looked familiar, I just couldn't place him."

"Yeah, usually you see him on the news. Never seen him come in here before. I need a tray of quarters, please."

Rosa made out a transfer slip and gave Frank a tray from her desk. She'd have to get some more from the vault.

She sipping her coffee, musing about the kachina. Frank hadn't mentioned him. She suspected she was the only one who'd seen him.

This made it more likely that her Kokopelli guy was a vision, and not just some old shaman. The thought didn't comfort her.

She took out her phone and called Cruz. "Could I come over after work? I want to talk to you about something."

"Kokopelli show up again?"

"Uh—no, but a friend of his, I think."

"Bring some *empanadas* and you can stay for supper."

"I will. Thanks, Cruz."

Rosa hung up and tried to focus on work. She went through

her "In" box, glancing up at the lobby now and then. The kachina didn't reappear, even when Arturo and Kyle Robbins came out after about half an hour. Arturo escorted Robbins to the door and shook his hand, grinning like a wolf.

Some big deal going down, Rosa guessed. Arturo looked pretty pleased with himself.

The rest of the day went slowly. At lunchtime Rosa drove to the Golden Crown Panaderia and picked up half a dozen of the little half-moon pies called *empanadas*. She chose three peach—Cruz's favorite—and three cherry for herself. The baker smiled as she handed Rosa the white paper bag.

"We'll have pumpkin ones soon."

"Already?"

"Fall's coming. Haven't you seen the yellow leaves in the *bosque*?"

Rosa laughed. "Maybe a couple."

The baker shrugged. "Maybe it's just the drought."

Rosa paused at the door, caught by the comment. Drought threatened the *bosque*, which needed high water to reseed and needed the river to survive. The cottonwoods stretched thirsty roots toward the Rio all along the valley. Rosa frowned, thinking about the snake swallowing up the river. She didn't understand it, not yet, but she had a feeling she was going to.

She went back to the bank and tried to keep busy so she wouldn't think about her visions. She kept expecting to see the kachina again, kept thinking she saw a striped leg around a corner, but she knew it was just her imagination teasing her.

When the lobby finally closed for the day Rosa breathed a sigh of relief. She helped the tellers balance their cash drawers and store them away in the vault for the night, and said goodbye as she let them out the locked lobby doors. Sandy had balanced out earlier and was working the drive-up, which would stay open until five. Rosa made sure Sandy had everything she needed, then spent the end of the afternoon at her desk doing paperwork, burying herself in the numbers.

At five she pulled her own cash drawer, locked her desk, and waited for Sandy to close so they could both put away their drawers. They went out to the parking lot together, heat blasting them as they left the air-conditioned lobby. Still a good two hours before sunset, Rosa thought, glancing westward.

Her house was on the way to Cruz's, so she stopped to feed Bruja, her cat, and change out of her work clothes. She put on a broomstick skirt and a light cotton top, and traded her stockings and heels for sandals. Much more comfortable, she gave Bruja a scratch behind the ears and left for Cruz's.

Cruz greeted her at the door, wearing a loose shift of undyed cotton. Rosa gathered from this that she'd been working. A hint of sage in the air confirmed it. Someone had come for healing today.

Rosa handed Cruz the bag of *empanadas*. Cruz opened it, stuck her nose in, and inhaled.

"Ah. Thank you, *hija*. We'll save them for dessert."

They went into the kitchen and made a salad to go with the chile stew simmering on Cruz's stove. Cruz mixed up some dough and cooked hand-made tortillas over an open burner. Today it was definitely too warm to eat outside, so Rosa set places at the kitchen table, where her vase of flowers from Saturday stood.

"So," Cruz said, bringing bowls of stew to the table. "What happened this morning?"

Rosa described the kachina she'd seen at the bank. Cruz listened, nodding.

"Sounds like a clown."

"Is that what the stripes mean? I couldn't remember."

"I think so. And the yucca whip sounds like something a clown would have. You know, they whip people at the dances sometimes. At Shalako if a *katsina* falls, the clowns come after the spectators with whips."

"Because it's supposed to be bad luck, right? You're not supposed to see a kachina fall."

"*Katsina, hija.*" Cruz nodded and took a sip of iced tea. "Every pueblo's clown *katsinam* are different, though. Maybe I'll call Joe Pino. He could tell us if it's a Sandia clown, at least."

"Why would a clown come into the bank?"

"I think the question is, why would a clown follow your manager and Kyle Robbins?"

Rosa shook her head and shrugged. "I don't know. I think Robbins has built stuff on the west side. At first I wondered if he's involved in the Paseo extension, but I don't think his company does road construction."

Cruz shook her head. "He builds houses. Whole neighborhoods. Even I know that."

Cruz didn't own a television and she never read the papers. She didn't want to be distracted from her work by bad news, and she said that almost all the news was bad. Rosa, who hadn't yet achieved this degree of separation from the mainstream world, occasionally told Cruz about an interesting news story, especially if it was one of the rare positive stories.

Rosa reached for the salad. "Maybe he was talking to Arturo about financing for some new project."

"Maybe so."

"I can surf the web and see if there's anything in the wind."

"You do that. You should also light a candle and meditate about this for a while, *hija*. Ask why you are having these visions."

"Yeah."

They finished supper and Rosa cleaned up while Cruz made some coffee to go with the *empanadas*. Retiring to the living room with mugs of steaming coffee and the pies on a little blue plate, they sat on the sofa. Cruz left the lights off, so the only light was the setting sun glowing through the back curtains. Rosa kicked off her sandals and tucked her feet up under her.

"Customer today?" she asked.

"Two. Need any eggs?"

Cruz's clients often paid her in trade. It was an old tradition, and Cruz was just as happy to get a dozen eggs and some cheese or a chicken in exchange for a session as she was to accept cash. It was mostly the older clients who paid this way. Younger ones wanted to pay with credit cards, and were sometimes offended when Cruz said she couldn't take them.

You lived in the world of your choosing, Cruz often said. Rosa knew how true it was. She had one foot in each of two very different worlds at the moment, and she never stopped being aware of the difference. It was disturbing, though, to have the spiritual world invade the banking world.

"Sure, I'll take some eggs."

Rosa often bought some of Cruz's surplus food. It was a way

of getting her some extra cash without offending her. Rosa paid cash for her lessons, too—a lump sum every payday. In exchange she got at least two lessons a week, and the benefit of Cruz's advice whenever she wanted it. The arrangement was casual, which was fine with Rosa. She liked the looseness of it, because it contrasted with the rigidity of banking.

She also helped Cruz in the garden and helped her put up herbs and tinctures. She always learned something new while they worked together. There were a hundred different ways she learned from Cruz.

Rosa took an *empanada* and bit off a corner. Sweet cherry inside the sugar-dusted crust.

"How's your mother?" Cruz asked. "You been to see her lately?"

"Yes, ma'am. Sunday dinner with the whole family, every week."

"Her arthritis any better?"

"A little. She likes the hot weather."

They chatted a while about Rosa's family, who were sometimes her guinea pigs. Her very first consultation had been with her mother about the arthritis, and with much coaching from Cruz she had actually been able to give her mother some relief.

When the *empanadas* were gone, Rosa carried the plate and mugs back to the kitchen. She slung her purse over her shoulder and kissed Cruz's cheek.

"Thanks for the supper, *maestra*. I'm gonna go do my homework now."

"OK. I'll call Joe and let you know what he says. You call me if you have any more visions."

"I will. Oh, here—" Rosa dug in her purse and came up with two dollars. "For the eggs."

Cruz pulled a small basket down from the iron ring and put in half a dozen eggs and a small chunk of farmer's cheese wrapped in wax paper. The cheese was homemade, and the eggs had probably been laid that morning. Fresh, fresh food.

"Here, have a couple of zucchini, too. I've got zucchini coming out of my ears."

Cruz took three squashes out of a full paper grocery bag on

the counter. Rosa grinned as she laid them carefully in the basket on top of the eggs.

"Zucchini bread. Thanks, Cruz."

"Bye, *hija*. Call me tomorrow."

"OK."

Rosa drove home with the sky overhead glowing blue. Bruja greeted her at the door and meowed like she was dying of starvation when she got a whiff of the cheese in the basket. Rosa gave her a little piece of it, then put the rest in her fridge with the eggs and zucchini.

Too hot to bake tonight. Maybe she'd make zucchini bread tomorrow.

She took a soda from the fridge and went to her computer desk, which was at the back of her dining room. Cruz had insisted she not have a computer in her work room, or in her bedroom. It wasn't just the electric fields, it was the distraction of technology. Computers were not restful, Cruz had said firmly, and Rosa had barely managed not to laugh.

No, they weren't restful, but they were very useful. Rosa fired up her machine and did a search for Kyle Robbins. She got back a lot of news stories, but the dates on them weren't very recent. She decided to check out his company's website. Robbins Corporation, not a very original name, but expressive at least of its owner's priorities.

The front page of the website featured a picture of Robbins and a couple of other guys in hard hats standing in front of a backhoe with the company logo on it. Rosa stared at the backhoe, frowning.

Land-eaters. It was a resonance, one she didn't like.

She clicked on "News Releases" and scanned the list of headlines. "Acquisition underway for Valle del Sol project" caught her eye, so she followed the link. The story was from several months ago, and didn't include much information. Just that Robbins Corporation was acquiring property for a new retirement community near Pena Blanca.

That was sort of in the middle of nowhere, she thought. She brought up a map and saw that Pena Blanca was a little town near Cochiti Pueblo, almost exactly halfway between Albuquerque and Santa Fe. She'd thought all the land out that way was tribal land, but it seemed she was mistaken. A little more surfing and she scored a land-use map that showed an irregular, shallow triangle of white surrounded by the brown of Indian reservations and a small chunk of green national forest. White would be private property, she assumed.

She stared at it a while, wondering why this bit of land had been excluded when the reservations were made. Influential property owner, she guessed, and maybe now the owner's heirs were ready to sell.

That white triangle looked small on the map, but it was a pretty sizable chunk of land. One of the short sides was about four or five miles long, by her guess. The piece was shallow, maybe only a mile across at the widest, but that was still a lot. There would be water rights issues, probably. Those got incredibly complicated, especially on old Spanish land grants along the Rio Grande.

The western tip of the white triangle lay across the river. A cold feeling settled in the pit of Rosa's stomach. She went back and read the news release again, but there wasn't much to it. No mention of how large the retirement community would be.

She searched a little more but didn't turn up anything else. Finally she shut down the computer and went into her work room to meditate.

This was where she saw the few clients she had worked with so far. The room had a couple of comfortable chairs, a small table, and a bookcase that held books on half the shelves and herbs, feathers, and charms on the other half.

In one corner of the room Rosa had made a little altar, with a framed poster of *La Guadalupana* on the wall beside an empty crucifix representing Christ ascended to heaven. The altar beneath was draped with a cream-colored shawl and covered with a scatter of silk and paper roses, red, white, pink, and yellow. Pictures of Rosa's family and tokens of prayer lay among the roses. A small vase of fresh roses stood toward the back, and in the center was a tall, white votive candle. Rosa lit the candle and lit some incense as well, then knelt before the altar and closed her eyes.

"Blessed Lady, Mother of Christ, please send me guidance. Help me understand these visions."

She prayed, then stayed quietly thinking over the visions. The hunchback flute-player was often a fertility figure, but that didn't seem to fit with what he'd said to her. He'd mentioned babies, yeah—but it seemed he was more concerned about the water.

The clown she had no idea about. The only thing she could think of was that he might be going to use the whip on Kyle Robbins, but if that was all there was to it, why did she need to see it? She hoped Cruz's friend at Sandia Pueblo would shed some light on that.

For a long time she sat thinking about the visions and the river. No new insights came to her, and when her feet started going to sleep she finally gave it up.

Leaving the candle burning, she went out to her living room and turned on the TV to watch the late news. No TV allowed in the bedroom either, so Rosa had developed the habit of brushing her hair out in the living room before going to bed. She sat on the sofa with her brush and watched the top news story—a big gang fight down in the south valley. One dead, four others in the hospital.

Rosa looked away as she brushed out her hair. No wonder Cruz avoided the news. Maybe it was wise to be aware of the troubles in the city, but the story left her feeling sad and helpless.

A couple more stories about crime, then a light piece about shifting weather patterns. Deforestation in South America might result in wetter summers in New Mexico. It sounded like good news, but at the bottom of it was the troubling trend of human influence changing Earth's climate. The reporter didn't mention global warming, but to Rosa the two effects were related.

Would global warming cause New Mexico to become hotter and drier, or hotter and wetter? Scientists and politicians didn't agree. There were a lot of opinions flying around, but not many solutions.

At the commercial break Rosa brushed her teeth, then changed into her nightclothes. She got back to the living room halfway through a story about a protest rally. She didn't know where it was or what it was about, but the signs held by the protesters in the background were about water. NO GOLF COURSE. RESCUE THE RIO. MINNOWS WILL DIE.

That one was a reference to the Albuquerque's fight over water from the Rio a decade or so back. The silvery minnow, an endangered species, needed a certain amount of water in the river in order to breed. There had been a big fuss about it, because the mayor wanted the water for the city and didn't care about the fish.

Rosa listened to the reporter interviewing the protest leader, trying to figure out where they were. This wasn't the minnow story being rehashed. The guy leading the protest—a bearded Anglo who looked normal enough and sounded reasonable— was talking about some new development.

"The water rights agreements were never intended to support this kind of development," he told the reporter. "This would only exacerbate the limitations we're already dealing with. Why should farmers in southern New Mexico have to go without water because Kyle Robbins wants a championship golf course?"

Rosa felt like she'd been slapped in the face. She put down her brush and leaned toward the TV, concentrating on the reporter's words, but the story was over and he was just signing off.

"This is Greg Garza reporting from Pena Blanca."

The weather came on. Rosa went back to her computer and searched for "Kyle Robbins" and "golf course." Skimming the results, she saw one titled "Valle del Sol to have World Class Golf Course."

She followed the link to a story in a Santa Fe paper that gave a few more details about Valle del Sol. Eighteen hole championship golf course. Country club with Olympic pool. Ten thousand homes, and that was just Phase One. Rosa shivered despite the warmth of the evening.

A link to a map brought up a familiar-looking shallow triangle, its western tip across the Rio Grande. Streets were laid out around the edges while the green swath of golf course twined along the center of the development, snake-like, its western end bumping up against the river.

Rosa stared at the map. It *did* look like a snake. Like a serpent. A chill of certainty ran through her.

"This is it," she said softly. "This is what it means."

Sean dragged himself out of bed Tuesday morning after spending most of Monday evening surfing the web. The book he'd bought had told him the basics about the Virgin of Guadalupe, but he wanted more information, so he'd gone looking online. The official website of the Basilica de Guadalupe down in Mexico hadn't provided any startling insights, but he knew a lot more about *La Guadalupana* now.

He stood in the kitchen eating cold cereal while he waited for coffee to brew, and thought about the woman he'd seen standing on the reservoir. It hadn't occurred to him at the time, but she did look sort of Hispanic.

The Virgin of Guadalupe, according to the earliest account which was supposed to be a transcription of Juan Diego's story, had been mestizo. She'd spoken to Juan Diego in his native tongue, Nahuatl. No wonder she was revered by Latin Americans all over. She was a deity of her people, literally.

Another thing Sean hadn't known was that the supposed original image of the Virgin, the peasant's homespun cloak on which the image had miraculously appeared, still existed. It turned out that a lot of the pictures he'd seen of *La Guadalupana* were photos of this image, which was now enshrined in the new Basilica de Guadalupe built in the 1970's when the old one was threatening to fall down. Most other images of *La Guadalupana* were based on the original, though there were sometimes color variations. He'd seen pictures where her starry mantle was green instead of blue, and where the pink robe didn't have any pattern.

He didn't know how miraculous it was that the image had survived since the 1600s. He did think the style of it was very like the iconography of that era in Spain. Probably the "miraculous image" had been painted not long after Juan Diego had seen the Virgin, maybe even to commemorate the event, and had gradually come to be accepted as the actual result of the miracle.

Or maybe it *was* the result of the miracle. Sean was hardly in a position to be skeptical. He'd seen her himself.

He rubbed his temples. Maybe he'd imagined it. Maybe the heat and the high of playing the flute had conspired to create an attractive hallucination. He would talk to Angel about it on the weekend, but until then he might as well put it out of his mind, because he'd done everything he could to try to figure it out, and come up blank.

He carried his breakfast out to the dining room, trying to shift his thoughts to the day's work ahead. Big project on his desk, an analysis of projected growth on the south side of Santa Fe, including the required infrastructure and environmental impact. The city was trying to curb growth, but it might not be trying hard enough, and there were developments outside the city limits that were impacting resources.

Sean took a sip of coffee and glanced out the window. He nearly choked.

The rosebushes in his back yard were covered with flowers.

Those scrawny old bushes hadn't put out so much as a bud all summer, yet here they were covered in pink and red blossoms. Sean stood up slowly and went out to the yard in his bare feet.

The dirt was cool underfoot. He walked over to one of the rosebushes and stood staring down at it.

He could smell the fragrance of the flowers without even bending down. He cupped a bloom in one hand, feeling the velvet softness of the petals.

He never had come out and watered the bushes. This wasn't his doing, and he doubted his neighbors had come over and dug up his neglected roses and planted blooming bushes in their place. Just to be sure, he glanced at the base of the bush, but the soil hadn't been disturbed.

Nope, this was *La Guadalupana's* doing. Just a little reminder that she hadn't forgotten about him.

Sean swallowed. The frustrating thing was, he couldn't make a fuss about this. If he called up Father Mahan and told him, it would only convince the priest that he was a nut.

My roses are blooming! It's a miracle!

Yeah, that would go over great. Too bad it wasn't December,

like when the original miracle had occurred. That would have had more impact.

Sean went back in the house and finished his coffee, then poured another cup. He didn't know what to do about the rosebushes. Just ignore them, maybe.

What did she want from him, anyway? She hadn't asked him to do anything. Just said "My children will die" — what was that about? He'd searched the web, but as far as he could tell, her "children" were all the Catholics in the Americas.

She'd been more up front with Juan Diego. Right from the start she'd told him she wanted a church. Sean didn't think this was about a church, but he could be wrong. He'd just have to wait and see, he supposed.

Great. He could expect another visit. Boy, he was looking forward to that. Why hadn't she picked someone who believed in her, anyway? She had thousands of faithful Catholics to choose from. Hundreds of thousands. Why him?

Feeling cranky, Sean cleaned up his breakfast dishes and went to dress for work. He tried not to think about *La Guadalupana*, since he couldn't draw any conclusions. He buried himself in the analysis project, not coming up for air or outside thoughts until early afternoon.

His company's office was in an old house northeast of the Santa Fe Plaza, so he could walk to lunch at any of a couple dozen restaurants. He had his favorites, of course, and he decided on the San Francisco Grill today. He could stop by the Palace on the way and ask Ruby if Angel would be coming into town before the weekend. The Madalenas didn't have a phone at their place out in Cochiti. Ruby had a cell phone, but Sean didn't know the number.

As he approached the plaza he saw that something was going on, some kind of rally. A lot of people with protest signs were crowded around the gazebo, where a guy with a PA was making a speech. Sean walked over to the corner of the plaza and stood listening until he figured out what it was — an anti-development rally. He'd seen plenty of those. Yes, uncontrolled development was a problem, but he didn't want to get involved in a big protest. It wouldn't look good for his employers, since developers were often their customers. The job he was working on at the moment was contracted by a developer, in fact.

He started to cross the street to the Palace, but was stopped by a pretty girl with curling red hair and big, silver hoop earrings. She held out a sheet of pink paper.

"No, thanks," Sean said.

"It's just about the town meeting on Friday. Please take a look. This is our best chance for influencing the Valle del Sol decision."

Sean took the page and stuffed it in the pocket of his jeans. Easier to take it than to argue.

He made his way over to Ruby's space on the *portal*, but she wasn't there. A blanket lay over her pottery. Her neighbor was keeping an eye on it, and he gave Sean a nod.

"Any idea when she'll be back?"

"Gone to get lunch and run a couple of errands. She left maybe half an hour ago."

"OK, thanks."

Sean crossed the plaza, giving the rally a wide berth, and went into the Grill at the southwest corner. The spacious, second-story restaurant was fairly busy, but he didn't have to wait long for a table. The waitress brought him his drink, and while he was waiting for his sandwich, he pulled the pink flyer out of his pocket.

Valle del Sol. He'd heard the name, but hadn't paid a lot of attention to it. Looked like it was a development out near Cochiti.

He frowned. That might have an impact on the Madalenas. Had they mentioned it? He couldn't remember. It wasn't like them to make a lot of fuss about their problems, at least not to Sean.

He scanned the flyer. Overuse of land that was intended for farming. Zoning changes made to accommodate the development, which the flyer claimed were illegal. Blah blah blah, protest hype. Come to the meeting on Friday and raise your voice!

The meeting was scheduled for Sweeney Center in Santa Fe, because it was expected to draw a crowd bigger than Pena Blanca's community center could handle. The governor's office was sending someone to talk about the land use issues. Some low-level assistant with a script to read and no authority, Sean figured. That was how these things usually went.

Reading between the lines, it sounded like the developer had greased the right palms in the state government to push the project through. The deal was already made. The meeting was just a formality, to let the protesters vent their objections. It wouldn't change anything.

Sean was about to crumple the flyer when a paragraph at the bottom of the page caught his eye.

> The Rio Grande is overtaxed and no longer reaches the Gulf of Mexico. Valle del Sol will place unacceptable increased demand on this endangered river. Water will no longer reach farms south of Socorro. Crops will wither. Children will die.

"Crap."

Gee, would those be *Guadalupana's* children? Oh, yeah.

It was hype. Probably no one would die, but farmers could lose their businesses. That was bad enough.

The waitress arrived with his sandwich. Sean stuffed the flyer back in his pocket and thanked her, then took a bite. Turkey with jack cheese and green chile that lit up his head. Good stuff.

He didn't want to get involved in the protest. He'd done his share of that kind of activism in California. It was heartbreaking, because it rarely succeeded. He had a sinking feeling, though, that he wasn't going to be given a choice.

He paid his tab and went back to the plaza. The rally was over, just a few of the protesters milling around while the leader packed up his PA. Tourists swarmed, making the little knot of protesters seem insignificant.

Sean skirted the plaza and entered the Palace *portal* at the west end, walking behind the shopping tourists to Ruby's space. She was back, sitting on her ice chest and taking discreet bites from a sandwich.

A frost-blonde woman in tight jeans and fringed leather jacket was crouched in front of her blanket, looking at the pottery while her bored husband stood waiting. Heavy silver and turquoise rings flashed on the blonde's fingers as she picked up a pot and turned it in her hands. Ruby watched, patient and sharp-eyed. She glanced at Sean, who smiled back. He'd wait til the customers were gone.

He let his gaze drift over the pottery. Ruby made figurines, like a lot of Cochiti potters, and she also made traditional pots, usually with at least one figure incorporated. Sean liked a pot that had a frog peeking over its rim. Another one had bean stalks climbing up its sides in 3-D, rather than just painted on.

The blonde picked up a *koshare* figurine. The striped clown held a huge slice of watermelon in its hands and looked like its mouth was full. It was smiling mischievously, ready to spit seeds. The woman put it down and picked up a storyteller instead.

Sean gazed at the *koshare*, wondering when watermelon had come to the upper Rio Grande Valley. Probably the Spanish had brought it. The Indians had grown squash, beans, and corn before colonization, but he didn't think they'd had watermelon. He doubted it could grow here without irrigation.

"I'll take this one," the woman said, holding out the storyteller.

Ruby wrapped the figurine in bubble wrap and completed the transaction, using her cell phone to authorize the woman's credit card. The woman strolled away with her husband, her prize held almost carelessly in one hand. Sean wondered if Ruby ever had a hard time parting with her work, seeing it carried away in the hands of a stranger.

"Hey, Sean."

He looked at Ruby. She picked up her sandwich.

"Hey. I was wondering if Angel would be in town before Sunday."

Ruby nodded and swallowed a bite of sandwich. "He's coming for the town hall meeting Friday night."

She poked around in her box of packaging supplies and brought out a pink flyer, offering it to Sean. He waved it away.

"I've got one, thanks. So you're both going to be at the meeting?"

Ruby nodded. "Got to make a stand. Won't do any good I figure."

"Won't do any good," Ruby's neighbor agreed.

"But Angel wants to go. He's all upset about this thing."

Ruby waved the flyer, then put it back in her box and put her sandwich on top of it. Another customer had stopped at her blanket.

Sean stepped back to make room. "Tell Angel I want to talk to him. I'll come to the meeting."

Ruby nodded, then turned her attention to the customer. "You can pick them up if you like."

Sean walked back to work, feeling slightly let down. He had trouble getting back into his project, kept getting stuck on the water issue. The general growth projection was for forty years in the future, and predicted a fifteen percent increase in Santa Fe's water use. Sean re-ran the figures and got the same result, then sat staring unhappily at the screen. Where was the water going to come from?

New Mexico was already up to its ears in water squabbles. Down near El Paso, wells on the Texas side were tapping into a big aquifer that lay mostly in New Mexico. The New Mexico residents who counted on that water had little recourse but to suck as much of it out of the aquifer as they could and store it elsewhere. And when it was gone?

Sean closed the general file and got to work on the code for a more specific projection of street and road construction expenses. He hammered at it for the rest of the afternoon and tried not to think about water. Driving home, his favorite local radio station was doing an interview with the guy who'd led the rally in the plaza—Tom Evans. Sean recognized his voice. He punched the buttons and found some mariachi music, which ordinarily he liked, but today it reminded him of *La Guadalupana*. He opted for rock and roll instead.

When he got home he glanced out the back doors to check on the rosebushes. They looked bigger, and there were more colors of flowers. The pink bush was sporting white roses as well, now, and the red bush also bore yellow blossoms with flame-tipped edges.

"OK," Sean said to the bushes. "You win. I'll do what I can."

6

Rosa brought her take-out lunch back to the bank, hoping to find Gerry, Arturo's secretary, in the break room. Gerry always brought a lunch from home, and Rosa had timed her lunch today to match when Gerry usually took hers. She found Gerry sitting at the round table, eating leftover enchiladas from a plastic food storage container.

"Hi, Gerry." Rosa set her lunch bag and drink cup on the table and sat down. She pulled out her sandwich and a large bag of french fries. Gerry loved fries, she knew, but with three kids at home her budget was pretty tight.

"Hi." Gerry's gaze strayed wistfully toward the fries. "Those look good."

"Help yourself. I forgot and said yes when they wanted to supersize. It's too much for me."

"Thanks." Gerry ate a fry, then another one.

Rosa unwrapped her chicken sandwich. "How are the kids?"

"OK. The usual. Tony sprained his ankle at football practice yesterday."

"Ay! I hope he's OK."

"He's fine, but you'd think he'd broken his leg, the way he carries on. His coach won't let him on the field again until next week."

"Football's starting up already? When does school start?"

"Couple of weeks."

"Man, the summer went fast."

"Yeah."

Gerry took two more fries and ate them slowly, a look of bliss on her face. Rosa finished a bite of sandwich and sipped her drink.

"Was that Kyle Robbins in here the other day?"

"Yeah."

"What was he doing here?"

"I don't know. He didn't have an appointment, he just dropped in on Arturo. They were talking about some land deal, I think."

"Oh."

Rosa ate a fry, then took another bite of her sandwich. She'd been hoping Gerry would know something about Robbins, but apparently not.

Gerry looked at her watch. "I gotta go. Have to run across the street and fill a prescription."

Rosa dumped half the fries on her sandwich wrapper and held out the rest to Gerry. "Take these."

"Thanks, girl!" Gerry blew her a kiss, then took her food container to the sink and washed it, leaving it perched on the over-full dish rack to dry.

Rosa finished her sandwich and picked at the fries. She was impatient for the day to end. Cruz had invited her to come for supper again, and this time there'd be another guest, Cruz's friend Joe Pino, from Sandia Pueblo. He'd expressed interest in Rosa's visions, and Cruz had decided it would be good for them all to talk together.

First there was the whole afternoon to get through, though. Wednesdays were usually slow, which didn't help. She glanced at the clock on the wall. Twenty minutes left of her lunch hour, and she didn't have anything to do.

The fries were cold now. Rosa rolled the rest of them up in the sandwich wrapper, stuffed it into the bag, and threw it away. She was just about to head out for a walk when Arturo came into the break room for coffee.

She paused at the sink and washed her hands, nerving herself to ask about Robbins. She didn't chit-chat much with Arturo, but this was worth making an effort.

"Say, was that Kyle Robbins you were talking to the other day?"

Arturo looked up from pouring sugar in his coffee and grinned. "Yes, it was."

"I didn't know he had an account here."

"He doesn't. Yet. We're working on a deal."

"Oh?"

"He has a new development project, and we're putting up

part of the financing."

"Really? Wow, that sounds great! Is it on the west side?"

Arturo shook his head. "It's a new retirement community. Valle del Sol."

Bingo.

Rosa tried to keep her voice casual as she threw away her paper towel. "I'd like to hear more about it."

Arturo didn't answer. She looked at him, saw him regarding her with surprise.

"My mom is thinking about retiring." That was true, though Rosa knew Mama would never leave her home.

"Oh."

"Did Mr. Robbins give you any brochures or anything like that?"

"Not that I can give away. You could come look at them in my office if you want."

"Thanks! I'd like to."

"Come on your break."

"Actually, I'm still at lunch. Would now be OK?"

Arturo watched her as he took a sip of his coffee. "OK. Come on, then."

Rosa followed him out to the lobby and across to his office. A light on Gerry's phone was blinking on the desk outside. Arturo ignored it and went on into his office, gesturing to Rosa to follow. He left the door open.

Being the branch manager, Arturo had a nice corner office with windows. He kept the blinds drawn on them, which Rosa thought was a terrible waste. He didn't even glance at them as he set his coffee mug down on his walnut desk.

"Here you go," he said, sifting through some papers on the desk and handing Rosa a glossy brochure. "And here's a map of Phase I."

Rosa took the legal-sized page. The map was the same one she'd seen on the web, with the green, serpentine golf course twining its way to the river. She glanced up at Arturo.

"Looks like a big golf course. Pretty fancy."

He grinned. "That's only the beginning. Look in the brochure."

Rosa sat down in one of his guest chairs and opened the

brochure. It was aimed at potential retirees. She scanned it, looking for details beyond what she'd seen on the web.

"Wow, country club, spa...a hospital?"

"Old folks like to have medical care close by."

All Rosa could think of was how much water all those things would use. She tried to work up the nerve to ask Arturo about it, but his phone rang. He answered it, then looked up at Rosa, who stood up at once.

"I'll bring these back," she mouthed as she moved to the door. Arturo nodded, and Rosa stepped out and pulled the door closed. She sat at Gerry's desk and read through the rest of the brochure. A couple of paragraphs at the back talked about security, water, and support services. Rosa reached for a sticky note to make some notes, then decided to just make copies of the brochure. Glancing toward Arturo's office, she got up and went to the copy room next to the teller line.

In five minutes she'd copied the whole brochure and the map, and returned the originals to Gerry's desk with a note thanking Arturo for letting her look at them. By then her lunch hour was almost over, so she went back to her desk and stashed the copies in the bottom drawer with her purse.

The afternoon dragged on, and finally ended. Rosa hadn't seen Arturo again. She and Sandy put away their cash drawers in the vault and headed out.

At home, Bruja was sitting in the front window, watching for her. Nice to have somebody waiting for her, even if it was just a cat.

She put down some food for Bruja and grabbed Cruz's basket and her garden shears, taking a couple of minutes to go out in the garden and fill the basket with fresh lavender. The pungent smell that rose up as she cut the stems helped clear her mind of the day's little stresses. She paused to inhale the scent of the blooms on her favorite rosebush, creamy yellow-white flowers with a rich perfume. She clipped three roses and carried them back into the house, put them in a vase and set it on the dining table, then grabbed her purse and headed over to Cruz's with the basket of lavender.

Cruz was sitting out front with an Indian man next to her, both sipping glasses of iced tea. For a moment he reminded Rosa of the flute player she'd seen at the cliffs, but he wasn't as old, nor as bent. Rosa gave him a shy smile as she came up the two steps to the *portal* and handed the basket to Cruz.

"Thank you, *hija*. Have you met Joseph Pino?"

Rosa turned to the man. "I don't think so."

"Joe, this is Rosa Marquez, my apprentice."

The man nodded and smiled back. His eyes were warm, with a glint of humor in them as if he were laughing at Rosa. It didn't offend her, because she sensed he looked at the whole world that way.

"Nice to meet you, Mr. Pino."

"Just call me Joe."

Cruz stood up. "Let's go in. The tamales should be ready."

Rosa followed the others in, holding the door for Joe. Cruz's kitchen was filled with the aroma of corn-scented steam. The table was already set for three. Cruz hung the basket of lavender up on the big iron ring, then went over to the stove.

"Can I help?" Rosa asked.

"Just fill the tea glasses. There's a pitcher in the fridge."

Cruz brought a platter of steaming tamales to the table and set a bowl of red chile sauce beside it. Another bowl of stewed beans, a dish of Spanish rice, and a basket of fresh tortillas completed the meal. Rosa filled the glasses and left the pitcher on the counter, close at hand.

They didn't talk much until about halfway through supper, when Joe shot a glance at Rosa while he helped himself to another tamale. "You're the one who's seeing clowns, eh?"

"Just one clown."

"What did he look like?"

Rosa described the figure she'd seen at the bank, aware that Joe was listening intently though he kept his gaze on the tamale as he unwrapped the corn husk from around it.

"The yucca whip is strange," he said when she'd finished.

"I've heard of clowns whipping people at Shalako," Cruz said.

Joe nodded and ladled chile sauce over his tamale. "I think those are mudheads." He glanced up at Rosa. "Different kind of clown."

Rosa poked her fork at her beans. She didn't know that much

about *katsinam*, but she knew they were sacred to the Indians. When a person put on a *katsina* mask, he became that *katsina*, that god, in a way that was as real to the Pueblos as the transubstantiation of the communion host. One of the things the clowns did was make sure the other *katsinam* were respected.

"I was hoping maybe you could help me understand why the clown appeared."

Joe chewed a bite of tamale, looking thoughtful, then sipped his tea. "A *koshare* is more than a clown. You know, they fool around and get in trouble, but there's a reason behind the way they act. They teach about what's not acceptable behavior. At the end of the day they get punished for the bad things they do. That's a lesson for everybody."

"This clown—this *koshare*—wasn't fooling around. He just followed two men into an office."

Joe shrugged. "They also keep people in line. The yucca whip seems to imply that's what your *koshare* was doing, or trying to do. Or maybe if he was hanging around with these men, he saw them as being like him, like *koshare*. Doing things wrong."

That made some sense, though not in a reassuring way. Rosa found herself staring at Joe and looked away, knowing he wouldn't be comfortable under her direct gaze.

"Who were the men that he followed?" Joe asked.

"The branch manager and Kyle Robbins. He's a developer."

Joe's face went flat, unreadable. He ate a bite of beans. Rosa watched, sneaking short glances at him. Finally Joe put down his fork.

"Robbins. OK, that makes sense. We have a name for Mr. Robbins. We call him the water thief."

Rosa exchanged a look with Cruz. "Why do you call him that?"

"He likes to build a lot of houses. He decided to make a development near our pueblo. Built a big neighborhood, sold all the houses, then went away. Couple years later the wells started going dry. Those people got stuck without water, so now they start looking around and they want their neighbors' water." Joe shook his head. "He builds problems and sells them as dreams. He's doing a bad thing."

"So you think that's why the *koshare* was following him?"

"I don't know why. Maybe you can tell *me* why."

Joe tilted his head and looked briefly straight at Rosa. His face looked tired, but his eyes were sharp and quick.

Rosa laid down her fork and put her hands flat on the table to either side of her plate, then closed her eyes. She thought about the *koshare* and held it in the front of her mind, focusing on it, letting all other thoughts and questions slip away.

Why?

In her thoughts she traveled with the *koshare* into Arturo's office. Inside, Arturo and Robbins were counting money, a big heap of gold coins. The *koshare* tried to chase them away, swinging his yucca whip, but they threw handfuls of money at him and with each coin that struck him, he grew smaller. He shrank until he was the size of a carved *katsina* doll, then shrank more and more until at last he disappeared. Arturo and Robbins went back to counting and stacking their coins, building a wall around themselves, until Rosa could no longer see them. But she could still hear the chink of the gold.

Rosa opened her eyes. Both Cruz and Joe were watching her.

"Greed. They're greedy. Arturo and Robbins both."

Joe nodded, looking unsurprised. Cruz watched and waited, wearing her *maestra* face.

Rosa glanced at Joe. "You said he was a water thief. I think he's getting ready to steal a lot more water."

"He's always doing that."

"Have you heard of Valle del Sol?"

Joe's mouth curved in a mirthless smile. "Oh, yes. Every pueblo on the river knows about that one. There's going to be a big town hall meeting about it in Santa Fe on Friday."

"Valle del Sol is what Arturo and Robbins were talking about in the office, I'm pretty sure."

"Mm."

Rosa looked down at her plate, her half-eaten dinner. She wasn't hungry any more.

"Joe, which *katsinam* are related to water?"

He chuckled. "All of them. They're all rain gods. When we dance, when we pray, we always pray for rain."

Rosa's heart sank. She had the feeling this time prayers weren't going to be enough.

"Have you seen the plans for the development?"

Joe shook his head. Rosa got up and fetched her purse, which held the copies she'd made of the brochure and map. She took her plate off the table and spread the map out at her place, facing Joe and Cruz, who leaned forward to look.

"This is just Phase One," she said.

Cruz traced the golf course with a fingertip. "Your serpent."

"Yes."

Joe glanced up, looking curious, so Rosa explained about meeting the hunchbacked flute player and the things he had said to her. Joe's brows rose as she talked, and when she finished he gave her a look of respect.

"So, what are you going to do?" he asked.

Rosa drew a breath. "I think I have to fight this development."

"Lot of people fighting it, not making much progress. How are you going to make a difference?"

"I don't know yet." Rosa gazed at the map, with the green serpent twining toward the river. "But I'm going to find out."

Friday afternoon, Sean left work right at five and hurried to the Palace *portal*. Ruby and Angel were both there, starting to pack up though there were still a lot of tourists around. Ruby only had a few pieces left on the blanket, and a couple she'd already wrapped and put away in a crate. The rest of the milk crates stood stacked by the back wall, empty.

Sean stopped in front of her and smiled. "Good day today?"

"Yeah, pretty good. People are getting excited about the Market, I think."

Indian Market was a week away, a huge outdoor market that took up all the streets near the plaza. Ruby didn't sell there; she said the booth fees were too high. Mostly it was the big name artists from all over the state who showed their work at the Market, charging top dollar for it. The rich collectors who flooded Santa Fe at Market time were willing to pay. Sean had once mentioned to Angel that he thought Angel's flutes would sell well there, but Angel had only smiled.

Now Angel glanced up at Sean with a similar smile and a nod. He unfolded a piece of wadded newspaper and handed it to Ruby, who used it to wrap a figurine.

"I have something I want to talk to you about," Sean said. "Can I buy you guys dinner?"

Angel traded a glance with Ruby. "Sure. Thanks."

Sean helped carry Ruby's things to her truck, parked in a lot a couple of streets away. He and Angel made the first trip with the empty crates. When they were away from the crowds on the plaza, Sean worked up the nerve to speak.

"I've had a vision, I'm pretty sure."

Angel shot him an interested glance. "A vision?"

"Yeah. The Virgin of Guadalupe."

"Oh."

Sean let Angel think about that for a while. The Madalenas

were Catholic, like many Pueblos. Sean didn't know how much the Indians revered *La Guadalupana*. He suspected it was more a Hispanic thing, but he could be wrong. The more he learned about her, the more it seemed she was a patron of all the native peoples in the Americas. The Indians down in Mexico sure loved her, but the Pueblo folk up north were a little different. Each Pueblo had its own patron saint.

"She made the roses in my back yard bloom."

Angel stopped, staring at Sean over his armload of crates. "Those scrawny old bushes?"

"Yeah. You ought to see them. They're going crazy."

Angel shook his head and walked on. Sean walked beside him, hoping Angel didn't think he was trying to put something over on him. He thought they'd known each other long enough that Angel would trust his word, but then, he never could tell what Angel was thinking.

They reached the parking lot and Angel opened the back of the truck. Sean set his crates inside next to Angel's. Angel locked it up again and turned to look at Sean.

"Where did you see her?"

"Up near the reservoir."

Sean explained about going up there to play, and described his vision to Angel. He also described his visit to St. Francis and his talk with Father Mahan. Angel's lip curved as Sean told him that the priest couldn't suggest anything except prayer.

"Well, he's right. You should pray."

Sean had never discussed religion with Angel, and wasn't hot to start. "I'm not much for praying," he said.

Angel gave him a troubled look. "If she's talking to you, you ought to listen. Try asking *her* to explain what she means."

Sean sighed. He hadn't considered that, but it made sense. He didn't really want to hear from *Guadalupana* again, he had to admit, but the roses seemed to indicate he wasn't going to get his wish on that point.

They started back to the plaza, walking in the shade of the buildings on the west side of the street. The late afternoon heat hadn't yet started to fade. Sean shoved his hands in the pockets of his jeans.

"I sort of think I know what she's getting at. I think its this

Valle del Sol development."

"Oh. So that's why you're coming to the meeting."

"Yeah."

"Ruby thought it was kind of strange. Most Anglos don't care about stuff like this. Except the tree-huggers, of course."

"I've hugged a tree or two in my day."

Angel laughed softly. They didn't talk any more about it, walking in silence back to the Palace. When they got to Ruby's space they found her packed up and waiting. Sean picked up the ice chest, Angel took the crate packed with pottery, and Ruby carried the blankets and her box of supplies.

They agreed to meet at Tomasita's for dinner, all of them ready to get away from the plaza. Sean jogged back to his office to get his car after seeing the Madalenas to their truck. Angel gave him a wave and a smile as he left, which Sean found reassuring. At least Angel hadn't totally written him off.

Over enchiladas and *chiles rellenos* they talked about the meeting and the development, but not about Sean's vision. It wasn't that he didn't trust Ruby—in fact he valued her opinion, down-to-earth as she was—but it just didn't seem right to discuss his vision in a public restaurant.

"I heard that golf course is supposed to go right down to the river," Ruby said in disapproving tone.

"Yeah, I guess," said Sean, watching her frown.

"She digs clay on the river bank," Angel said.

"Oh. Well, this probably won't stop you from doing that, at least."

Ruby stabbed a bean with her fork. "I don't want a bunch of golfers watching me."

"It's a sacred activity," Angel said after a moment. "Taking gifts from the earth."

"Oh. I see."

Sean had a sense of feeling left out, something he got now and then around the Madalenas. Their lives were driven by spirituality, especially Angel's, but there was a strange duality to it because they practiced not only Catholicism but also the traditional rituals of their tribe.

It hadn't occurred to Sean that digging clay could be a sacred act, but it made sense. The clay went into Ruby's pottery, which was her livelihood, and also her means of artistic expression. Why wouldn't it be sacred?

Sean didn't have anything as rich to attach to his work. He earned his living pushing electrons around.

Maybe *Guadalupana* could advise him about that. Maybe she'd have something mystical to say about electrons.

Shaking off the thought, Sean finished his meal and paid the bill, then promised to meet the Madalenas over at Sweeney Center. He found a place to park not far from the building and hurried to join the people thronging in.

Sweeney Hall, the main meeting hall in Santa Fe for decades, had recently been torn down and rebuilt as a huge, new conference center. The town hall meeting was in a secondary meeting room, a modest auditorium with a simple stage at one end of the large, rectangular room. The place still smelled new.

The auditorium was crowded. Most of the people Sean saw looked Indian or Hispanic, with a few Anglos sprinkled through the mix. He noticed the redhead who'd given him the flyer up near the stage, setting up poster-board displays. One of them looked like a map. Sean edged closer, trying to see it, but the place was too packed for him to get near enough. He gave up and looked for Angel and Ruby instead, spotting them against the back wall.

"Quite a turnout," he said as he joined them.

Angel nodded, but didn't say anything. He wasn't much for crowds, Sean knew. He tended to fade into the background when there were more than a few people around.

Sean noticed a table with two huge coffee urns at the side of the auditorium. People were buzzing around it like bees at a honeysuckle vine.

"Can I get you some coffee?"

Ruby nodded. "Cream and sugar."

"Want help?" Angel asked.

"No, I can get it. Be right back. Save me a piece of wall."

Sean worked his way over to the coffee and filled three cups, black for him and Angel, cream and sugar for Ruby. A pretty Hispanic girl asked him for the cream, and Sean gave her a second look as he passed it to her.

She was slim, with long, dark brown hair caught back from

her face in a comb, and gold hoop earrings. Nice shape, and the red blouse she wore showed it off, with ruffles at the v-shaped neckline and at her wrists. Below the blouse she had on a broomstick skirt with big roses all over it, and sandals.

The roses caught Sean's attention. He frowned.

"Something wrong?"

He glanced up at her with a belated smile. "No. Nice skirt."

She gave him a wry look, but smiled back. "Thanks."

An amplified voice made a feeble attempt at cutting through the babble of the crowd. Sean glanced toward the stage and saw the same guy who'd been giving a speech on the plaza the other day, talking into a microphone. Turning back to the table to pick up his three coffees, Sean saw that the girl in the rose skirt was gone.

For a moment he had a panicky feeling it had been *Guadalupana* again, then he spotted the red blouse in the crowd as the girl moved toward the displays at the front of the room. He edged his way back to the Madalenas, managing to keep from spilling the coffee. Ruby stepped to one side, making room for him, and smiled as she accepted her cup. Sean took a sip from his. It was wretched, but it gave him something to do.

"If I could have everyone's attention," said the speaker, still barely audible.

The talk settled down to a low murmur.

"Thank you all for coming to this town hall meeting. I'm Tom Evans, with the People for Responsible Development. Let me just quickly run down what we're going to talk about tonight. We have David Fenway here from Robbins Corporation—"

Evans paused while a couple of "boos" subsided. The crowd muttered, and Evans raised his voice.

"Mr. Fenway is going to give us an overview of the Valle del Sol project and address some of our concerns. Then we have Ben Lucero from the New Mexico Department of Water, Minerals, and Natural Resources; and Councilor Richard Jaramillo from Sandoval County, who will give us their perspective. After that I'll suggest some ways we can all work together to make sure our concerns are addressed, and then we'll have open discussion. OK, so now let's please welcome Mr. David Fenway."

A smattering of applause was accompanied by more catcalls.

Evans handed the microphone to a man in a pale linen suit and sky blue tie. He looked about Sean's age, though his brown, short-curt hair was already receding from his temples.

"Thank you, Tom. Good evening, ladies and gentlemen. I'm glad to have this opportunity to assure you that Robbins Corporation takes your concerns very, very seriously."

"PR guy," Angel said to Sean, who nodded.

They listened while Fenway ran down the details of the development. The more Sean heard, the less he liked it. Fenway said over and over again that the corporation had gone through all the proper procedures to ensure that the development met state land use standards. To Sean that meant that they'd greased the right governmental palms.

A flash of color caught Sean's eye. The girl in the red blouse had raised her hand. Fenway continued his spiel until he reached its end, then pointed to her.

"Yes, ma'am?"

She lowered her hand. "What are you doing to address concerns about the amount of water this development will use?"

"We have taken that into serious consideration. The development is designed to conserve water in every possible way."

"Then why are you building a golf course?" someone shouted.

Fenway held up a finger, waiting for the chorus of agreement to subside. "The golf course will be maintained with gray water."

"*Whose* gray water?"

"Yeah, where you going to get the water?"

Fenway stepped forward until his toes were at the edge of the stage. "We will be using gray water from the Valle del Sol community."

"What about before the community is occupied?" shouted someone else.

A general rumbling broke out. Fenway waved his hand, trying to get the crowd to quiet down. At last they subsided.

"I assure you, we are being very careful about the water. We're working very closely with the Natural Resources Department." He glanced at one of the other two men waiting to talk, who nodded back.

"Toady," murmured Sean.

Angel glanced at him, then looked back at the stage. Sean pushed away from the wall and held up his hand.

"Yes—there in the back," Fenway said.

"Has there been an environmental impact study?" Sean said.

"I'm going to let Ben Lucero address that issue."

Someone else asked a question about traffic, and Fenway gave another non-answer. Sean finished his coffee and crumpled the paper cup. He was getting annoyed, and the meeting wasn't half over.

Fenway dodged a couple more questions, then handed the microphone back to Tom, the organizer. Tom thanked him for coming and introduced Ben Lucero. Sean watched Fenway disappear off the stage, and noted that he didn't come out into the auditorium. Probably escaping through a back door, into a cushy limo.

Lucero accepted the mike and stepped forward. He was older, with a liberal sprinkling of silver in his black hair, a white shirt, black-rimmed glasses, and a bolo necktie. Flashing a brief smile at the audience, he launched into a string of vague statements about the development. His voice was a politician's mind-numbing drone, the kind used in legislature sessions when the speaker wanted to slide things past his hearers. Sean concentrated on his words and found them lacking in meaningful content.

Lucero finished his spiel and called for questions. Sean raised his hand again.

"The environmental impact study?"

"Yes. That is underway."

"Isn't it a little late? The groundbreaking's a month away."

"The study will be completed before the end of September."

"Who's conducting it?"

Lucero became conveniently deaf and pointed to another raised hand. Sean stifled a temptation to repeat his question at a yell. The mood in the auditorium wasn't exactly content, and he didn't want to contribute to making it ugly.

After answering a few more questions, Lucero yielded the mike. Next to speak was Commissioner Jaramillo, whose speech was even more vague, though it was filled with lots of upbeat talk about benefits to the neighboring communities such as hospital access, a fire station, and other emergency services.

Sean noticed a grim look on Angel's face. After a couple of minutes he leaned closer to Angel and asked, "Who is this clown?"

"His family has a house in Pena Blanca," Angel said quietly. "That's how he could be on the County Commission, but he actually lives in Albuquerque most of the time. The Jaramillos used to own a lot of the land that's going into the development."

"Oh."

The sellouts, in other words. Sean watched Jaramillo go through his song and dance. The man didn't even attempt to answer questions, just handed the mike back to Evans and disappeared backstage like Fenway and Lucero.

"OK, thank you, Commissioner Jaramillo." Tom peered at a handful of papers he held. "Now, a couple of suggestions for those of you who want to make sure the Valle del Sol development doesn't degrade your quality of life. Call your representatives in the state legislature at the numbers on the handout that's going around now. There's also a clipboard going around. If you put down your name and phone number and your email, we'll contact you about future meetings and some demonstrations that are being organized. Questions? Yes, in the green shirt."

An older Indian man in the front of the room lowered his hand. "Are there any plans to file a lawsuit to stop this thing?"

"We're looking into it. In order to file a suit we have to have legal grounds for complaint. Right now we're not sure we've got a solid basis. I'd be especially interested to hear from those of you who are landowners in the area and anyone from Cochiti or Santo Domingo who'd like to be involved in a legal action. Please come and talk to me before you leave."

Sean glanced at Angel and Ruby, who looked worried and stubborn, respectively. They'd be staying to talk to Evans about the lawsuit, probably.

As the discussion continued, Sean slipped out of the auditorium and headed for a drinking fountain in the lobby. The girl in the rose skirt was there ahead of him. She looked up as he approached, and Sean smiled.

"No more of that coffee for me."

She nodded and laughed as she stepped aside. "It's pretty bad."

The sound of her laughter set something ringing inside him, and he had an impulse to follow it up. Before he could chicken out, he spoke.

"Can I buy you a better cup of coffee, after the meeting?"

Her dark eyes opened a little wider. "Oh. Um, I have to drive back to Albuquerque."

"Oh, I see." Sean nodded and smiled.

"But if it doesn't take too long, I'd like to."

"Great!" Sean thought madly through the coffee-type places nearby. "There's El Cañon. It's close, and they serve espresso. We could walk."

"OK."

"I'm Sean, by the way. Sean Carpenter."

She smiled and offered him a hand. "Rosa Marquez."

"Oh, so that's why the roses."

He glanced at her skirt as they shook hands. Her hand was small and soft, and her grip light.

"Yeah, I like roses. You'd think I'd be sick of them, but no."

Sean wanted to offer her some of the ones in his garden, but he thought that would probably be too much right now. Instead he started to shove his hands in his pockets, then realized he was still holding his crumpled coffee cup. He looked around for a trash can.

"So, um, you drove all the way up here from Albuquerque. How come?"

"Well, I'm very concerned about the river."

Sean glanced back at her sharply. "The river?"

"Yeah. You know the Rio Grande is endangered."

"Yeah, I know."

"Well, this could kill it."

A slight frown had creased her smooth brow as she gazed distantly at the wall behind Sean. She looked concerned, and a little helpless. Pretty much how he felt. She glanced up at him and gave a small, nervous laugh.

"I don't understand why the government people aren't getting upset about it."

"They've been bought off."

Rosa looked shocked. "You think so? That's horrible!"

"I've seen this kind of thing happen before. I was pretty active in environmental stuff in California."

"Is that where you're from?"

"No, actually I was born here. I had a job out in San Jose for a few years."

"But you came back."

He shrugged and glanced around. "This is home. New Mexico, I mean. I grew up in Dixon, not Santa Fe."

Rosa smiled. "I'm sorry, I just assumed you'd moved here from out of state."

"Can't blame you for that. Most of the Anglos in town did just that."

She stayed there smiling at him for a moment, then glanced toward the auditorium. "Well, I guess I'd better put my name down on that clipboard."

"Yeah, me too."

He started to follow her back in, but she paused, looking amused. "You forgot to get a drink."

"Oh. Guess I got distracted."

He grinned, then walked backward toward the drinking fountain, keeping his eyes on her all the way. She laughed again and went into the auditorium. Sean took a quick drink from the fountain, then pitched his crumpled cup into a trash can across the lobby, scoring a hit from fifteen feet away. Feeling a pleasant buzz of anticipation, he went back into the auditorium.

Tom Evans was still fielding questions, but the meeting was starting to break up. Small groups of people were talking together, and the noise level in the room had gone up again. The people trying to listen to Evans were crowding at the front of the room.

Sean searched for Rosa's red blouse. He spied it in a cluster of people waiting to sign the clipboard. Rather than join them right away and maybe make Rosa uncomfortable, he looked for the Madalenas. They were at the front of the room, looking at the displays. Sean made his way toward them.

Angel was staring at the big map, and Ruby was listening to Evans. She had a couple of brochures in her hand, looked like marketing materials. Maybe Fenway had brought them.

Sean joined Angel and exchanged a nod with him, then turned his attention to the map. He hadn't seen a detailed visual depiction of the development before, and he couldn't help whistling. It was impressive. Scary impressive.

His brain started calculating water use for the number of lots platted out. This was the kind of stuff he did at work, and though he'd need a computer for accurate numbers, he could make a ballpark guess. Assuming conservative two-person families, since the development was designed for retirees, the amount of water needed to support the community was still staggering, and that didn't include the golf course or other facilities. And this was just the first phase of a planned four phases.

"They're talking about building a city," Sean said aloud. "It's a city of ten thousand people, right in the middle of the Rio Grande Valley."

Angel was watching him. Sean met his gaze.

"The impact would be enormous."

Angel nodded, then looked back at the map. His gaze was sad, almost resigned. Sean had a strange desire to fight the development just for Angel's sake. He didn't like seeing his friend and teacher look so hurt.

Ruby was now talking to Tom Evans, who had given up on the microphone and was sitting on the edge of the stage, surrounded by a clot of mostly Indians. Sean glanced over his shoulder.

"I'm going to go find that clipboard."

Angel nodded again but didn't say anything. Sean left him and went in search of the errant clipboard, which was being passed around near the table with the coffee urns. Rosa was standing nearby, talking with a white guy in a Willie Nelson t-shirt, but she flashed Sean a smile as he came near. He smiled back, then waited his turn for the clipboard. When it was handed to him he glanced up the page and found Rosa's name. Her email was rosam@cybersky.net. It burned itself into his brain before he even registered it.

He wrote down his own name and contact information, then handed off the clipboard to Ruby, who had come up behind him, looking even more like a bull ready for a fight. Sean noticed that she wrote "Cochiti" next to her name.

She glanced up at him. "We're going to join the lawsuit, if it happens."

Sean nodded. "I would too, if I lived out there."

"Is this a friend of yours?"

Sean looked up to see Rosa standing before him. Ruby shot him a wry glance, then handed the clipboard to the next person waiting.

"Uh, yeah. Rosa Marquez, meet Ruby Madalena."

Rosa smiled. "Hi. We have the same name."

"No we don't," Ruby said flatly. "Yours is a flower, mine is a gem."

"But they both mean 'red,' too. It's nice to meet you."

Rosa held out her hand, and Ruby shook it, unbending a little. She gave Sean another sidelong glance.

"Are you coming for coffee with us?" Rosa asked.

Sean stifled a sigh. If Rosa felt more comfortable in a group, he could live with it.

"We're going over to El Cañon," he said.

Ruby's brows rose. "Oh. OK, sure. Be nice to get the taste of that crud out of my mouth."

Ruby gestured toward the urns, and Rosa laughed. Her laugh was like music, Sean thought.

"I'll go find Angel," Ruby said. "He's still staring at that map, I think."

She bustled away, leaving Sean alone with Rosa. "Angel's her brother," he said. "They're from Cochiti Pueblo."

"Ah. They must be concerned about Valle del Sol, then."

"More than concerned, and rightly so."

"It just amazes me that the politicos are willing to let this happen."

Sean gave a resigned shrug. "A lot of people don't bother to think beyond the short term."

"That amazes me, too."

Ruby came back with Angel, and they all headed out to the street. It was around nine, by now, and the evening was beginning to cool down. Rosa paused, looking up at the sky.

"So many stars. We only see a few in Albuquerque."

"You should see them from our place," Ruby said. "Too much light here in town."

"It must be beautiful." ·

"It is. But it won't be if they build that development with hundreds of street lights."

There was a tinge of resentment in Ruby's voice. Sean hoped Rosa wouldn't be put off by it. The two women walked side by side with the men behind them. Ruby was solid, no nonsense and looked like you couldn't move her if she didn't want to be moved. Rosa floated in her skirt and ruffled blouse like a flower on the breeze.

El Cañon was a café and bar, tucked into the northeast corner of the Hilton Hotel. There were a couple of old cowboys in there talking and drinking beer. The decor was Santa Fé nouveau, with careful rustic touches to give an exotic flavor for the tourists. Sean picked out a table by the window, far enough from the bar to give them a little privacy. He and Angel ordered espresso, and the girls ordered lattés.

"Do you think that meeting will do any good?" Angel asked.

Sean shrugged. "Maybe a couple of demonstrations will help, and maybe the phone calls will at least make the politicians tread carefully. That Tom seems to be a good organizer."

"But it isn't enough," Rosa said firmly. "It isn't enough to save the river."

Angel looked at her as if he hadn't noticed her before. Sean realized he'd forgotten to introduce them.

"Oh, sorry. Rosa, this is Angel Madalena, Ruby's brother. Angel, this is Rosa Marquez."

Rosa nodded, and smiled shyly. "Hi."

"Hello." Angel was still gazing at her as if trying to understand why she was there.

"She came up from Albuquerque for the meeting," Sean said.

"Why?"

Angel kept looking straight at Rosa. She stared right back at him, and her chin rose a little.

"I had a vision," she said.

Everyone was silent. Sean glanced at Angel, but Angel was looking at Ruby now. Had he told her about *La Guadalupana*, Sean wondered? And what the hell was Rosa having visions about?

"Let me guess," Sean said. "The Virgin of Guadalupe."

Ruby shot him a sharp glance that told him yes, Angel had talked to her. It must have been while they were in the truck, driving to dinner or to the meeting afterward.

Rosa gave Sean an ironic look. "No. Actually it was a clown. A ko-, *koshare*?"

She looked to Angel for confirmation, but Angel didn't move. Sean thought he'd stopped breathing for a minute, then Angel let out a long, slow exhalation.

"You saw a *koshare* and that's why you came to the meeting?"

"I saw a *koshare* following Kyle Robbins into a bank manager's office."

Sean felt like he'd missed something somewhere along the line. He opened his mouth to ask a question, then quickly closed it as the waiter came up with their coffees. It took a minute to sort out the drinks, and when the waiter left no one said anything. Ruby poured sugar into her latté and stirred it, then licked foam off the spoon.

"OK, wait," Sean said. "I'm confused. You saw Kyle Robbins

in a bank?"

Rosa shifted her gaze to him. "I work at a bank in Albuquerque. Kyle Robbins came in the other day—Monday—and went with the branch manager into his office. And I saw a *koshare* follow them in."

"How do you know it was a *koshare*?" Angel asked.

"I talked to a guy from Sandia Pueblo about it, a friend of my teacher's. I'm apprentice to a *curandera*."

"And this *koshare* inspired you to come to the meeting?"

"Well, partly. It was also the flute player." Rosa glanced from Angel to Sean. "I saw him up by the petroglyphs a couple of days before I saw the *koshare*. I know it sounds crazy, but you asked why I came here. That's why."

"Wait a minute—a flute player?" Sean asked incredulously.

"Yes. An old, hunchbacked flute player. Like Kokopelli," she added, sounding resigned. "He said a lot of stuff about the land-eaters ruining the world, and a serpent swallowing the river and how babies would starve."

Sean felt the last words like a smack in the face. He leaned back in his chair. "This is too weird."

"I'm not asking you to believe it," Rosa said, sounding defensive. "Let's talk about something else."

"That's not what I meant—"

"He's a flute player," Angel said, nodding toward Sean.

Rosa turned her head to stare at him. Sean felt his cheeks coloring.

"So are you! You're the master," he said to Angel, then glanced at Rosa. "Angel's teaching me to play the flute."

"And he's seen a vision, too," Angel said.

Great. Thanks, Angel.

Sean couldn't think of what to say, so he picked up his espresso and took too large a sip, scalding his tongue. He winced and set the cup down again, wishing he'd asked for a glass of water.

Rosa was staring at him, her eyes slightly narrowed in suspicion. If she had known Angel she'd know he wouldn't make fun of her, but she didn't know him. Sean cleared his throat and lowered his voice.

"The Virgin of Guadalupe."

Rosa frowned. "You saw her?"

"Up near the Santa Fe Reservoir. She said 'my children will die,' and then she disappeared. And no, I'm not Catholic."

"Santa Maria!" Rosa whispered.

"That's the one."

Rosa pressed her lips together, looking annoyed. She picked up her latté and sipped it.

"Tell her about the roses," Angel said.

Sean shot him a look, wishing he'd let the whole subject drop. This was all too strange, and Sean needed time to think about it and figure out how he felt.

"What roses?" Rosa asked.

He swallowed. "I have a couple of old rosebushes in my back yard. I haven't been watering them or anything. They were just bare, but after I saw—you, know, *her*—they started blooming."

Rosa's eyes widened. "May I see them?"

"Uh—sure, I guess. I mean, they're just rosebushes."

"I'd like to see them too," Angel said.

"And so would I," said Ruby, "but first I want to finish my coffee."

Sean picked up his own cup and took a more cautious sip. They all sat in silence, drinking their coffees and thinking. Sean couldn't decide if he was happy or perturbed that Rosa was having visions, too. Nice to know he wasn't completely nuts, but kind of frightening when he wondered about why it was happening.

It was also a little disappointing to think that he hadn't just met her by chance, that she was more than a pretty girl he wanted to get to know. While everything else was unclear, it seemed plain to him that he'd been supposed to meet her tonight.

When they'd finished their coffee, Sean asked for the check. Rosa opened her purse and pulled out a five, but he shook his head.

"I invited you."

"Let me pay for Ruby and Angel, then. I invited them."

"Why don't we all share?" Angel said gently, making Sean feel foolish for quibbling over the bill.

They paid and left, walking back toward Sweeney Center.

Everyone drove their own cars, Sean leading Rosa with the Madalenas coming up behind in Ruby's truck. He pulled into his garage, leaving room for the truck and Rosa's car in the driveway.

He led them through the living room to the glass doors that opened on the back yard. There was a floodlight, but he left it off, because the moon was rising over the Sangre de Cristos. He stepped out into the yard and walked toward the back wall, watching the golden half-moon peer over the edge of the mountains. The others followed him out.

He heard Rosa say, "Oh," then no more. They all stood and watched until the moon had cleared the mountains. Angel stepped up to one of the rosebushes, then, and cupped a blossom in one hand.

"These were bare last Sunday. I remember."

He knelt down and smelled the flower. Sean watched as Rosa slowly approached the other rosebush. She touched a red flower, then a yellow-and-red flaming one. She bent down to smell it.

"Beautiful," she said, straightening. "My roses only have a few blooms right now. It's too hot, they usually go dormant in August."

Sean bit back an offer to ask *Guadalupana* to give them a boost. Rosa probably wouldn't find it amusing.

"May I cut some for you?" he said instead.

She stared at him, her dark eyes and hair looking black in in the moonlight. She shook her head.

"I don't think you should cut them."

"Why not?" Angel said, standing up again.

Rosa looked at him. "They're a miracle."

"I think if he cut some to give to you, they'd grow even more flowers. You are a miracle, too."

Damn, that was a good line. Sean wished he'd thought of it.

Rosa turned back to the rosebush, her hands drifting over it, touching the petals of each bloom. Sean went into the house and found some scissors and an empty olive jar he'd set aside to recycle. He filled the jar with water and carried it back out to the yard, then set it down on the ground and started clipping roses, taking some from each bush, some of each color. When there was no more room in the jar he handed it to Rosa and looked back at the bushes.

"See? You can't even tell any are missing."

Rosa glanced at them, then buried her face in the roses she held, inhaling their fragrance. She looked up at Sean.

"Thank you."

"You're welcome."

He stood gazing at her, taking in her face, hair, eyes, her figure—slender, but with just enough curves. He was still attracted to her but he was confused, too. What now?

"I have a picture of *La Guadalupana* in my work room," Rosa said. "It's a photo of the image in the Basilica—do you know the one?"

Sean nodded. "I've been brushing up on my *Guadalupana* lore."

"Did she really look like that?" Rosa asked shyly.

"Yep. Blue robe with stars. Halo of light. The works."

She bent to smell the flowers again. "I wish I had seen her."

"I wish you had, too," Sean said before he could stop himself.

Her eyes flashed. "You should be honored!"

"I am. I'm tremendously honored. I'm also deeply confused. How come I get the lady you care about, and you get a clown?"

"Why don't we go inside?" Angel said, glancing at the fence that separated Sean's yard from his neighbor's.

"Yeah, good idea," Sean said. "I can make some more coffee if anyone wants it."

"I do," said Ruby.

The moon was well clear of the mountains now and had gone white and small. Sean led his guests back into the living room, then went to the kitchen to put away his scissors and put the coffee on. He came back out to find Ruby and Angel sitting on the couch and Rosa in the armchair. Sean pulled up a dining room chair and sat on it backwards, folding his arms over the top and resting his chin on them.

Rosa had set her jar of roses on the coffee table. She was leaning forward with her elbows on her knees, her hands clasped together. She looked uncomfortable.

"I wish I knew what the heck was going on, but I don't," Sean said.

"You've been called," Angel said. "Both of you. Called to

fight Valle del Sol."

"Yeah, but why?" Sean said. "Why me?"

"You must each have special gifts to bring to the fight." Angel looked from Sean to Rosa. "You said you were a *curandera*."

"An apprentice. I've only been studying a few years."

"But you are treating people."

"A little, yes." She blushed and gazed down at her hands.

"So you have medicine."

Rosa looked up at him sharply. "That's what the flute player said."

Angel nodded at this confirmation. "Medicine is important. It must be needed for the fight."

Sean stared at him. He meant medicine as the Indians used the word. Medicine was power, supernatural power. A medicine man was a seer as well as a healer. Sean didn't know much more than that.

"Do you have anything else that would help?" Angel asked Rosa.

"Um, I'm not sure. Maybe my job? Why else would I have seen the *koshare* at the bank?"

"He was following Robbins, you said."

She nodded. "Robbins and our branch manager. I think the manager's working on a deal to finance part of Valle del Sol."

Angel leaned back. "So you might have access to information about it."

Rosa looked troubled. "Maybe. It's not the sort of thing I usually hear about, except in a general way. I wouldn't want to spy, you know?"

"Not even to save the river?" Ruby said.

She'd been quiet until now, and everyone turned to look at her. She gazed steadily at Rosa.

"I don't know," Rosa said in a small voice.

"You may not need to," said Angel gently. He looked at Sean. "How about you? What are you bringing to this fight?"

Sean shrugged. "Search me. I don't have a clue why I got tapped."

Angel gazed at him thoughtfully. "The madonna came to you while you were playing. I think maybe your music is important."

"How the—excuse me, but I don't see how music can help us!"

Angel shook his head. "Music is important. It must be, or why would she have seen the flute player?"

"Maybe—" Rosa began, then hesitated as everyone looked at her. She cleared her throat. "Maybe your music could bring people together, set the tone for working together at a meeting or demonstration. I use gentle music when I'm treating clients, flute music sometimes. It's very soothing and peaceful."

"Peaceful is not going to win fights," Sean said.

"But she's right about it bringing people together," Angel said. "When everyone's listening to music, they're thinking together. We are going to need that if we want to win fights."

"That meeting tonight wasn't like that," Ruby pointed out. "Everyone was scattered in little groups."

Rosa nodded. Sean felt restless, so he went to the kitchen to check on the coffee. The last few drips were falling into the carafe. He put some mugs, sugar and milk and spoons on a tray along with the coffee.

Rosa smiled as she accepted a mug from him. "Thanks. I'm going to need this to keep awake on the drive home."

Sean handed her the milk, then glanced at his watch, surprised to see that it was almost eleven. "Maybe we should call it a night."

"In a little while," Angel said. "We should decide what to do next before we go."

"There's another PRD rally on the plaza on Sunday afternoon," Ruby said. She pulled a folded flyer out of her pocket and smoothed the page on the coffee table. "That Tom guy is leading it. Maybe we should call him. He said this is his number."

She stabbed a finger at the flyer. It was a lot like the one Sean had been given, the one advertising the meeting they'd been to that evening.

"Call him and say what?"

"Offer to play at the demonstration," Angel said. "I'll play if you will."

Sean looked at him. As far as he knew, Angel had never

performed publicly outside of Cochiti. Sean had only heard him play in private.

"You mean, play together?"

Angel appeared to consider the question, then nodded. "That would be best. Two together have a stronger voice."

"That would get people's attention," Rosa said. "People who might just walk past a demonstration would stop to hear you play."

Ruby nodded. "And then they'd hear Tom talk, and maybe get the message. I'll call Tom tomorrow."

"But what would we play?" Sean asked. He felt uncomfortable about performing. Usually he and Angel improvised together, and that was precarious enough even when they were alone.

Angel grinned. "The rain chant. Seemed to be pretty powerful for you."

"Oh, man."

Sean could just picture *Guadalupana* showing up in the back of a crowd of demonstrators. Actually, it would be a relief if somebody else saw her, too, but he doubted he'd get that lucky.

He reached for the coffee carafe and topped off his mug. He was unhappy about losing his Sunday lesson to this rally. He wanted time with Angel, alone. After all the strangeness of this week, he needed even more to clear his head and get centered.

Angel picked up Ruby's flyer. "The rally is at one o'clock. That would give us time to practice beforehand." He met Sean's gaze over the page, and Sean had a weird feeling Angel had read his thoughts.

"OK."

"Should I come?" Rosa asked. "To the rally? I don't know what I could do, but—"

"You would help direct the thoughts of the people there," Angel said. "All of us should be there."

Ruby nodded. "I'll get Luis to watch my space during the demonstration."

"How can we direct people's thoughts?" Rosa asked.

"By giving our attention to the speaker," Angel said. "Others will follow. When no one is speaking, we can talk with those around us, encourage them to think about the survival of the river."

"You know, Tom didn't mention the river at all," Ruby said. "He just talked about the neighbors, quality of life and that kind of thing."

"You're right," Rosa said. "He never said how the development would affect people lower on the Rio Grande. Nobody cares about us folks in *Rio Abajo*."

Rio Abajo. Downstream. Sean, who had grown up much farther upstream, was familiar with the attitudes represented by the terms *Rio Arriba* and *Rio Abajo*. The farther north people lived, the closer to the Rio Grande's headwaters, the more self-importance they had. There was even a county in northern New Mexico named *Rio Arriba*.

"Maybe that should be our first goal," Angel said. "To shift the conversation from the development to the survival of the river."

Rosa nodded. "There are a lot of people who don't care about developments, but would care very much about the river. I think Joe Pino at Sandia Pueblo would be interested. And there's Isleta, too."

"I'll make some phone calls," Ruby said, turning over the flyer. "You got a pen, Sean?"

He fetched her one from the kitchen, then picked up the coffee tray and carried it back. Rosa followed him, bringing her empty mug.

"Thanks for the coffee."

"You're welcome." Sean picked up the carafe and swirled its contents. "You want to take the rest with you for your drive?"

She smiled. "That would be great, if you don't mind."

"Not at all."

He put the coffee in the microwave to warm it up, and dug a seldom-used travel mug out of a cupboard. Rosa poured in the coffee and added milk, took a sip, then screwed down the lid.

"Mm. Good coffee, by the way."

"Oh, thanks. Get it at the health food store."

"I'll bring your mug back on Sunday."

She leaned against the counter and gazed at him. Sean gazed back, aware again of her attractiveness, and newly aware of her determination. There was a quiet strength in her that he hadn't seen at first, probably because he was distracted by her looks.

"I'm glad we met," he said.

"Me too. I think we can make a difference, the four of us." She nodded toward the living room.

"I hope so. Hate for perfectly good visions to go to waste."

Rosa laughed softly. Her smile stayed behind.

"This feels right," she said.

"Yeah?"

"When you're a *curandera* you pay a lot of attention to how things feel. On my way up here and at the meeting I just felt worried and frustrated. Now I feel like we have a direction."

Sean smiled back at her, glad to be included in the "we." For his part he still felt pretty confused, but he would just take things one step at a time. Playing the flute at Sunday's rally was enough to think about for now.

Angel poked his head around the doorway. "We're going to go. I'll see you Sunday morning, right?"

"Right."

"I'll call you after I talk to Tom," Ruby said. "What's your number?"

Sean fetched a notepad from the kitchen and a flurry of number exchanging followed. Ruby gave him her cell phone number, and Rosa wrote down her phone and the email address he'd already memorized. She wrote them again on another page and gave it to Ruby, glancing at Angel as she did so.

Sean followed Angel and Ruby to the door and said goodnight. Rosa was close behind, with her purse slung over one shoulder and the travel mug in her hand.

"Wait," Sean said, and hurried back to the living room. He returned with the olive jar. "Your roses."

"Oh, thank you. So beautiful."

She bent her head to smell them again. The gesture reminded Sean of an obeisance. She looked lovely and graceful, devout, bowing over the flowers, and it gave him a sudden pang of regret that he wasn't religious. She glanced up at him shyly.

"See you Sunday."

"Yeah. Drive carefully."

"Thanks, I will."

He watched from the doorway as she got into her car. Ruby's

truck had already rumbled halfway down the street. Sean waved as Rosa started the car and backed out. He watched until she turned the corner and was gone from sight, then went back in. The fragrance of roses seemed to linger in the house, and he smiled to himself as he finished cleaning up.

9

Saturday dawned warm and sunny, with still no sign of rain in sight. Cruz was booked up with clients all day, so after breakfast Rosa started a load of laundry, then put on jeans and a t-shirt and went to the Rio Grande Nature Center to walk in the *bosque*. She liked visiting the herb garden there, which featured many of the plants she was learning to use in *curanderismo*. Some of these she had growing in her own garden, like lavender, rue, rosemary, and *yerba buena* or mint. Others were a little more obscure.

There were yellow leaves scattered among the green overhead in the boughs of the cottonwoods, a hint of fall coming on even though it was still high summer. Rosa listened to the rustling of the leaves in the warm breeze as she strolled the path through the *bosque*. She reached the Nature Center itself, a concrete slab of a building, and went in to get a drink from the water fountain and leave a dollar in the donation box.

The place was full of kids, laughing and bouncing and making a lot of commotion which their parents struggled to keep to a dull roar. Rosa smiled, but she wasn't in the mood for their rowdiness, so she slipped into the observation room, hoping to find a little quiet.

The room doubled as a library, with bookcases all along the back wall and a glass wall on the north side that overlooked a large pond where dozens of wild birds gathered. They made their own kind of racket, picked up by microphones mounted on the outside of the building and broadcast over speakers in the room. Rosa sat on one of the sofas facing the window and watched the geese and ducks playing for a while. Pretty wood ducks, with their mandarin-looking bobtails, swam in and out of a tangle of bare branches that draped down to the water near the shore. A half-submerged log near the window was covered in sunbathing turtles.

All these creatures would be affected if the river died. She didn't know how the pond was maintained, but she assumed it

85

was fed by the Rio Grande, which wasn't far away.

Thinking over last night's meeting in Santa Fe and the people she'd met there—Sean and Ruby and Angel—she wondered for a moment if she was getting in over her head. She did want to help save the river. It was pretty plain that was why she'd been having visions. She'd been reassured to learn that Sean was having them too, though she had to admit she was a little jealous. She would have liked to see *La Guadalupana*.

That was an unworthy thought, she knew, and she shook her head to clear it. There was a reason for her seeing what she had seen, and for Sean seeing what he'd seen.

The door opened, letting in noise and a dad with two kids. Rosa got up to make room for them and went back outdoors, pausing to peer through a square observation window cut in a concrete wall that overlooked the pond. Unamplified, the birds' calls seemed quieter, just part of the flow of sound that was normal in the *bosque*.

To the west was a bridge over the irrigation ditch that paralleled the river. Rosa crossed it, peering down at another turtle the size of a dinner plate that was lying beneath the clear flow of water only a few inches deep.

Beyond the bridge was an asphalt path for joggers and bikers. Other people were out on the path, getting in their exercise before the day got too hot. Rosa walked along it toward the head of the nature trails that ran up and down the *bosque* beside the river.

She was north of the pond, now, and houses with big back yards could be seen on the east side of the ditch, some with horses and even a llama or two. When she reached the sign marking the trails, she turned west off the path and chose the north-running trail. It was a short walk, about a mile round-trip. Sometimes she brought a picnic and sat staring out at the river, but today she was just here for the walk.

Dry leaves crackled underfoot, sending up a faint, dusty, leftover autumn-leaf smell. The fire danger was high, and she knew other parts of the *bosque* were closed to the public at the moment. The mayor had closed them before the fourth of July, and had never reopened them. If things got really bad even the Nature Center's trails would be closed.

The path angled toward the river, then turned north again, close enough now that Rosa could glimpse the Rio through the trees and the underbrush. The water looked low. No surprise—it was usually low this time of year, with farmers irrigating their crops through the hot season. Still, it bothered her.

Rosa followed a path that turned off the trail and headed for the riverbank. She stood on the edge of the river, gazing westward. A high bluff rose on the far side of the river, with fancy houses overlooking the *bosque*. Beyond it the volcano cliffs marched in the distance. Rosa thought about the petroglyphs and the flute player, then glanced around, worried she might see him again.

Nothing but the river trickling by. It was so low that more of the riverbed was taken up with sandbars than with water. The mighty Rio Grande ran in trickles that snaked among the sandbars. She didn't think it looked more than a couple of feet deep anywhere.

Feeling a sudden urge to get wet, Rosa looked down at the bank beneath her feet. A tangle of tree roots stretched toward the water below. It was muddy, but she thought she could get back up again. So what if she got dirty. It was mother earth, right?

She sat down and took off her sneakers and socks, tucking them under a bush a little way off the path. Sitting on the bank and dangling her legs down, she peered into the eddy below, looking for anything that might hurt her if she stepped on it. The water was a pale muddy brown like all of the Rio, obscuring her view of the bottom, but she knew it was sandy, not rocky. Glass was always a possibility but she doubted there'd be any here. Most of the people who used these trails were pretty responsible, and folks from the Nature Center monitored them, so the kind of people who liked throwing bottles into the river tended to go to other places.

A sandbar was only a couple of steps away. Rosa pushed off the bank and jumped for it, landing short with a splash in the eddy. Mud sucked at her feet and she flailed her arms to keep from toppling, then slogged her way up onto the sandbar.

She'd forgotten to roll up her jeans, and now they were muddy and wet. She reached down and rolled them up anyway, then strolled out toward the middle of the river. A small rivulet separated the sandbar from another, larger one. Two ducks startled up into the air as she hopped over it. She watched them fly away south, then kept walking.

About a third of the way across the riverbed she reached a larger, faster-running stream. Peering across the maze of sand and water, she decided this was probably the main channel of the river. It actually looked like it might be three or four feet deep in the middle, and she decided not to risk crossing it. Instead she strolled north up the sandbar until she reached its tip. Here there was a shallow place where the water eddied indecisively before splitting itself to go around the bar.

Rosa stepped into it, letting the cool brown water run over her feet and swirl around her ankles. She closed her eyes and inhaled, listening to the murmur of the river, the calls of water birds, the breeze in the cottonwoods on the shore. Beneath it all was the constant hum of the city, the whoosh of traffic, the throb of the airport to the south. Rosa acknowledged those sounds, then let go of them, turning her attention to the river, to the gentle lapping of the water on the sand, to its near-silent gliding and the space it created in the air between the river banks—a breathless space, a holy space.

This water wasn't just important, she realized. It was sacred. The Rio Grande meant the difference between life and death for those who lived along it. For centuries it had meant this, long before the Spanish colonists had brought *La Conquistadora* up to Santa Fe. Indians had lived along the Rio Grande forever, and Rosa knew they considered it sacred.

Every day they prayed for rain, she remembered hearing Joe Pino say. Rosa prayed for rain, too, now. She prayed for the river to thrive, to rise above the small flow that she could easily step across, to fill its banks from side to side and feed the thirsty roots of the *bosque*.

In her mind she saw a circle of Indian men dressed in black loincloths, their faces painted, feathers braided into their long, black hair. They were standing in the river as she was, bending down to cup handfuls of water and then raising them to the sky. They were singing, a low, rhythmic, plaintive song whose words had no meaning for her but flowed as smoothly and gently as the river itself.

One by one the men knelt in the water and lowered themselves to let it flow over them, a curious quasi-baptism. They didn't rise again, but lay turtle-like in the stream, making Rosa wonder how they were breathing. The last one standing turned to look over his shoulder directly at Rosa, and she gasped as she realized it was Angel. He faced away again, knelt down, and disappeared beneath the muddy water.

Rosa's eyes flew open. She was standing alone in the river, sunshine reflecting from the water in blinding white brightness. She blinked a few times in confusion.

It hadn't been a vision, exactly. She'd started out imagining it, but she'd never meant to picture Angel. Had her subconscious taken a hand?

A shriek of childish laughter broke her reflections. Glancing downstream, she saw three kids hopping from sandbar to sandbar in the middle of the river. Nearby a small, yellow, inflatable raft lay abandoned on one of the bars.

She looked across to the western shore, trying to recapture the feeling she'd had a moment before, but it was lost. The mud was starting to suck at her feet. You could get caught in quicksand here if you weren't careful. She pulled herself free of the riverbed and returned across the sandbars to where she'd left the trail.

The bank looked higher from this side. Rosa managed to scramble up it by hanging onto roots that dangled in the water. She got mud up to her elbows, and all over her jeans. Her feet were so caked with mud she didn't want to put her shoes back on. She sat on the river bank, looking out over the Rio while she absently rubbed the dirt from her feet.

Tradition had a lot to do with her feelings about the Rio Grande. Her people had relied on it for centuries. So had the Indians. The white men...not so long, less than two centuries. New Mexico hadn't become a part of the U.S. until 1846. It hadn't become a state until 1912.

So it shouldn't surprise her that white people didn't care so much about saving the river. They just wanted to use it to make their golf courses, and didn't care what happened to the people downstream.

That wasn't entirely fair, she knew. There were Anglos who

did care. Tom Evans cared, obviously. Sean cared, and she thought he probably would have cared even if he hadn't had the vision.

She felt a stab of envy. Part of her wanted to doubt that he had actually seen *La Guadalupana*, had been honored by the blessed Virgin's appearance. Why him? Why not herself?

Rosa shook her head. If she wasn't careful she'd drag herself down with *envidiar*. Maybe she should talk to Cruz about it.

She gazed out over the riverbed, feeling an echo of the hush she'd sensed while standing in the middle of the river. If that feeling could be captured—that quiet, sacred feeling—and given to everyone in the city, *that* might make them care.

She had no idea how to do that. All she could do was pray for it to happen, and for guidance.

Her feet were dry now, and she'd rubbed most of the dirt off them. She put on her shoes and stood up, looking out at the river and saying a silent farewell.

She was starving by the time she got home, and very thirsty. She poured a tall glass of water and chugged it, then made herself a sandwich and refilled her glass with iced tea, emptying her sun tea jar. She took the time to wash the jar and fill it with fresh water and tea bags, then set it out on her back steps to let the sun brew the tea.

There was a Siberian elm tree in the little fenced back yard—a junk tree, Cruz called it, but at least it gave some shade. Rosa had a lawn chair under it with a little side table beside it, and she sat there to eat her lunch, gazing at her garden. The fence was waist high and made of chain-link. Rosa had put up taller bamboo screens near the house on both sides, to give herself and the neighbors a little more privacy. The back fence, which faced an alley, she'd left alone, and had planted tomatoes and basil along it.

She had a couple of rosebushes back there, too. Roses liked heat, but they were looking a little bedraggled in the relentless August sunshine. She couldn't help comparing them with the ones in Sean's garden in Santa Fe.

Well, it was cooler up there, and wetter.

But Sean said he hadn't watered his roses at all. Rosa watered hers faithfully every day, with the soaker hose that ran all along the back fence and fed all those plants.

While she was thinking about it, she got up and turned on the hose, then went to check on the bird bath by the statue of *La Guadalupana* on the east side of the yard. She had put up privacy screens here, and had planted rosebushes to either side of the statue, and rosemary plants nearby. She kept the bird bath here because she felt the Virgin would like to have birds singing around her. Rosa added fresh water to the bath, and threw a scoop of bird seed into a little feeder she had hanging from another elm tree that leaned over the fence.

She smiled and stepped back. It felt good to putter in her garden. She had let herself get stressed this week, worried over the visions and the river. If she let herself get out of balance she wouldn't be any good to anyone, she knew.

She took her dishes in the house, then returned with her garden shears and a basket and trimmed the rosemary, which had a tendency to sprawl. She would dry the trimmings and put them up for cooking, maybe share some with friends who didn't have gardens. Her mother liked rosemary, and so did Gerry at the bank.

The phone rang, calling her back to the mundane world. Rosa turned off the hose, then carried her basket inside and left it in the kitchen as she went to the living room to answer the phone.

"Rosa? It's Sean Carpenter."

"Oh. Hi."

"Um, I was wondering if you'd like to have dinner with me after the rally tomorrow."

Rosa pressed her lips together. She wasn't sure if she wanted to complicate the situation with Sean.

"I mean, since our coffee kind of turned into a planning meeting last night," he added, laughing a little.

"I don't know. I have to be at work Monday morning."

"We could make it an early dinner. I doubt things will go much past four."

Rosa's gaze fell on the jar of roses in front of her on the coffee table. They were even more stunning in daylight—red, yellow, pink, white. She reached out and touched one, its petals velvety soft against her fingertips.

"I guess that would be all right. I can't stay late, though."

"Sure, sure. Do you like Italian?"

"Yeah."

"I'll make us a reservation at Pranzo. Five o'clock sound good?"

"OK."

"Great! Thanks, Rosa. I'm looking forward to it."

She smiled. He was nice, and good looking in a slightly nerdy way. She'd been interested in him when they'd met at the meeting. She didn't know why she felt hesitant now.

"I am too," she said, mostly because she knew it would please him.

She thought about telling him how she'd seen Angel in the river, then decided against it. It didn't feel right to mention that over the phone. She could tell him tomorrow. It would give them something to talk about at dinner.

Should she tell Angel about it? Her instinct was not to. She felt shy even thinking about talking to Angel.

"So I'll see you on the plaza tomorrow," she said. "One o'clock, right?"

"Right. See you then."

"Bye."

She put the phone down and sat looking at the roses. She'd have to call her mother and let her know she wouldn't be there for Sunday dinner. Most weeks the whole family got together, but Mama would understand when Rosa explained why she was going up to Santa Fe.

Rosa got up and fetched Sean's travel mug from the dish drain in the kitchen and put it on the little table by the front door so she'd remember to take it tomorrow. The roses deserved a better container than an old jar, so she took them to the kitchen and put them in a vase. Even though the vase was bigger than the jar there were so many roses that they were still crowded, so she pulled out a few and arranged them in a smaller vase to put on the altar in her workroom.

Stepping into the room, she paused to drink in the peaceful feeling there and let go of the tension she felt. She had worked hard to make this room a peaceful place, and Cruz had taught her to shift her mental state whenever she came in, leaving the outside world behind.

She set the roses on the altar against the east wall. Muted sunlight came in the window beside it through the decals of a cloudy sky she'd put on the glass for privacy. Lace curtains hung over it, another layer of protection from the world outside. A hanging planter on the far side of the window held one of those plants that everyone called a philodendron but wasn't, its green leaves dangling in long coils from the terra cotta pot.

Rosa lit a tall candle with *La Guadalupana*'s picture on the glass and set it beside the roses. Every rose was a miracle, she thought, smiling, but these were truly remarkable. Even if she hadn't believed Sean about them, she had to believe Angel. His reaction when he'd seen them had been striking, especially for an Indian. Most Indians she'd been around were pretty guarded with their emotions. They would laugh and kid around, but the things that mattered deeply they kept to themselves.

And these roses mattered deeply, to Rosa as well. They were a brush with the miracle Sean had seen, an echo of *La Guadalupana's* blessing. Rosa leaned forward to smell them. Their scent was as rich as it had been last night, maybe richer in the warm midday air. It gave her a feeling of peace, a feeling of quiet bliss, a little like the river.

Rosa opened her eyes. Maybe the roses were a way to take that feeling to other people.

A tingle flowed through her. These were miracle roses. Sean had commented on how many flowers the bushes bore, how they seemed even to be growing. Maybe there were enough to bring some to the demonstration and hand them out to people?

It would be a way of getting their attention, a different way than just talking over a microphone. Like the flute music Sean and Angel were going to contribute.

Rosa felt a growing excitement. She wanted to share the idea with Sean, but she felt hesitant to call him. Calling him on the phone was personal, and she wasn't sure she was ready to take that step.

Getting up, she made a little bow of thanks to the Virgin, then went out in the living room to find her purse. She dug inside it for the slip of paper with the Madalenas' phone number. Yes, Sean had written his number on the bottom of the page, and also his email address.

Rosa carried the paper to her desk and turned on her computer. She opened her email program and started to type a new message, smiling as she did so.

"Hey Sean — I had an idea."

10

Sean played with his eyes closed, floating on the music like an eagle on the wind. His flute and Angel's blended into one voice as the rain chant circled again and again.

It had taken him a little while to remember it at first, because he hadn't played it since last Sunday, at the reservoir. He'd been afraid to. He hadn't wanted to conjure any more apparitions.

But the tune rolled through him easily, now. He could play it without thinking about it, which left him free to listen more closely to Angel and notice some of the subtler nuances. A flip of a grace note here, a falling off of a held tone there. Each said something, added feeling to the chant.

Finally Angel slowed the last phrase ever so slightly, and they ended together on a held note that fell away into breathless silence. Sean opened his eyes and saw Angel nodding.

"Good. I think we're ready to play it for people."

Sean glanced at his watch. No time for a full lesson today. He'd fixed sandwiches ahead of time for lunch, so they could be back in the plaza before one.

"Shall we eat?"

"OK."

Sean brought out the sandwiches and a couple of sodas, and sat with Angel at the dining table. Angel stared out the window at the rosebushes.

"Man, those are incredible."

"Rosa suggested we cut a bunch and hand them out today."

Angel looked at Sean in surprise. "Cut them?"

"You can't even see where I cut flowers on Friday night. In fact I think there are even more now."

Angel gazed at the bushes again. "Miracle roses."

"She thinks it would get more people to pay attention."

"It might."

Sean took a bite of his sandwich and watched Angel, who seemed to be far away, thinking. Angel did that a lot. He would forget completely about his lunch, sometimes.

Sean took a sip of soda. "How do you feel about *La Guadalupana*? I mean, does she mean a lot to you?"

Angel shrugged. "Not especially. There are other images that mean more. *La Guadalupana's* around, but she's not as big a deal for us as she is for the Mexicans."

"She's pretty popular with the Central American Indians."

"Yeah, but that's not us."

Sean wondered what images meant more. Some other version of the Virgin? Probably not. He couldn't picture Indians getting very enthusiastic about *La Conquistadora*, for example. Catholicism had been imposed on them, and though it was part of their culture now, he suspected the older Pueblo ways were more important.

Angel finished his sandwich and took a long pull at his soda. "You know, Cochiti's gone mainstream, pretty much. A lot of the older traditions have gone by the wayside. Everyone's got cable TV and a phone nowadays. Half of us don't live at the pueblo any more."

Sean nodded. Angel was doing the mind reading thing again.

"You still have dances, though, right?"

"Yeah."

"I'd like to come to one some time."

Angel gave him a curious look. "Yeah? You just missed the big one. San Buenaventura feast day, in July. But there are others. I can let you know if you like."

"I would like, yes."

"You should come for all day, though, not just to watch for half an hour."

"OK."

"I mean, if you really want to understand the dance."

"I do."

Angel smiled, looking pleased in his mild way. He finished his soda and stood up.

"We should probably get going if we're going to cut those roses."

Sean cleared away their lunch plates and found a couple of plastic buckets to hold the flowers. He put some water in each of them and got two pairs of scissors, then headed out to the back yard. He gave a bucket and scissors to Angel, and they each took on one rosebush.

"We might have to pull thorns off of them."

"I don't see any thorns," Angel said.

It was true. The roses had straight stems and no thorns to speak of. It was as if they'd been cultured specifically to be given out as cut flowers. Sean was a little creeped out by this, but he decided to ignore the implications.

He was cutting from the pink and white bush. He tried to take flowers evenly from all around it, so it wouldn't look denuded. When he'd filled the bucket with as many flowers as it would hold, he stepped back to look at the bush.

"Jesus."

"No. Mary."

Angel met his gaze, smiling slightly. His bucket was full, too, and his rosebush was still covered with flowers. Both of them were. They looked perhaps slightly less dense than before, but that was all. Sean shook his head in amazement, then peered into his bush, trying to see where he'd clipped flowers. There had to be thirty or so in his bucket.

"What, are they growing new ones from the cut stems? Is this a hydra rosebush?"

Angel laughed softly. "I don't know, but I know my mom would kill for a bush like this."

"Too bad I'm not in the flower business. I'd clean up."

They carried the buckets back in the house. Sean locked up, then they took their flutes and the roses and piled into Ruby's truck. The heady scent of the roses filled the cab, even with the windows open.

Sean thought idly about his joke about selling them. Miracle roses. Flowers that rejuvenated when you cut them. If he set up a booth on the plaza he could make a lot of money, but he had a feeling the bushes wouldn't put out like this for commercial purposes.

Rosa's idea had plainly been approved by *Guadalupana*. Those two really ought to get together.

The plaza was hopping, and Tom and his crew were already in the gazebo, setting up. Angel dropped Sean on the corner with the two buckets of roses and went off to park the truck. Sean made his way to Ruby's space, and found Rosa there talking with Ruby. She was wearing a summer dress, blue with white and yellow flowers all over, and sandals again. Sean's travel mug dangled from her hand. She turned and brightened with a smile when she caught sight of the roses.

"Oh, good, you got my email! Wow, they're beautiful! I hope you didn't wipe out the bushes."

"Not even. You ought to see them. We could have cut twice this many."

"Wow!"

Rosa leaned closer to smell the flowers, and Sean's pulse increased at her nearness. She straightened up again and offered to take one of the buckets off his hands, holding out Sean's mug.

"Here, trade you."

"Mmm. I could just hold these all day."

Sean looked at her dreamy face above the red and yellow flowers and couldn't help grinning. "You look beautiful."

She gave him a startled glance, then a fleeting, self-conscious smile. "Thanks."

She took a step away, just a shift of her feet, and looked down at Ruby's pottery. Sean mentally kicked himself. Too fast, damn it! He'd said it without thinking.

"Ruby, you have a lot of turtles," Rosa said.

"Uh-huh. I'm a member of the Turtle Clan."

"You are? Um, is Angel in the same clan?"

The question seemed casual, but her tone had an underlying intensity that caught Sean's attention. He watched Rosa set down her roses and crouch to pick up a pottery turtle.

"Yes, we're both Turtle Clan. Turtles bring good luck."

Rosa smiled. "To anyone, or just to members of the clan?"

"Well, my turtles are lucky for anyone, of course."

"Of course."

Rosa turned the turtle figure around in her hands. It was white, with black designs and touches of earthy red-orange.

"I saw some turtles yesterday, at the Nature Center."

Sean watched her face, which had a faraway look, as if she was thinking of something else. She came back after a moment, and held the turtle out to Ruby.

"I'd like to buy this one. Will you save it for me?"

Ruby wrapped the turtle up in newspaper, wrote Rosa's name on it with a marker, and set it aside in her supply box. Rosa picked up her bucket of roses and stood up, just as Angel came up to join them. He handed Sean his flute.

"It's almost one. Guess we should go over there."

"Right. Um, Ruby, can I leave this with you?" Sean gestured with the mug.

"Sure." Ruby held out a hand for the mug, and stashed it in one of her crates. "I'll be there in a minute."

Sean, Angel, and Rosa crossed the street to the gazebo, where Tom was talking with the redhead, who held a posterboard sign that said "WHERE WILL THE WATER COME FROM?" Other signs were stacked against the gazebo steps. Tom smiled and reached out a hand to Angel.

"Glad you could make it. Thanks again for offering the music. I think it's a wonderful idea." His glance shifted to Sean, then landed on Rosa. "Pretty flowers."

"We thought we could hand them out, if that's OK," Rosa said.

Tom faced her and a slight frown creased his brow. "You're not from a religious group are you?"

"No, no," Sean said. "They're from my back yard."

Tom glanced at him with a raised eyebrow. Rosa took a step closer.

"We just want to give them to people passing through the plaza," she said. "It might get a few more of them to stop and listen."

"Yeah, OK. They're visual, and that's good because the TV stations are here."

Tom nodded toward the center of the plaza, where two news crews were milling around with their equipment by the Civil War memorial. A lot of other people were in the plaza, some eating takeout lunches on the benches, some just strolling through, a handful of kids playing hacky sack on one corner. As Sean watched, a police squad car pulled around the corner and cruised to a stop just before the planters that blocked off Palace Avenue to vehicle traffic. Two cops got out and sidled over to the gazebo.

"What's going on here, folks?" said one, a lean Anglo with

his hair in a buzz cut. "Putting on a show?"

"A rally to raise awareness about land development issues," said Tom. "We have a permit."

"Let's see it."

Tom picked up a clipboard from the gazebo steps and leafed through the papers on it. He pulled one out and showed it to the cop.

"Here you go."

The Anglo cop perused the paper while the other cop, an Hispanic, looked Rosa up and down. She appeared not to notice, and Sean took a deep breath to quell the urge to step between them.

"This is just for a meeting," said the Anglo cop, glancing at Angel, "not for a musical performance."

"The music is just an introduction," said Tom. "Just a couple of minutes, before we start talking."

The cop shook his head. "Sorry, it's too disruptive. You'll have to leave out the music."

"It'll be very quiet," Tom said. "It's Native American flute music, it's appropriate for the plaza."

"Maybe, but your permit doesn't cover music."

"Shall I ask Nelson to step over here?" Sean asked Tom, nodding his head toward the news crews and the well-known reporter waiting with them. "He might find this interesting."

The cop shot him a dirty look, then handed the permit back to Tom. "If it's just a couple of minutes we'll let it pass, but if you guys get too rowdy you'll have to disperse."

Tom gave him big, friendly smile. "We won't be rowdy. Thanks."

The cops retreated to their squad car and leaned against the fender, glowering at Tom and his people. Sean hid a smile.

Tom grimaced as he returned the paper to his clipboard. "Every time we have a rally here some cop comes and bugs us about our permit."

"Maybe they do that to everyone who uses the gazebo," Sean said.

"No, they don't," Ruby said, joining them. "I see people using it all the time, and no cops bother them."

Sean met Tom's surprised gaze. "You're being harassed."

Tom shrugged.

Sean gave his bucket of roses to Ruby and she and Rosa went to stand closer to the middle of the plaza, past Tom's protestors with their signs. Sean drifted that way to watch. Rosa offered a rose to a silver-haired woman passing by with her husband.

"A rose for the Rio?" she said, smiling.

The woman stopped and accepted the flower. "For what?"

"For the Rio Grande. The river's endangered, and we're going to talk about ways to save it."

"Here's some information," added the redhead from Tom's crew, hastening up to give the woman a flyer.

"Oh. Thanks." The woman glanced at the flyer, then at the redhead's sign. Turning away a little, she smelled her rose and smiled at Rosa. "Thanks," she said with more warmth, and walked on.

Rosa looked at the redhead, who shrugged and said, "Can't hurt."

Sean wasn't so sure. People stopped listening if you got too pushy. He thought Rosa had been doing fine, but maybe he was biased.

One of the reporters strolled up to Rosa. He was dressed for summer in slacks and a short sleeved sport shirt, and had a button in his ear and a power pack at the back of his waist.

"Hi there, I'm Greg Garza. You with the rally?"

Rosa smiled. "Yeah."

"Pretty roses."

"We're handing them out. Roses for the Rio."

Garza's brows rose. "Oh? I thought this was about development."

"It is. The Valle del Sol development is threatening the Rio Grande."

"Oh, I see." Garza nodded, then smiled. "Would you mind me asking you a few questions on camera?"

Rosa glanced over her shoulder toward the gazebo. The redhead had gone back there and was talking with Tom.

"Well, I'm not really one of the organizers. I'm just here to help."

Garza smiled. "We'll be talking to them, too, but I'd like to get a shot of you with the flowers."

Rosa glanced at Sean, eyes a little wide. He smiled to encourage her.

"OK, I guess."

Garza turned toward his crew and waved a hand. "Leo. Over here."

Sean watched a cameraman come over and set up to tape the impromptu interview. Before they began, he heard his name called from the gazebo. He glanced that way and saw Angel beckoning to him. Throwing Rosa an apologetic smile, he hurried over.

"We'll be starting in a few minutes," Angel said. "We should warm up a little."

"Yeah, OK."

Sean looked back toward Rosa and the news guys. Ruby was standing with them now, and Garza was talking with both women while the camera guy fiddled with his lens.

Sean took his flute from under his arm and blew some long notes with Angel, closing his eyes and focusing on the sound, letting everything else go. After a while Angel stopped, and Sean opened his eyes.

"We're ready for you guys," Tom said. "We have to keep it short, I'm afraid. Those cops are still here."

Sean glanced toward the squad car. The Anglo cop was still leaning against it. The other one wasn't around.

"We'll just play twice through," Angel said, and Sean nodded.

"You want me to introduce you?" Tom asked.

Sean shrugged and looked at Angel. Angel shook his head.

"That isn't necessary. Let's just start with the music, to set the mood."

"OK. You can stand about as far from the mike as you are from me now, and it should pick you both up."

Tom looked from Angel to Sean, gave a nod, then waved them toward the gazebo. All the protest signs had been picked up now, held by various familiar-looking people who were milling near the gazebo. The redhead flashed Sean a smile as he followed Angel up the steps to the stage.

They stood in front of the mike together, facing the plaza. The group of protestors seemed bigger from up here. Sean noticed a few people around the edge of the crowd holding roses. He looked for Rosa and saw her near the middle of the plaza, handing a rose to a young Hispanic woman with a baby stroller. The news crews had their cameras pointed at the stage now.

Sean looked away from that distraction, and instead watched Angel. When Angel raised his flute and took a deep breath, he followed. The first note came out strong and resonant, sounding like one flute, and Sean knew it would be a good play. He closed his eyes again, enjoying the music for its own sake, letting the rain chant ripple over him, around him and through him. He wanted to play it more than twice, but Angel slowed the final notes on the second time through, and they held the last note a long time, resonances swelling and ebbing and finally fading.

A smattering of applause made Sean open his eyes. He'd just played his first public performance, he realized with mild surprise. Hadn't planned on that.

Tom joined them on the stage, applauding against a sheet of paper in one hand. Angel and Sean stepped back and let him have the mike.

"Thank you, Angel and Sean, for that beautiful introduction. Welcome, everyone, and thanks for taking a moment out of this fine Sunday afternoon to stop and listen."

Tom went on into his spiel, much like what Sean had heard him say before on the plaza and at the meeting at Sweeney. He and Angel quietly left the stage and drifted into the crowd. They came across Ruby, who was handing out roses right and left. Sean glanced at her bucket and had a suspicion that the dang flowers were multiplying. She still had a lot left.

"Roses for the Rio," she said cheerily, giving flowers to a gaggle of teenage girls. "Come and listen, you can help save the river."

One of the girls broke the stem off her rose and tucked it behind her ear. Her friends giggled. They moved away, but then paused and listened to Tom for a minute before wandering off.

Even that little shift could make a difference, Sean realized, watching them play with the roses. Next time they heard about this issue, on the news or wherever, they might pay a little more attention. The time after that they might start talking to their friends and family about it. Later on they might even get involved.

Angel came up next to him. "I'm going to go watch Ruby's space," he said. "Do you want me to keep your flute over there?"

"Yeah. Thanks."

Sean handed Angel his flute and watched him walk over to the Palace, disappearing into the constant crowd of tourists milling along the *portal.* Here and there a shopper carried a rose.

Rosa was still busy handing out flowers. Deciding not to bother her, Sean moved a little closer to the gazebo and listened to Tom. The redhead from Tom's crew sidled up to him.

"Your music was beautiful," she said quietly.

"Thanks."

"What's this 'roses for the Rio' stuff?"

"Oh—we just thought it would be a way to get more people's attention."

"Makes it sound like we're about the river."

"We are, aren't we? I mean, water is the biggest concern."

She tilted her head and gave him a quizzical look. "I don't know about that."

Sean glanced up at the sign she was holding—"WHERE WILL THE WATER COME FROM?"—and grinned. She blushed, her freckles darkening.

"OK, yeah, the water's a big part of it, but it's not the *only* issue."

"True."

She faced the gazebo again, seeming absorbed in what Tom was saying. Sean did the same.

"I'm Pam, by the way," she said after a minute. "Pam Weston."

"Sean Carpenter."

"Hi." She flashed him a smile, then returned her attention to Tom.

Sean listened for a while, thinking about the focus of the campaign. To him it made sense to make it about the river. Lots of people identified with the Rio Grande, whereas the scrap of land near Pena Blanca mattered mostly to the immediate neighbors, Cochiti and Santo Domingo Pueblos. Make it about the Rio, though, and you get people from Albuquerque interested. You get people all the way down to El Paso interested.

Tom was a good speaker and showed no signs of flagging even though he'd been at it for more than an hour. He paused to answer the occasional question from someone in the crowd, and went on smoothly from there into the points he kept emphasizing—the impact on the pueblos, the negative effects of large-scale development, and of course, the water issue.

Sean wandered off to buy a soda from the fajita cart on a corner of the plaza. He returned and sat on the flagstone bench that circled the Civil War memorial, leaning his back against the short wrought-iron fence that kept kids and vandals away from the memorial itself. One of the plaques on its sides had been vandalized in the 70s, causing a great hullabaloo. The word "savage" had been chiseled away from a plaque honoring the heroes who defended New Mexico from "savage Indians."

Interesting debates had followed. No one really wanted to defend the attitude represented by the language on the plaque, but there was an interest in preserving the history it represented, warts and all. Sean had been just a kid when it had happened, but he remembered his mom being upset about it. He hadn't understood why until years later.

Rosa came over and sat down beside him, setting her bucket of roses on the ground between them. Sean glanced at the flowers.

"How many of those have you given away?"

Rosa met his gaze. "Um, a lot."

"That's what I thought."

Her lips curved in a secret smile. "Miracle roses," she said softly.

Sean nodded and looked toward the gazebo, crossing his arms. Miracles creeped him out.

"How did the TV interview go?" he asked.

"Oh, fine I guess. I wasn't expecting it."

"Didn't surprise me."

She glanced up at him, gave him a shy half-smile, and looked away. A woman wearing a gaucho hat and a lot of turquoise heishi necklaces over a black sleeveless blouse paused to look at the roses.

"What pretty flowers!"

Rosa hopped up and handed her one. "A rose for the Rio."

She was off again, passing out more roses to people coming through the plaza. Sean watched her move among them, her blue dress looking cool despite the increasing warmth of the day. He was starting to feel hot, himself. He'd put on a good shirt since he was taking Rosa to dinner, but it was long-sleeved and kind of warm.

He got up and made his way to the Palace, thinking to find a bit of shade. The sun was headed west now, and the *portal's* deep shadow offered some relief from the heat, though the bodies crowded inside didn't help. Sean went to Ruby's space and crouched at the corner of her blanket, waiting for a chance to talk to Angel, who was wrapping a piece of pottery in bubble wrap. Two others sat in front of him, their shapes already obscured by layers of plastic bubbles. Sean waited until he had finished the transaction and the customer was strolling away with her purchases in a big shopping bag.

"Business is good?"

Angel nodded and waved a hand over the dozen or so pieces on the front of the blanket. "This is all that's left."

"Excellent."

"Had a couple of people ask if we had a CD."

Sean gazed at him with interest. "No kidding?"

Angel nodded. Sean couldn't tell from his face whether he was pleased by the request, but since he'd mentioned it he must be flattered at least.

"You should record one. It worked for Carlos Nakai."

"Hm. But Carlos Nakai is out there for people who want flute music."

"Yours is different. There's room for more than one flute player on the market."

Angel smiled and his eyes crinkled with amusement. "There's probably already a dozen on the market."

"So what?"

"I don't know if I want to tie my music down like that."

Sean dropped the subject, knowing he'd lose that argument. Angel did what Angel wanted to do, and despite his mild temper, he could be as hard to move as a boulder.

A family of tourists in shorts and matching lime green t-shirts stopped to admire Ruby's pottery. Sean got out of the way, watching with slight anxiety as one of the kids reached for an owl figurine. Angel leaned forward and picked it up before he could grab it, then turned it around in his hands, telling the kid about the painted designs.

Sean smiled at Ruby's neighbor, who nodded back. For something to do, Sean squatted to look at his jewelry. A small silver Kokopelli pendant on a chain caught his eye. It was a simple execution of the common design, with a tiny turquoise bead for the flute-player's eye. Sean picked it up, dangling it from its chain.

"How much?"

"Thirty-five."

High price for such a small piece, but then this was the plaza. Sean pulled out his wallet.

"I'll take it."

He handed the pendant to the jeweler, who put it in a little white box. Sean gave him two twenties, then tucked the change in his wallet and the box in his shirt pocket.

The tourist family had moved on, so he sidled back to Ruby's blanket. The owl was gone.

"Made a sale."

"Uh-huh. Looks like things are winding down over there."

Sean glanced toward the gazebo, realizing that Tom's voice was no longer droning over the PA. The TV crews were long gone, and the protestors were stacking their signs. Ruby came across the street and joined them, looking slightly heated but cheerful.

"I should have worn a hat. Here's your bucket." She handed Sean the empty bucket that had held her roses.

"Thanks."

"People really liked the roses. We should do that again."

"Fine by me," Sean said. He suspected it would be fine with *Guadalupana*, too. He looked toward the plaza. "I'd better go find Rosa."

Angel stood up to make room for Ruby. "Want your flute?"

"Um—not yet, if you're staying here. I'll pick it up on the way out."

Sean crossed back to the plaza, looking for Rosa in the crowd. He saw roses in the hands of some of the people, but couldn't spot Rosa's blue dress. Getting concerned, he glanced toward the cop car and saw her standing near it, talking with the Hispanic cop. A couple of roses were left in the bucket she held in one hand.

Sean drifted that way, but slowly. He didn't really want to talk to the cops. He was pretty sure they'd been sent to hassle Tom's people, and such tactics pissed him off.

Reminded that he had wanted to talk to Tom, he turned toward the gazebo. Tom was coiling the power cord he'd used for his PA system. Sean went over to him.

"Thanks for having us play. This was a good rally, I think."

Tom nodded. "Yeah. Can you play again at the next one? Tuesday at five."

"Have to talk to Angel, and see if I can get off work a little early. I'll let you know."

"OK." Tom glanced toward the squad car, which was pulling away from the plaza at last. "I'll make sure our permits include music in the future."

"Good idea."

Rosa was coming toward them, swinging the bucket as she walked. She looked happy, and Sean found himself smiling. He turned to Tom.

"Now isn't the time, but can we talk some time about your message strategy? I'd like to explore some different angles."

Tom gave him a wry look. "Like 'roses for the Rio'?"

"Well, yeah."

"We can talk, sure. I think it's important to keep our focus, but I'm open to new ideas."

Sean nodded. "I'll call you, then."

"OK." Tom offered a hand, his grip firm as they shook. "Thanks again for your help."

"Need a hand with the PA?"

"No, I've got it. Thanks."

Pam came up and traded a glance with Tom. She was carrying a box half full of the flyers she'd been handing out. Turning to Sean, she smiled.

"Thanks for joining us. Good to see you here today."

"Yeah. Well." Sean felt awkward suddenly. He glanced toward Rosa, who reached them in the next moment. She was smiling. For a moment no one said anything, then Pam held out a hand toward Rosa.

"We haven't met. I'm Pam."

"Hi, Pam. I'm Rosa."

Pam's eyebrow rose. "That's why the roses?"

"Not really. Oh, you didn't get one. Here."

Rosa pulled out the last two roses and set the bucket down at her feet. She offered a red-and-yellow rose to Pam, who looked nonplussed, as if she'd been ready for a challenge, not a gift. Rosa gave the other rose, a red one, to Tom.

"The flowers were a nice idea," he said.

"Might be better uses for the money, though," said Pam.

Rosa's smile faded a bit. "They didn't cost anything."

"They came from my yard," Sean added, hoping to avoid an argument.

"You must be a master gardener," Tom said, grinning. He picked up the PA. "See you Tuesday, maybe?"

"Maybe. I'll call."

Tom and Pam walked away together. Sean wondered if they were a couple, then decided probably not. Pam wasn't giving out that kind of signal.

"What's Tuesday?"

Sean turned to Rosa. "Another rally, five o'clock. Would you be interested in coming up for it?"

"I don't know. I couldn't get here before six at the earliest, and it's a weeknight. Is there anything next weekend?"

"Not here. Indian Market."

"Oh, yeah."

"I'll ask Tom what else is on the schedule and let you know."

"OK."

Sean checked his watch. "It's a little early for dinner, but Pranzo has a patio bar. Can I buy you a drink?"

She smiled. "Sure."

Sean picked up her bucket, poured the water from it onto one of the plaza's struggling patches of grass, and stacked it with the other bucket. "I need to get my flute from Angel."

"Oh, and I need to pay Ruby for my turtle. Thanks for

reminding me."

They crossed to the Palace together and made their way to Ruby's space. Angel was standing up, leaning against the wall and twiddling on a flute, too quietly to be heard. He stopped and smiled as Sean and Rosa came up.

"Good day today," he said.

Sean nodded. "Yeah. I talked with Tom a little. He's open to discussing new strategies. He also wants us to play at another rally if we're interested. Tuesday at five."

Angel looked mildly surprised. "Tuesday."

"Yeah. If this keeps up we're going to have to learn another song."

It took a moment for Angel to register the joke. He smiled and laughed softly.

"I'll have to think about it."

"Sure. Just give me a call when you decide, and I'll let Tom know."

Rosa had pulled a slender leather billfold from the little embroidered purse she wore slung over one shoulder and was handing some cash to Ruby. She smiled as she accepted the newspaper-wrapped figure in exchange, and cradled it in her arm.

"You want some bubble-wrap?" Ruby asked.

"No, it'll be OK. Thanks."

Sean retrieved his flute from Angel and his mug from Ruby, stashing the latter inside the empty flower buckets. They all said goodbye, then Sean strolled away with Rosa. She headed east up the *portal*.

"You want to bring your car over to the restaurant?" he asked.

"Yeah, it's parked at the library. I couldn't find a space on the street."

"You know how to get to Sanbusco?"

Rosa nodded. "Is that where Pranzo is?"

"Yeah, it's across from the parking lot in front."

Sean walked her to her car, then hurried to his own, which was stashed behind Sena Plaza. He'd skipped his walk on this occasion, figuring he'd want the car for the evening.

He drove over to Sanbusco Marketplace and parked a couple

of spaces from Rosa, who had pulled in just before him. He admired a flash of her long calf as she stepped out of her car. She was wearing sunglasses, and a rising breeze stirred her hair.

The restaurant was quiet, deserted for the moment except for a couple of waiters setting tables. Vague preparatory noises issued from the depths of the kitchen. Sean led Rosa upstairs to the patio bar, where shade and the breeze cut the intensity of the heat. Choosing a small table next to a planter rioting with purple and white petunias, Sean pulled out a chair for Rosa.

"Oh, a gentleman!" She smiled, accepting the courtesy.

"Out of fashion, I know, but my mom drilled it into me."

She laughed. "Viva your mom."

A waiter came up and greeted them. "What can I get you folks?"

Sean glanced at Rosa. She took off her shades.

"Well, since I'm wearing my margarita dress I'd better have a margarita."

"Two," Sean said, glancing at the waiter. "Top shelf."

The waiter retreated. Sean watched Rosa put her shades away in her purse.

"Margarita dress?"

She looked up at him, then touched a flower on her shoulder. "Daisies. That's what 'margarita' means."

"Oh. All these years and I never knew that." Sean smiled. "It's a pretty dress."

"Thanks."

"So you don't just wear roses."

She laughed wryly. "No."

A lull of awkwardness fell over them, the dreaded "what do I say next?" moment. Sean searched for a topic and latched onto the first thing he thought of.

"What were you talking to that cop about?"

"Oh, I was just saying hi. He and my brother were in the same class at the academy."

"Your brother's a cop?"

"Mm-hm, so you better watch out. Treat me right or he'll come after you."

"Yes, ma'am!"

Their drinks arrived, causing a momentary distraction. Sean

licked salt off a spot on the rim of his glass and took a sip. Cold, tart, and strong, the lime almost overpowering the sweet. He watched Rosa taste hers and then lean her head back, closing her eyes.

"Mmm."

Her throat looked amazingly long, and he couldn't keep his gaze from following its line down to the neckline of the margarita dress. It wasn't a plunging neckline, but it was low enough to give him a glimpse of her cleavage, enough to stir the imagination. She wasn't wearing a necklace, which reminded him of the pendant he'd bought. He put down his glass and took the jewelry box out of his pocket.

"On the subject of treating you right, I saw this and it made me think of you."

Rosa blinked in surprise at the box. "Oh—you shouldn't have done that."

"It's just a little thing. You don't have to wear it if you don't like it."

He offered her the box. She took it, looking slightly reluctant, and opened the lid.

"Kokopelli," she said with a small, exasperated laugh. She lifted the chain from the box and let the little dancing flute player dangle. "You know, this whole thing is so strange. Two days ago I didn't even know you, or Ruby or Angel."

"Yeah. Pretty wild, huh?"

She met his gaze. "Yeah."

She caught the Kokopelli charm in her hand and stared at it, frowning slightly, rubbing her thumb across the silver. After a minute she unhooked the clasp and fastened it around her neck. Kokopelli dangled just above the neckline of the margarita dress. Sean took another sip of his drink.

"Thank you," Rosa said quietly.

"You're welcome. Hope he brings you luck."

She smiled and picked up her glass, turning her head to gaze at the mountains beyond the rooftops of Santa Fe. Her eyes had that faraway look again.

Sean took another hit off his margarita. The tequila was starting to give him a bit of a buzz. He sensed Rosa didn't really want to talk at the moment, so he looked at the mountains too and thought about the afternoon. They'd done OK, but even if they did this every Sunday it probably wouldn't be enough to stop Valle del Sol. He wasn't sure there was anything that would stop the development.

Maybe he was being too cynical. Maybe enough people would make phone calls and something would tip the balance. He just had the feeling that it was a done deal and nothing would stop it short of a bomb in Kyle Robbins's equipment yard.

"What are you thinking?" Rosa asked.

He looked at her. Man, she was pretty. There were little flecks of gold in the brown of her eyes—he hadn't noticed that before.

"I was thinking we're fighting an uphill battle."

"A losing battle, you mean."

Sean shrugged. Rosa sipped and regarded him over the glass.

"Why are you doing it, then?"

For you, he wanted to say, but that was probably not a good idea. It wasn't the only reason, either. Certainly not the original reason. He picked up his drink.

"It's kind of hard to ignore a miracle."

She tilted her head. "Do you really think it was a miracle?"

"I don't have a logical explanation."

"Me neither."

Sean smiled. "Do *you* think it was a miracle?"

She glanced at him sidelong, shifted in her chair and took another sip of her margarita. "I think what you saw was a miracle."

"But not what you saw?"

"*Koshare.* Kokopelli." She shook her head, frowning. "I don't know."

"They're sacred to the Pueblos."

"That's different."

"Why? How is it different?"

"They're not sacred to me."

"Well, and the Virgin isn't sacred to me, either."

Rosa looked shocked. "You don't believe in her?"

Sean bit back his exasperation. He had the feeling he was digging himself into a hole.

"I'm not a Catholic."

"You're not a Christian at all, are you?"

"I'm not religious, OK?"

Rosa's expression changed to dismay, with a big dose of pity mixed in. Sean found that really annoying. He should never have gotten into this discussion. So much for getting to know Rosa better.

"Are you an atheist?" she asked in a small voice.

"No. I don't have any opinions on the subject."

"Agnostic?"

"Fine. Sure. Can we talk about something else?"

"I'm sorry."

She picked up her margarita but didn't drink, just held the glass in her hands. It reminded Sean of a priest holding up the chalice or whatever they called it. He looked away.

"I can be pretty nosy sometimes," Rosa said. "It's a habit from my work in *curanderismo*."

Sean relaxed a little. He picked up his glass and glanced at her.

"What does being nosy have to do with healing?"

"I ask my clients about themselves. Take a history, like a doctor would."

"Oh, I see."

"But not just a medical history. *Curanderismo* treats the spirit, the soul, as well as the body. They're inseparable, even though modern medicine ignores the soul and tries to treat only the physical body."

"Hm."

Sean drank, and found that his margarita was down to mostly ice. He tipped it back to get the last of the liquor, then set it down, ice rattling.

"So if I came to you with a broken ankle, you'd ask me how my soul was doing?"

Rosa made a wry face. "Not exactly. But I might ask what you were doing and thinking when your ankle got broken."

"What difference would that make?"

Rosa's eyes lit with interest. "If there's a cause—some reason, even a subconscious one, that you placed yourself in danger of getting hurt—then just treating the injury won't cure the cause and you might put yourself in harm's way again."

Sean gave her a skeptical look. "What if I'm just accident prone?"

"Well, to me accident prone is a condition that probably has an underlying cause."

"A spiritual cause."

"Yeah. Or emotional."

"Like wanting to punish myself or something."

Rosa shrugged. "Could be a lot of things. That's one possibility."

"Sounds like psychology."

"It is, partly. *Curanderismo* has a lot of facets. I actually took a psych class last year, night school. It gave me some interesting insights."

She was getting to the bottom of her drink as well. Sean watched her turn the glass and close her lips over a fresh patch of salt on the rim.

"So you'd try to figure out why I broke my ankle. Would you at least strap it up while you were doing that?"

She flashed a smile. "I'd send you to your doctor to fix up the ankle, then maybe we'd talk about why it happened. Actually, you'd probably just go to your doctor to begin with and not come to me."

Her tone was joking, but he heard an underlying self-doubt that made him want to deny her very sensible conclusion. He felt a sweeping desire to gather her in his arms, so strong it surprised him, and scared him a little.

"Rosa, sweet Rosa," he said, almost whispering. "If I hurt myself will you heal me?"

She met his gaze and answered just as quietly. "I can only heal people who have faith in the divine."

"People of your own faith?"

"People of any faith. Or no faith, if faith means religion. When I say faith I mean a belief that there is a divine power that watches over us. You have to have something to pray to."

"You'd heal me if I believed in *katsinam* and Kokopelli?"

"I don't care if you believe in little green men from Mars, as long as you believe in *something*."

He leaned back in his chair, his gaze drifting again to the

mountains. "I believe in music."

She was quiet for a moment, then leaned forward, resting her elbows on the table. Her hands closed around the foot of her glass and she began to turn it, spinning it slowly on the table top.

"Music as more than just notes and rhythms?"

Sean nodded. "There's power in music. I have to believe that. I know it."

"Well, that's something."

There was power in Angel's rain chant. He was certain about that. Playing it gave him extraordinary feelings. And playing it was what had brought *La Guadalupana* to him. He knew that, too, though he couldn't explain why he was sure. There wasn't any logic to it.

"You folks ready for another round?"

The waiter's voice seemed loud, forcedly cheerful. It shattered the mood between Sean and Rosa like a rock through glass.

Sean glanced at his watch, then at Rosa, who shook her head slightly. "No thanks. Our table's probably ready by now."

"OK. Have a great evening!"

They went downstairs and were seated by the hostess. Over pasta and risotto they talked about their jobs, movies, gardening and so on, carefully steering clear of anything that mattered deeply. The restaurant filled up around them and the background noise increased proportionally. Sean wished they were back up in the patio bar, though by now that would be crowded and noisy, too.

Rosa turned down dessert but accepted an offer of coffee, saying she'd need it for the drive home. Sean wanted to ask if she'd like to come home with him, but he was seriously afraid she'd say no. He wasn't sure at all of how she felt about him. He wasn't getting any strong signals either way.

Maybe she hadn't made up her mind. Time for him to be charming and gallant and irresistible. Sadly, he found himself unable to channel Cary Grant at the moment. Maybe he cared too much.

Time came for him to pay the bill and walk Rosa to her car. The sun was setting as they came outside, and they both paused to gaze at the Sangre de Cristos, the peaks gone dusty pink and blue in the slanting sunlight.

"Beautiful," Rosa said.

"Yeah. Like you."

She hesitated a moment before thanking him. Too strong, too fast. She hadn't made up her mind, or at least he hoped not, because if she had he was out of luck.

"Thanks for the dinner," she said. "I enjoyed it."

"Me too. Let's do it again some time."

She smiled at him but didn't say anything. Sean walked her to her car, feeling helpless, as if she was slipping away.

"Can I call you if I break my ankle?"

She laughed. "Sure."

"OK." He smiled as he watched her get in the car. "Drive safely. Watch out for the wackos."

"I will, thanks."

Want to have dinner again? He couldn't say it.

Chicken-hearted. He didn't want her to say no to his face. He smiled and waved as Rosa pulled out of the parking lot, and stood watching until her car passed out of sight.

Well, there was always email. With email no one could see you cry.

Rosa pulled onto the Interstate and relaxed as she accelerated into the Sunday night traffic. The sunset was fading, down to an orange blur at the edge of a sky that was deepening to the magical glowing blue that Rosa loved so much.

She felt bad about Sean...a little. She hadn't even given him a kiss on the cheek when they'd said goodbye. She didn't want to encourage him too much, because she wasn't sure she wanted to get any closer to him. She liked him, but not as much as she suspected he liked her.

Her mother would raise an eyebrow to hear that Rosa was seeing an Anglo. If she learned that he wasn't a Catholic or even a Christian, her eyebrows would go through the roof.

Rosa laughed, picturing Mama's reaction. She doubted it would come to that.

Mama wanted Rosa to marry and give her some more grandkids, of course. Rosa had pretty much the same idea — she liked the thought of having a family — but she hadn't found a guy she wanted to marry. She had saved her virginity for marriage, because she believed it was right to do so. She was still waiting to find a man who would appreciate the gift.

Would Sean? She didn't know. He had good manners, which was very nice and pretty rare these days, and she liked his dedication to saving the river. She just didn't know if she could ever love a man who had no faith in God.

Maybe *La Guadalupana* would change his mind. He didn't seem too happy about having seen her, though. In fact, he seemed a little resentful. Rosa could understand that, she guessed, because she felt more or less the same about the *koshare*.

It was dark by the time she reached her exit in Albuquerque. The city traffic was crazy as usual, and she had to be on the alert to avoid being hit by some idiot. The drunks were out.

Rosa breathed a sigh of relief as she turned onto her quiet little street in the North Valley. She slowed down to go over the speed bump that would eat the bottom of her car if she drove any faster than a crawl. As she started to turn into her driveway, her headlights fell across a black and white striped figure and she stomped on the breaks.

Koshare! He stood right there in front of her, brandishing his yucca whip. She could hear the brittle yucca leaves rattling together.

Breathing hard, she stared at the apparition. The *koshare* turned to look at her house, waved his whip in that direction, and vanished.

Rosa sat blinking. What did it mean? She glanced at her living room window, the curtains glowing warm and white from the light she'd left on that morning. Bruja wasn't sitting there, which was odd. Usually the cat was waiting in the window when she came home.

Something caught her eye—a movement in the shadows by the front of the house, near a Rose of Sharon tree.

Someone was there!

Rosa gasped and threw the car into reverse. She backed out of the driveway without even looking for traffic. Fortunately no one was driving by, or she'd have hit them.

The shadowed figure came running toward her. A man, dressed in dark clothes, with something shiny in his hand. Knife or gun, she didn't stick around to find out which.

She gunned the engine, flew over the speed bump and landed with a painful thump, then drove like crazy back out onto the main streets. She watched nervously in her rear view mirror for someone following her. There was too much traffic to tell, really, and she was too frightened to think straight. She drove to her mother's house, a few blocks away in the Duranes barrio. Mama had big dogs to keep people away from the house.

Rosa left the car running as she got out and hurried to open the gate. Pancho and Mimi barked joyfully at her, jumping up on the chain link fence. She glanced nervously down the street, but it looked like no one had followed her.

She pulled her car inside the fence next to her mother's sedan and shut off the engine, closed the gate again, and went back to the car for her purse. Suddenly she felt her knees give out. She sat down sideways in the driver's seat and sobbed until she could breathe again.

The door of the house opened. "Rosa? Is that you?"

Rosa coughed and reached for a tissue. "Yes," she called, then blew her nose.

"What's the matter?" Mama came hurrying up to the car, wearing an apron over her nice Sunday dress. Her eyes filled with worry as she reached Rosa. "Oh, *Mijita*, what happened? Are you hurt?"

"I'm all right. Let's go inside."

Rosa stood up and was immediately enfolded in Mama's warm, soft embrace. Mama's arms were big and strong and could hold the whole world. She led Rosa into the house and made her sit in the big armchair that had been her father's and brought her a cup of coffee.

"Gloria and the kids just left. I've got some *natillas* left over from supper. You want some?"

Rosa took a sip of the coffee, then nodded. "Yes, please."

The *natillas* were still warm. Custard with frothy egg whites and cinnamon—comfort food. Rosa ate half the bowl, then set it down to keep from gobbling the rest and told her mother about the stranger in her yard. She left out the part about the *koshare*. Her mother was fairly open-minded, but Rosa didn't feel like explaining the whole *koshare* Kokopelli thing.

"*Pobrecita!*" Mama said. "You should call Miguel. He was here for supper, but he left early. I think there's a game on."

"I don't want to bother him. Whoever it was is probably gone."

"You know he'll be angry if you don't call. Let him go check out your yard."

"OK, but let me finish this."

Rosa took a big swallow of coffee, then picked up the *natillas* and stirred them around with her spoon. She wasn't really hungry. She was wondering who could have been in her yard.

It wasn't a burglar. A burglar would have just broken in the house, taken what he wanted, and left. No, this person had been waiting for *her*. Her stomach clenched.

"We saw you on the news," Mama said. "You looked beautiful. Where did you get those roses?"

"They came from a friend's yard."

"What is all this about the Rio?"

"It was a protest rally. I told you about it."

"I thought that was about some development."

"It was."

Rosa took another bite of *natillas*, then put the bowl down again as her stomach protested. She didn't feel like explaining about the rally just now.

Mama went to fetch her cordless phone and brought it back. She sat on the couch, dialed a number and waited.

"Hello, Miguel? Your sister wants to talk to you."

Mama held out the phone. Rosa sighed and took it.

"Hi, Miguel. Sorry to bother you."

"What's the matter?" Miguel's voice had an edge to it. He picked up on things quickly.

"There was someone in my yard when I got home tonight. I drove over to Mama's instead."

There was a pause, and Rosa thought she heard Miguel mutter a curse. "How long ago?" he said sharply.

"Maybe half an hour."

"OK, stay there. I'll come over and follow you home."

"Thanks, Miguel. I'm sorry—"

"Don't even worry about it. I'll be right over."

"Thanks. Bye."

Rosa turned off the phone and set it down on the side table next to her coffee and *natillas*. She leaned back in Papa's chair, crossing her arms over her stomach. Mama was watching her, looking worried again.

"Do you know who it was?"

Rosa shook her head. "No idea."

"You didn't break up with a boyfriend or anything?"

"I don't have a boyfriend. You know that."

"I just wondered if there was someone new, maybe. Someone you hadn't told me about."

Yeah, there is. He's got black and white stripes all over.

Thinking about the *koshare*, Rosa suddenly realized why it had appeared in her driveway. It had been warning her away. If it hadn't been there, she might not have noticed the stranger hiding in her yard. She might have got out of her car and walked right into a trap.

Cold poured through her arms. Maybe she owed the *koshare* her life.

She wanted to talk to Cruz, but it would have to wait until she was home and Miguel had checked out her yard to make sure it was safe. She closed her eyes, wanting this day to be over.

After a few minutes the dogs announced Miguel's arrival. He came in wearing a muscle shirt and jeans and his belt with his gun and all his cop gear. He looked half-cholo, half-cop, and ready for a fight. There was usually an underlying tension in him —that was just part of being a cop—but tonight it was higher.

"Tell me exactly what happened," he said, sitting down on the couch.

Rosa went through the same explanation she'd given Mama, with a little more detail. She finished her coffee and handed her mug and the *natillas* bowl to Mama.

"You're not going to finish?"

"I'm full. Thanks."

Mama carried the dishes off to the kitchen, shaking her head. When she was out of earshot, Rosa leaned forward toward Miguel.

"He had something in his hand. A weapon, I think," she said softly.

Miguel's frown deepened. "You don't know who it might have been? You didn't argue with anyone?"

She shook her head. "No."

"Hm. Well, he's probably gone, but let's go check it out."

Rosa said goodbye to Mama and received another sustaining hug before going out to her car. Miguel insisted on opening the gate for her. She waited for him to get in his squad car, then drove home slowly, checking frequently for his headlights behind her. His car should be enough to frighten away the intruder if he was still there.

Her pulse increased as she drove over the speed bump again. No *koshare* this time. She parked on the street as Miguel had ordered her to do, and waited inside her car with the doors locked and the windows up.

Miguel parked his squad behind her and got out, long black flashlight in hand. He stood at the end of her driveway and scanned the beam across her house, then all around her front yard. She watched him approach the house, shining the light at the Rose of Sharon and the other shrubs. He worked his way around the east side and disappeared.

Rosa waited in silence, afraid to turn on the radio in case it prevented her from hearing a shout or, God forbid, a gunshot. It wasn't unusual to hear gunfire in the neighborhood now and then. On the fourth of July and New Year's Eve every idiot who owned a gun felt compelled to fire it off. Sometimes people got hurt.

Rosa frowned, gazing at her house. She didn't like feeling afraid of her own home. She felt restless, and shifted in her seat, waiting anxiously for Miguel to return. Her gaze fell on the little newspaper bundle on the passenger seat.

Her turtle. She glanced toward the yard but Miguel wasn't back yet, so she picked up the bundle and carefully unwrapped Ruby's work. The smooth, slightly cool pottery felt good in her hands. She could see the designs painted on in the light from the lamppost down the street. Cheerful designs, rain and flowers. She held it close to her heart, cradling it to her for comfort.

At last she saw the flashlight beam dancing around the west side of the house. Miguel climbed over the back yard fence and came up to Rosa's window. She put the turtle in her lap and rolled the window down.

"Nobody around. There are some footprints in your flowerbed by the front window, where you said. He stepped on some of your flowers."

Rosa thought of some names to call the intruder, but didn't say them. She never cussed in front of Mama or Miguel. She tried not to cuss at all.

Miguel shut off his flashlight. "I didn't see any sign of forced entry, but let me come in with you and look around."

"OK."

Rosa got out of her car and handed Miguel her house key, bringing the turtle and her purse. Miguel unlocked the front door and brought his flashlight up to his shoulder again as he started to search the house. Bruja peered out at Rosa from beneath the coffee table, eyes wide.

"Police," Miguel said loudly. Bruja disappeared.

Miguel went into the short hallway that accessed Rosa's

bedroom, her workroom, and the bathroom. Rosa put her things on the coffee table, then scooped up Bruja and petted her, making little soothing sounds as much for her own comfort as the cat's. Bruja purred loudly, an anxiety purr. Cats knew when things weren't right.

Miguel came out of the workroom and looked at Rosa. "Looks OK. I'll check the kitchen and the laundry room."

"Thanks."

Rosa sat on the couch with Bruja. After a minute the cat crawled off her lap and stretched. Rosa stroked her back and gave her tail a gentle tug. Bruja mewed a half-hearted complaint.

"Everything's fine," Miguel said, coming out of the kitchen. "I checked the shed out back, too, but nobody'd been in there. Whoever it was must have left right after you did."

"Thanks for checking, Miguel."

"Sure. You keep all your windows closed and locked, OK? I don't care about the swamp cooler."

"Yes, sir."

"I'll ask the guys in your district to run a nightly watch on your street for a couple of weeks. I'll cruise it too. You see anything else, or hear anything, you call me right away, OK? Day or night."

"OK."

"I'm going to get my camera and take pictures of those footprints. Might help get an ID."

Rosa walked with him to the door. He handed her keys to her, then gave her a fierce hug.

"You be careful, Rosa."

"Yeah. Thanks, Miguel."

He stood back, holding her at arm's length and peering into her eyes. His concern for her showed in the tautness of his face. She smiled, though she still felt a little afraid.

"If you think of who it might have been, let me know."

"I will."

"OK. Take care, sis."

"You too."

She went out with him and moved her car into the driveway under his watchful gaze, then went back in the house and locked the door. Peeking out the front window, she watched Miguel come back with his digital camera and take a half-dozen flash pictures of the flower bed, then return to his car. As his squad pulled away the spotlight swept the other yards along the street.

She let the curtain fall and went into the kitchen to put on the kettle. No more coffee, but she wanted a hot drink, even though the evening was still warm. She took out a little jar of *yerba buena*—mint—that she'd dried from the garden and put some in her small teapot. While she waited for the kettle to boil she put some food in Bruja's bowl, then called Cruz and told her what had happened.

"You need a *limpia*," Cruz said.

"I do, but I'm not going out again tonight."

"You want me to come over?"

Rosa hesitated. She felt like asking Cruz to come over would be asking her to come into a danger zone. She didn't like feeling that way.

"No, it's OK. I'll give myself a *limpia*, and I'm going to smudge the house, too."

"And your yard. It needs cleansing too."

"I'll do it in the morning."

"Good. I'll light a candle for you, *hija*."

Rosa smiled. Just knowing Cruz would be praying for her made her feel better.

"Thank you, *maestra*."

"Why don't you come over for supper tomorrow? We can talk about it some more."

"That would be great. Thanks."

"Goodnight, *hija*. Be safe."

"Thank you, Cruz."

Rosa hung up the phone and turned off the fire under the steaming kettle. She poured hot water over the mint leaves, and tidied the kitchen while she waited for the tea to steep. She heard the sound of a car out front and looked up, frozen for a moment, until it passed down the street.

"Silly, Rosa. Can't jump at every noise you hear."

She poured herself a cup of tea and went out to the living room. It was past ten—the evening news had already started. She turned it on, hoping to see the story about the rally. About midway through the broadcast it came on, Greg Garza standing in the Santa Fe plaza introducing the story as "a fight for the Rio Grande."

Rosa raised her eyebrows. That wasn't how the rally had been described by Tom. The scene switched to her interview and she leaned forward.

The bucket of roses in her hands was a blaze of red and yellow, complemented by the blue and white of her dress. She saw herself smiling, and thought how strange that she'd been so happy and carefree just that afternoon.

"The roses are to remind people that our water is precious," she said to Garza on the television. "The Rio Grande is a lifeline for people all the way down its length, for hundreds of miles. We have an obligation to make sure there's enough water for everyone on the river, not use it all for a golf course up north."

Rosa winced. She hadn't realized how specific she'd been. Of course, the whole rally was about fighting Valle del Sol, but seeing herself dis the development on TV made her wish she'd been a little more cautious.

Garza asked her a couple more questions, then switched to an interview with Tom, who said the same things he'd been saying all along, that development on the middle Rio Grande should be carefully planned to ensure quality of life for neighboring communities. It was doublespeak. Easy to forget. Less dangerous, too, than what Rosa had said.

Could this be why the stranger had been waiting in her yard? She had a cold suspicion that it was. Her name had been right there on the screen.

The story ended and the weatherman came on. Rosa finished her tea and carried the mug to the kitchen, then checked the back door to make sure it was locked and checked all the windows. Miguel must have closed the ones in her bedroom and kitchen, which had been cracked to help the swamp cooler move cool air through the house. Everything was secure.

Rosa watched the weathercast until she saw that there was no chance of rain in the coming week, then turned off the TV and went into her workroom to give herself a *limpia*. Usually she used fresh rosemary for the ritual cleansing, but she'd have to go outside to cut some and she was reluctant to do so. That made her sad.

She could do a *limpia* with incense and a feather, or with an egg for finding blockages in her energy. Her gaze fell on the roses from Sean's miracle bushes on her altar, and on impulse she reached up and took one from the vase.

Flowers were good for *limpias,* too. She held the rose to her nose and inhaled deeply. Its scent was as sweet and fresh as if it had just been picked. Its petals were dark, rich red. She set it down while she lit a candle and prayed to *La Guadalupana.*

"Holy Mother, free me from fear and bless me with your protection."

She picked up the rose and brushed it over her head, her face, her neck and down her limbs, going over her whole body, smoothing and cleansing her energy. The feel of the velvet petals on her skin was soothing. She felt lighter as she continued brushing away all the fear and dark thoughts that had collected in her. When she was finished she shook the rose toward the east to get rid of the negative energy, then laid it on her altar. She would let it dry overnight, then scatter the petals at the feet of her statue of the Virgin in her garden in the morning.

Feeling better, she said prayers for her family and friends as she did every night. She added Sean, Ruby, and Angel to the list of friends for whom she asked the Virgin's protection, and as an afterthought included Tom and his people. She had a feeling everyone fighting Valle del Sol needed protection.

She hesitated before closing her prayer. She felt she hadn't given adequate thanks for being saved from the intruder.

"Holy Mother, thank you for sending the *koshare* to warn me," she whispered, then crossed herself and said "amen."

She gazed at her poster of *La Guadalupana* on the wall. Had the Virgin sent the warning, or had it been someone else? Whatever its source, she was grateful.

She checked to make sure the candle was burning safely, setting on a tile to keep it from overheating the wooden altar when it burned low in the glass. She put her face in the roses one last time, drinking in their fragrance, then left the workroom.

She was tired, and got ready for bed, undressing and tossing the margarita dress in the laundry bag in her closet. The little Kokopelli caught against her chin as she pulled off the dress. She'd forgotten she was wearing it, and now she unhooked it and held it in her palm.

Could this little thing have brought the bad man to her house? No, she didn't think so. If anything, Sean's wish that the Kokopelli would bring her luck amounted to a prayer. Maybe Kokopelli had sent the *koshare*.

She wasn't entirely comfortable with that thought. She put the necklace in her jewelry box and changed into her nightshirt, then brushed her teeth and hair. She was ready for bed, but she kept thinking about the Kokopelli necklace. She'd forgotten to thank Sean again for it at the end of their dinner. She really had left him without much of a thank you.

On impulse, she went out to the dining room and turned on her computer. She'd send Sean an email to thank him. That felt like the right thing to do.

Her email program showed several messages waiting, mostly spam. One had the subject "about the Rio Grande." She didn't recognize the address. Maybe it was from Tom, setting up when they'd do another rally. She deleted the spam messages and opened the one about the Rio Grande.

DON'T GIVE ANY MORE INTERVIEWS, OR YOU'LL GET ANOTHER VISIT. JUST A FRIENDLY WARNING.

12

Rosa's hands shook as she dialed her brother's number. Her heart started thundering again. She leaned toward her computer monitor and looked more closely at the address the email had come from. It was from one of those free email services. Probably a disposable address.

"Hello?" Miguel's voice sounded sharp and anxious.

"Um, Miguel, it's Rosa. I got an email — it's sort of a threat."

"Shit. From someone you know?"

"No, I've never seen the address before."

"Forward it to me. We'll track down where it came from."

"OK." Rosa clicked the forwarding button and entered Miguel's address.

"Was it because of you being on the news?"

"Uh, yeah. Looks like it was."

"Don't go on TV again."

She gave a weak laugh. "That's what the email says."

"You OK? You want me to come over?"

Rosa took a deep breath, tempted to say yes just because she wanted a hug. "No, I'm fine. It's just an email."

"Make sure you leave your porch light on."

"I always do, like you told me."

"You want me to drive you to work in the morning?"

"Thanks, but I'll be all right."

"OK." There was a pause. "I love you, sis. We'll find this guy."

"Thanks. Love you too."

"Call if you need me."

"I will. Good night."

Rosa put the phone down. No way she was going to get to sleep, at least for a while. She sent off the forwarded email, then thought about emailing Sean as well. She ought to let him and the others know about the threat. She wished Angel and Ruby had email.

She looked up Sean's address and opened a new message.

After a short debate, she decided to tell him about seeing the *koshare*. She described the vision, then the intruder at her house and the threatening email she'd received, and suggested he alert Tom about the threat.

Restless after sending the message, she went into her workroom, said a brief prayer asking for protection from the Lady and her Son, and lit a smudge stick. She had made it herself, from sage she and Cruz had gathered in the hills and rosemary and lavender from her own garden. Now she carried it through her house, room by room, smudging each door and window with the fragrant smoke, praying for protection. When she was finished she carefully extinguished the smoldering smudge stick and left it in a pottery bowl in her workroom.

Feeling better, she went to the kitchen to fix another mug of mint tea. The house smelled of sweet herbs and pungent sage. Rosa considered turning on the TV, but decided not to. She noticed Ruby's turtle sitting on the coffee table and picked it up.

She should find a safer place for it, one where Bruja couldn't accidentally knock it on the floor. There was a nicho in one wall of the living room, but it was too shallow for the turtle, and she liked keeping a candle in it. Maybe in her bedroom? That didn't feel right either.

She carried the turtle into her workroom and put it on her altar. For now, it could stay there to remind her of the river. Gazing at it, she thought of the turtles she'd seen at the Nature Center and how she had walked in the river that day. A quiet stirring in her reminded her of the power she'd felt from the river. Power she sensed, but didn't fully understand.

She went out and checked her email one more time to see if Miguel had sent her a confirmation. He had, and so had Sean. Rosa sipped her tea as she read Sean's message.

Rosa—

I was just about to send you an email. Damn, I'm so sorry this happened! I hope you've already called your brother about this threat. I wish I was there so I could track down the bastard that stalked you and give him what for. It was probably some thug working for Robbins. They're just trying to scare you.

"Yeah, well it's working," Rosa said to the screen. She took another swallow of tea.

I'll let Tom know. We're going to have to talk with him anyway, I think, about the direction of the campaign. It's OK if you decide you don't want to participate any more, though I hope you won't let these a**holes intimidate you.

Rosa chuckled. Sean's indignation made her feel better. She considered withdrawing from the campaign, but knew immediately that she didn't want to.

It was a little frightening to realize this. She'd never thought of herself as a crusader. That's what this was, though—a crusade.

The rest of Sean's email was about how he'd enjoyed their dinner and hoped to see her again, whether or not she continued in the campaign. She sent a short reply assuring him that her brother was looking into the threat, and that she wasn't going to back out of the fight for the river. She added her thanks for the dinner and the Kokopelli pendant, then sent off the message and shut down her computer.

After she finished her tea and cleaned up the kitchen, she got into bed with her Bible. Bruja came and curled up beside her, purring.

Rosa liked to let the Bible fall open and read whatever was on the page it opened to. Tonight it opened to Psalms, and she found comfort in the words that caught her eye:

> *Guard me, O Lord, from the hands of the wicked;*
> *preserve me from violent men,*
> *who have planned to trip up my feet.*

She read the psalm softly aloud, making it her own prayer, from her heart. Comforted, she put the Bible aside and turned out her light, lying back and stroking Bruja's fur as she stared at her darkened ceiling.

The river needed her help. She'd been sent visions for this purpose, a holy calling. Never mind that she hadn't been called by the Virgin herself. In a way, the fact that it was the *koshare* who came to her — something she never would have expected — made it clear that the visions were not just creations of her own imagination. She had been called, and she knew she must continue, threats or no threats.

Rosa woke to the sound of bird song from her radio alarm clock, which she kept tuned to the classical station even though she didn't really like classical music. Every morning they played birds singing and it was a beautiful, peaceful way to wake up.

She stretched, amazed at how well she had slept, and got up to get ready for work. When she was dressed and had the coffee on, she went into her workroom for the rose she had used for her *limpia* last night.

She had expected the rose to be withered and faded after having lain on her altar all night. Instead, it was as fresh as if it had just been cut. Rosa picked it up, gazed at it for a long moment, then hesitantly smelled it. Its perfume was as sweet as ever.

A miracle rose. She looked at the rest of them in the vase. She had a handful of miracles on her altar.

She wondered if all the other roses were like this, the ones she had handed out on the plaza yesterday. How many people had taken the roses home with them, and how many of them had noticed their continued freshness? And how long would it last, for that matter? Only way to tell was to wait and see.

Rosa laid the bloom down again. She felt awed by this demonstration of the Holy Virgin's power.

Roses for the Rio. She had made it up on the spot, but maybe that's what they really were, the Lady's gift to the campaign to save the river.

She left the rose lying on the altar and went to eat some breakfast, then glanced at the kitchen clock as she washed up her dishes. She had time to do a quick cleansing of the property around her house before she went to work.

For this she used her eagle feather, fetching it from her altar. Walking the perimeter of the yard, holding the feather so that it swept any evil influences off the property, she silently prayed for protection. Bruja came with her and followed her along the edges of the back yard, then lost interest when Rosa went through the gate to the front and headed off on her own investigations of the garden.

Rosa went around the front yard and the driveway, and stood for a moment by the flowerbed where the intruder had damaged a plant, waving her feather back and forth through the air above it. She crouched and pulled off the broken stems, scattered them over the footprint, then continued her tour of the property. When she had been all around the house and both yards, she returned to stand before her statue of the Virgin in the back garden.

"Thank you, Blessed Mother, for your protection. Please keep your mantle over me."

It was one of those little cement statues from a local greenhouse, and Rosa had painted it to look like the image of *La Guadalupana* from her poster, with a blue star-studded robe and pink gown. She had even painted on the gold designs of the gown, and had carefully painted the Virgin's face and hair in the right colors, and the little cherub holding the crescent moon on which the Virgin stood. The corona of light that surrounded the Lady was white and gold. She looked down at Rosa from her pedestal in the flower bed, another garden-store find. Rosa felt enveloped with peace and didn't want to move, didn't want to leave.

She had to go, though, or she'd be late for work. She went inside and gave Bruja some breakfast, then put her feather away on the altar. The roses caught her eye, and on impulse she took one out of the vase to take to work. She got a bud vase from the kitchen and put a little water in the bottom of it, though she suspected the rose wouldn't fade without water.

As she got out of her car in the bank's parking lot, Sandy's purple Saturn pulled into the space next to hers. "Hey, it's the Rose for the Rio lady!" Sandy called, grinning. "Complete with rose!"

"You're early," Rosa said as she used her key to let them into the lobby.

"I have a dentist appointment, remember?"

"Oh, right."

Rosa had forgotten that she'd agreed to let Sandy leave early today for her appointment. It meant that Rosa would have to cover the drive-up for the last hour of the day.

She went to her desk and set the bud vase on it, leaning over to smell the rose before sitting down and going over the work schedule for the week. Two more tellers arrived, and Rosa took everyone to the vault to get their cash drawers.

"Hey, I saw you on TV!" Frank said.

"Yeah," said Margo. "You looked beautiful!"

"Thanks."

"What's that all about, with the roses?"

"We're trying to save the Rio Grande. It's endangered."

"It is? I didn't know that."

Rosa hesitated to say more, which made her angry. She had taken up this crusade, and she should make the most of any opportunity to spread the word that the river was in trouble. The memory of a moving shadow in her yard made her hold her tongue.

She carried her own cash drawer back to her desk and stashed it in its drawer, leaving the cover locked until she needed to open it. It was Monday, so there was plenty to do, and the morning went by quickly. Frank wanted to switch lunches with her so he could run an errand uptown. Since he usually went to lunch at eleven it meant a long afternoon for Rosa, but her afternoon was already disarranged. She accepted it with a shrug and a smile.

On her way out to lunch, she passed Kyle Robbins coming in the lobby. He turned and gave her a startled look, and Rosa's heart jumped with fear. Had he ordered that man to wait for her in her yard?

She hurried out without meeting his gaze and jumped in her car. Paranoia made her check the mirror to see if she was being followed, but if she was she couldn't tell. She went through a fast-food drive up, then parked by a pre-school playground to eat in the car, hoping that if there *was* anyone watching her they'd be bored silly. She sat sipping her drink and watching the kids play in the dusty school yard until it was time to go back to work.

She worked Frank's station during the midday rush, taking transactions back to her desk to complete them. Gerry came through the line with a deposit for opening a new account.

"Hey, Mr. Robbins was asking about you," she said as she handed the paperwork to Rosa.

"He was?" Rosa felt her chest tighten with fear.

"Yeah. Said he wanted to take you to lunch."

"I thought he was married."

Gerry gave her a sly look. "He is."

"Well, I'm not interested."

Rosa printed out a receipt for the deposit and stamped it with her teller stamp, then handed it to Gerry. Gerry leaned forward in the teller window.

"I think it's cause you're famous."

"What?"

Gerry nodded toward the vase on Rosa's desk. "Everybody saw you on the news. Pretty girl with an armful of roses. No wonder he wants to take you out."

"That's sick."

"Hey, there's nothing wrong with going to lunch! Maybe he wants to offer you a job as a spokesperson or something."

Rosa gave a derisive snort. "I doubt that."

"You'd get a nice meal out of it, at least. He took Arturo to the Rancher's Club."

Rosa stood on tiptoe to catch the eye of the next customer in line. "I can help you over here."

Gerry shrugged and strolled away with her receipt. Rosa smiled at the customer, thankful that the lunchtime rush was enough to keep her busy.

A couple of customers mentioned they'd seen Rosa on television. She brushed aside their curiosity, feeling guilty for doing so instead of encouraging them to think about the river. She was glad to return to her desk when Frank got back from lunch. She didn't want to talk to anyone about the roses. She was sorry now that she'd brought one to work, and considered throwing it away, but couldn't bring herself to do it. She couldn't treat a miracle with that much disrespect.

Maybe this was a test of her determination. Was she really willing to devote herself to this cause? Or was she too frightened by the boogie man in her yard?

During the afternoon lull she got a phone call from Miguel. She glanced at the lobby, not wanting to be overheard by Arturo or Gerry.

"We tracked down the email," Miguel told her. "It was sent from a free account that was set up with bogus information."

"I thought that might be what it was. Thanks for trying."

"Everything all right at your place this morning?"

"Yeah, except for one smushed chrysanthemum."

"Sorry about that."

"You didn't do it. It'll be all right, it just lost a few flowers."

"OK. You going straight home after work?"

"Yeah, but then I'm going over to Cruz's for supper."

"Want an escort?"

Rosa smiled. "No, thanks. I think I'll be OK."

"Call if you change your mind."

"All right. Thanks, Miguel."

The afternoon wore on. When it came time for Sandy to leave, Rosa helped her put her cash drawer away and moved her own drawer to Sandy's station at the drive-up. She could have gone back and forth to her desk, but she preferred to sit out of sight of the lobby.

Closing time came and she sighed with relief as she sent out the last receipt and shut down the drive-up. She hadn't seen Arturo all day, for which she was grateful. She took her drawer to the vault, and she and Gerry locked the vault for the night.

She supposed she ought to try to find out what was going on with Robbins. Reluctantly, she looked at Gerry as they headed for the parking lot.

"So, what was Mr. Robbins doing here today?"

"Meeting with Arturo. They're going over some financing."

Rosa nodded. Valle del Sol.

"They talked in Arturo's office for a long time. He's coming back later in the week."

Rosa considered coming down with a cold for the rest of the week. That would just be a cop-out, she knew.

Gerry gave her a sidelong look. "So maybe you'll have another chance at that lunch."

Rosa managed to laugh. "Come on. Why should I want to go

to lunch with some married white honcho?"

"You never know. It could be a golden opportunity."

"If he's looking for a honey on the side I'm the wrong girl."

"I don't think that's what he's after."

Rosa turned her keychain in her hand, finding the car key. "What else would he be after?"

"I don't know." Gerry paused beside her minivan. "He said you have presence."

"Presence?"

Gerry nodded. "'That girl has presence,' he said. I don't know what he meant, but he sounded impressed."

Rosa felt uneasy about this. She tried to laugh it off. "Eh, he's just *loco*."

Driving home, Rosa checked her mirrors a lot. She worried about being followed, though she didn't see anyone. She didn't like that she'd attracted Robbins's attention. She couldn't think of any good that might come of it.

She drove slowly when she got to her street, watching for any sign of an unwelcome visitor. She pulled into her driveway and sat with the motor running while she stared hard at every shrub in the front garden and especially near the house. Bruja was sitting in the window, watching her. When Rosa was satisfied that no one was hiding in the yard, she turned off the car and went inside the house.

Bruja meowed and rubbed against Rosa's ankles. Rosa gave her some food, then changed into comfortable clothes and went into her workroom. The rose she had left lying on the altar was still fresh and perfect. She picked it up, smelled it, and glanced at *La Guadalupana*.

"Thank you, Lady, for your many blessings."

Cruz should see this rose. She'd take it with her, she decided. She picked three more out of the big vase on the dining table to take as well—a pink, a white, and one of the yellow and red ones. She wanted to show them to her teacher and tell her about the miracle bushes in Sean's yard. A lot had happened since the last time she'd seen Cruz.

On the drive over she thought she saw a little blue car following her, but it turned off at a gas station a couple of blocks from Cruz's street. Frowning at the mirror, Rosa turned early and wound her way through the neighborhood to Cruz's house.

Cruz met her at the door, wearing her white cotton work shift. She closed the door and gathered Rosa into a hug.

"*Pobrecita*. Come and tell me."

Rosa smiled as they stepped apart. "Have you been with a client?"

"No, this is for you, *hija*. You need a *limpia* and a massage."

"Oh, that sounds so good!"

"Let me put those flowers in some water, and you go on into the treatment room."

"OK, but I have to tell you about these. These are miracle roses."

Cruz raised her eyebrows. "Miracle?"

"Yes. This one has been out of water for almost twenty-four hours."

Rosa handed her the red rose. Cruz looked at it, then smelled it.

"That can't be true. It's too fresh."

"I know. It's true, though. I used that to give myself a *limpia* last night, and left it to dry out on the altar. Only it didn't dry."

Cruz frowned. "Where did this rose come from?"

"It's a long story. Let's sit down."

"OK. *Plática* first. Want some iced tea?"

"Yes, please."

They went into the kitchen where Cruz fixed them glasses of tea with fresh mint leaves. She insisted on putting the roses in water whether they needed it or not, and carried the vase into her treatment room.

Cruz's room was bigger than Rosa's. It had once been a garage, and was now carpeted and furnished with a comfortable couch for the *pláticas*, the heart-to-heart talks that were such an important part of *curanderismo*. Cruz's altar was on the east wall, and near the west end of the room stood her massage table. A fountain in one corner gave a quiet, soothing sound of trickling water. Plants hanging near the shaded windows filled the room with a gentle glow of life. Rosa loved Cruz's treatment room and tried to give her own workroom something of the same comfortable feel.

Cruz set the vase of roses on the little table before the couch.

"OK, tell me about the miracle roses."

Rosa explained how she'd met Sean and the Madalenas at the meeting in Santa Fe Friday night, how Sean had seen the Virgin of Guadalupe and how the Lady had made his rosebushes bloom. She then told Cruz about handing out the roses at the rally in the plaza on Sunday, and how she'd been on TV.

"That's why there was someone in my yard last night. I got a threatening email, warning me not to go on TV again."

Cruz frowned. "That's very bad. I told you TV is a bad influence. It only brings unhappiness."

Rosa didn't fully agree, but they'd hashed through that discussion often enough. She knew Cruz had a point, especially about the news.

"I don't think it matters if I go on TV or not," Rosa said, looking at the roses. "So many people have these roses now. Sooner or later they're going to notice that they're not fading."

"And then what?"

"They maybe they'll think some more about the Rio."

"OK. So you got the message out. You don't need to send it out any more, and the bad guys can't do anything about it."

Rosa frowned slightly. "I don't know about not sending it out any more. I think I need to keep going until we know the river is safe."

Cruz leaned forward. "Whoever sent that thug to your house isn't going to like it."

"Maybe not. But he can't complain if I don't go on TV. That's all he said in the email. No interviews."

"You're playing with fire, *hija*."

Rosa took a swallow of tea. "I know. But this is important. Don't you think so?"

Cruz reached out and traced a fingertip along the petals of the pink rose. "The river is important. Yes."

Rosa considered telling Cruz about her walk to the river and how she'd seen Angel in a circle of men in the water. She decided not to. That felt different—it wasn't like the *koshare* or the old flute player. Angel was a real person, for one thing. She didn't understand what she'd seen, but she had an instinct that it was something private. Maybe it was a secret ceremony of the Turtle Clan. Maybe she shouldn't have seen it at all.

"Come on, *hija*. Let's give you a *limpia* and a rubdown. Shake all the shadows away."

Cruz led Rosa to her altar and lit a candle and some incense, then used the smoke and a feather to give Rosa a *limpia*. Rosa closed her eyes and let the comforting smell of copal lift her spirits while Cruz brushed her body to cleanse it of unwanted energies. She tried to let go of all the fears and doubts that had pursued her in the last day and night. Breathing deeply, she gradually relaxed.

After the *limpia*, Cruz took her over to the massage table and gave her a long massage. Cruz's hands were full of healing, and she knew just how to rub to get the tension out of Rosa's neck and shoulders and her back. She left Rosa lying on the table with sweet music playing—Rosa hadn't noticed when she'd turned it on—and murmured that she was going to check on supper, and that Rosa should relax as long as she wanted.

Rosa lay drifting, thinking of turtles and roses. She felt peaceful and safe. In this place she could believe in a bright future, that the river would be saved and all would be well. She hung onto that thought, treasuring it as long as she could, praying that it would come to be.

Finally she had to get up and use the bathroom. Straightening her clothes, she came out into Cruz's living room. Cruz had set the dining room table for supper, and the light glowing through the curtains had a golden tone to it. Rosa peeked out the glass doors and was surprised to see how low the sun hung in the sky. It was getting late.

A clank from the kitchen drew her to the doorway. Cruz was pouring gravy into a bowl. A platter of carved roast chicken sat on the counter. Rosa could smell the rosemary and sage it had been rubbed with.

Cruz glanced up. "There you are. Feeling better?"

Rosa gave a contented sigh. "Yes, thank you."

"Take that out to the table, will you?"

Rosa carried out the chicken, and returned for a bowl of roasted potatoes. Cruz brought the gravy and a big bowl of salad, and they sat down in the green-gold light to share the feast.

"This is wonderful. Thank you, Cruz."

"You're welcome. I figured you needed a good home-cooked meal."

Rosa grinned. She wasn't a bad cook herself, but somehow it was always better if someone else did the cooking.

"Thank you for the treatment, too. I should pay you for it."

"You pay me enough."

"But this wasn't a lesson."

"Maybe it was."

Rosa tilted her head to look at Cruz, who was cutting her chicken. She looked up and returned Rosa's gaze.

"You need to slow down, Rosa. You need to be careful."

Rosa blinked. "I know I'm doing the right thing. That's what the miracles are saying."

Cruz raised a shoulder in a half-shrug. "Maybe they're not your miracles."

"Some of them are mine. The *koshare* in the driveway is mine. And anyway, I think all of us are meant to work together."

"All of you?"

"Me and Sean, and Angel. And Ruby."

"You only met them on Friday."

"Haven't you ever met someone and known instantly that you'd be friends?"

Cruz gazed at her thoughtfully, then smiled. "Yes, I have."

Rosa felt herself blushing. She knew what Cruz was thinking. The first time the two of them had met, they had clicked. From that moment Cruz had been her substitute mother. Not that her own mother was deficient — Rosa loved Mama dearly — but Cruz was a mentor, a guardian. Cruz had vision, and Rosa had wanted to be like her.

Well, Rosa thought, a small shock running through her veins, now I am. I have visions. Important visions. Maybe I have finally learned enough to truly begin my work.

All the times Cruz had told her to listen to her heart, to open herself to visions, and now Cruz was urging her to be cautious. Maybe Cruz had seen her own visions, and was trying to protect her.

"*Maestra*? Do you think I am on the wrong path?" Rosa asked humbly.

Cruz's brow creased a little. "No, not the wrong path. But it is a dangerous path, *hija*. Be careful to keep your balance."

"I will. With your help."

Cruz smiled, and stabbed a potato with her fork. Rosa glanced toward the glass doors beside them. She could feel the sun's last heat glowing through the glass, and as she gazed, she felt it slide below the horizon, leaving a cool whisper of peace in its wake.

13

Sean woke to the sound of his doorbell, rubbed his eyes, and looked at the clock on his nightstand. It was six-fifteen, half an hour before he usually got up. Groaning, he hauled himself out of bed and pulled on his robe, then shuffled out to the front door. A glance through the peep hole showed him his neighbor, Mrs. Trujillo, a nice little old Hispanic lady who brought him homemade tamales at Christmas. Sean pulled his robe tighter and tied the belt, then opened the door a crack.

Mrs. Trujllo looked up at him, smiling, her eyes very bright. She was wearing slacks and a striped short-sleeved blouse, and her hair was a curling cap of salt-and-pepper.

"Did I get you out of bed?"

"It's OK, I was about to get up."

"I saw you on the news last night, and the roses they were handing out at that meeting looked like those ones in your back yard."

"Um, they were, actually."

"My granddaughter was in the plaza and got one. She loves it!"

"Oh." Sean wondered where this was leading, and whether he should ask her in.

"Her little sister wasn't at the plaza, though, and she wants a rose, too. You know how kids are. I was wondering if you'd mind...?"

"Oh. No, of course not. Uh, come in."

He went to the kitchen and got his scissors and a paper cup of water to put the rose in, then led Mrs. Trujillo out to the back yard. She made a beeline for the red and yellow rosebush.

"Santa Maria! They're beautiful!"

"Um, thanks."

"I never noticed them before!"

"Well, they've been here." *Haven't bloomed like this, but they've been here.* "What color would your granddaughter like?"

"Oh, I don't know." Mrs. Trujillo's hands hovered over the

blossoms, touching them reverently. "She loves pink, but the red ones are so pretty, and Alma's is red."

"Why don't you just take one of each?"

She glanced up at him with a hopeful smile. "If you don't mind."

"Not at all."

Sean cut four roses and put them in the paper cup. "There you go."

"Thank you! Oh, they're so pretty." She held them to her face and closed her eyes as she smelled them. "So beautiful."

Sean smiled, glad to have made her happy. He glanced at the rosebushes, thinking maybe he should give them some water. Or maybe not—if he actually watered them, they might turn into trees.

Mrs. Trujillo started toward the house. "I'll get out of your way, let you get ready for work. Thank you so much!"

"No problem. Nice to see you."

"I'll make sure the girls include you in their prayers."

Sean gave an embarrassed chuckle. "OK. Thanks."

He saw her to the front door, then went back to the kitchen to put away his scissors and start a pot of coffee. Since he was up early he took a long shower and emerged feeling more awake.

It was Tuesday, but he and Angel wouldn't be playing at the rally. Angel had decided against it, and had called Sean on Ruby's cell phone the night before to tell him. Their conversation had been short and strained. Angel didn't like talking on the phone, Sean knew, so he didn't take it personally, but he wondered if there was something else on Angel's mind.

Hoping to shake the slightly troubled feeling that came with these thoughts, Sean picked up his flute and stepped out in the back yard. He began to play softly, just improvising, gazing at the roses and thinking about Angel. He valued Angel's friendship and didn't want to jeopardize it. If playing at rallies would endanger it, then forget the rallies.

But Angel had wanted to play on Sunday, and had enjoyed it. That wasn't the problem. It must be something else.

Sean found himself toying with the starting notes of the rain chant. He gave in and played it through, just once, then stood looking at the roses. Trying to see an answer to an unknown question.

Well, he'd see Angel on Sunday. Maybe he'd find out then. Maybe it was nothing.

It was time to leave for work. Sean put away the flute, locked up, and headed for the office. He kept thinking of the weekend, of Rosa and the rally and the whole Valle del Sol thing. Working with the projections he was doing for the city, he remembered how the politico, Ben Lucero, had brushed off his questions about an environmental impact study for Valle del Sol at the town hall meeting.

He frowned. Wasn't an EIS required by law for that kind of project? He thought so, but wasn't sure. If a study was being done at all it was probably under contract to some buddy of Lucero's, who'd write it up the way Lucero wanted and get it rubber stamped by the Feds. There might be a document labeled EIS, but it wouldn't mean a thing.

Well, Sean could do his own estimates, informally. He had enough data in the flyers he'd collected at that meeting to draw some general conclusions, at least. Halfway through the morning he took a break and went out to his car to fetch the papers, then spent a few minutes plugging numbers into the projection software and running an analysis.

The results made him sit back. He stared at the screen, which estimated water use of 10,000 acre feet per year for the completed development. All he had put in were the homes, the golf course, and the major facilities like the hospital and fire station. No lawns for the houses, though for all he knew Robbins had planned them.

He looked at the brochure. Phase I and the golf course were supposed to open the first year. Then Phase II the third year, and so on. Sean saved his first analysis, then ran another of just the first year. The numbers were much lower, of course. By doing the development in stages, Robbins was hiding the total impact it would have.

The entire volume of the Rio Grande was about 480,000 acre feet per year. Valle del Sol was looking to suck up about two percent of that, an enormous amount for one development. An enormous amount considering the number of people competing for the river's water. Two percent didn't seem like much, but it could be the straw that broke the camel's back. He did some checking on the Internet, and confirmed that ninety-five percent of the Rio Grande's flow was already claimed by cities and agriculture.

Sean scanned the Valle del Sol brochure for anything he might have missed. A waste-water treatment plant was mentioned, so he added that to the mix, basing the volume and costs on the stats of a water treatment facility down in Albuquerque. He deducted the treated water from the amount the golf course would suck up from the river, but the difference was minimal, three percent of the total. Essentially the result was unchanged.

A little core of excitement started burning in Sean's gut. This information might be a way to block the development. If it was disseminated the right way—which included getting the media to take interest—it might rouse enough opposition to stall Valle del Sol.

Tom would know more about how to do it than Sean would. Sean saved his files, burned them onto a CD, then called the number on Tom's flyer. He didn't recognize the exchange. It was probably a cell phone.

"Tom Evans."

"Hi, Tom, it's Sean Carpenter."

"Oh, hi."

"Two things. First, Angel and I won't be able to play at the rally tonight."

"That's OK. Turns out those cops were right—the city won't authorize music under the kind of permit we have. They'd want us to apply for a whole different permit, a performance permit, that really isn't appropriate for what we're doing. I'm sorry."

Sean sat back in his chair, disappointed. "Yeah, me too. I thought it got a good response."

"It did."

"Well, the other thing is this. I ran an analysis of Valle del Sol's projected water use based on the development plans. It's pretty astounding. Ten thousand acre feet per year."

Tom was silent. Sean felt pleased with himself for impressing him.

"How'd you come up with that number?"

"I used the projection software developed by my company. I do this kind of thing for a living."

"Oh. What company is this?"

"Analysis Visions. We do a lot of work for the county. I'm working on a city project right now that's similar to Valle del Sol. Much smaller scale, but the same type of thing, except no golf course or hospitals or any of that."

"Well. Ten thousand. That's very interesting."

"I thought so. I figured you'd know how to pitch the water use angle to the media. If they pick it up, we could raise quite a stink. Might be enough to put a stop to the development."

"Maybe. Let me think about it, talk to a couple of people."

"OK. You want me to email you the numbers?"

"Sure."

Sean said goodbye, fired off an email, then got back to work. He felt more positive than he had before running the analysis. He wanted to talk to Tom some more—they still needed to discuss the focus of the rallies, and he'd forgotten to pass along Rosa's warning about the threat she'd received. He decided to drop by the plaza after work and try to catch a few minutes with Tom.

On impulse, he called a friend who had a background of working with water rights in small communities around the state. These days Forrest worked for the Forest Service (which got him endless jokes), and Sean reached him at his office in Santa Fe.

"Hey, Sean, good to hear from you! Long time no see."

"Let's correct that. You free for lunch?"

"Ah...sure, if we can make it a late one. I have a meeting at eleven-thirty."

"How about one-thirty? The Shed?"

"Done."

The Shed was one of his favorite restaurants, though he tended to avoid it this time of year because it was generally overrun with tourists. One-thirty wasn't quite the end of the lunch rush. Sean got there a little early and put his name on the reservation list, accepted the pager the hostess handed him, and went back out to the little courtyard to wait for Forrest.

The building was old, old adobe, hundreds of years old,

probably one of the oldest buildings in town. It had been a hacienda, one of a series built in a long row northeast of the plaza and now all converted to shops and restaurants. The interior courtyard of this particular hacienda was surrounded on three sides by shops, with the fourth side, the farthest from the street, serving as the entrance to the Shed. The restaurant had put a few tables out in the courtyard to accommodate a few extra patrons, and at the moment every table was full.

The food was New Mexican, mostly, plus sandwiches and soups and wonderful desserts including Sean's favorite, lemon soufflé. The place had been open since the sixties and a lot of the decor reflected that era—bright, psychedelic floral designs that were also reminiscent of Mexican folk art. The quaintly narrow front doors were glass in a purple-painted wood frame.

The waiting room inside was packed and Sean preferred to be out in the fresh air. He hung out under one of the trees in the courtyard, avoiding looking at the people sitting nearby so as not to make them uncomfortable. Instead he watched the *zaguan*, the tunnel-like passage that led to the street, originally built so a wagon could pass through into the courtyard. After a few minutes, he saw Forrest stroll in.

Forrest had light hair and the kind of friendly face that could set anyone at ease. His attitude matched his looks. Sean had met him in college and had seen him in all kinds of environments, and he always seemed comfortable and happy to chat with whatever company he was in. He grinned as he walked up to Sean.

"Hey, I saw you on TV a couple of nights ago!"

Sean shrugged. "Oh, yeah. It was a rally."

"I didn't know you played the flute."

"Yeah, I'm taking lessons from the other guy who was playing."

"The Indian guy? Cool! Sean discovers hidden talents."

"What about you, what have you been up to? How's the new job?"

"Pretty good. I spend a lot of my time trying to arrange land swaps. It's amazing how complicated it gets."

"Political?"

"*Mui* political."

The pager Sean was holding went off, so they headed inside the restaurant and were shown to a tiny table in one of the back rooms. Soft light filtered through a stained-glass window, supplemented by a wagon-wheel chandelier. Purple and turquoise flowers, accented with touches of metallic gold paint, sprawled across the whitewashed adobe walls. A slightly harried waitress took their order and brought them glasses of the Shed's specialty iced herbal tea. Forrest stirred a packet of sugar into his and glanced up at Sean.

"So, how's the analysis biz?"

Sean shrugged. "Pretty good. Actually, I'm doing a little side project that I wanted your opinion on. You know that rally where I was playing the flute? It was about a new development proposed out by Pena Blanca."

Forrest nodded. "Valle del Sol. Another Kyle Robbins special."

"So you know about it."

"Oh, yeah."

Sean took a sip of his tea. "I ran some numbers. It looks like the development would suck two percent of the Rio's volume, once it's all built."

"Ouch."

"I'm working with People for Responsible Development. We're trying to find a way to block this one, and I think my analysis might get people motivated, if we can get it out through the media. What do you think?"

Forrest shrugged. "Grassroots is hard. There's an easier way, though it isn't as flashy."

"What's that?"

"This group—People for Responsible Development? If they have enough resources, they can initiate legal proceedings that would lead to a general stream adjudication on the Middle Rio Grande."

"Adjudication?"

"It's something the State does to settle water rights claims. You know how the old Spanish land grants and the Pueblo charters and all have different claims."

Sean nodded. "Yeah. It's a can of worms."

"A major can of worms. In a general stream adjudication, the

State sues every landholder on a given watercourse to make them prove their water rights. If that happens on the Rio Grande —I should say when it happens, because it will—then we're talking fifty, sixty thousand landowners. Maybe more. The cases could be tied up in court for decades."

"And Valle del Sol could be on hold all that time."

Forrest nodded. "Robbins's investment would just be sitting there, not earning him a dime. Costing him money, probably."

"Sweet."

"Of course, you wouldn't make any friends by setting this in motion."

Sean sighed. "I'm not out to make friends. I'm out to save the Rio."

"Good luck to you. Wouldn't want to take it on, myself."

"I sort of don't have a choice." Sean pulled an old receipt out of his wallet and took a pen from his shirt pocket. "I'd better make some notes. Tell me how this adjudication works."

Forrest went over the details while they ate their lunch, and Sean's notes filled his receipt, then spilled onto a paper napkin. He folded them together and stuffed them in his pocket, debating whether to mention his visit from *La Guadalupana* to Forrest. He decided against it. Not that he thought Forrest wouldn't give him the benefit of the doubt, but he didn't really want to talk about it in public.

When the waitress offered dessert, they both passed. Sean would have liked a lemon soufflé, but waiting for a table had eaten up a chunk of his lunch hour, and anyway the soufflés were best earlier in the day, when they were fresh out of the oven.

Sean insisted on picking up the tab. "Least I can do to thank you for the advice."

Forrest smiled. "I'll get the next one, then. Next week?"

"Sounds good. And we'll catch a hike too, one of these weekends."

"Deal."

Back at work, the rest of the afternoon went by quickly. At five, Sean shut down his computer and walked to the plaza. A breeze had picked up, gusting now and then, hard enough to throw a cloud of dust in his face. He strolled along the *portal* at the Palace, but Ruby's space was empty.

"She sold out," her neighbor said. "Went home to make more."

"I see." Sean nodded, smiled a thank-you and moved on.

He crossed the street to the plaza, where Tom and his gang were milling around the gazebo. No signs today. That must have been for the media's benefit on Sunday. The redhead—Pam, he remembered—glanced up at him and smiled.

"Hi, Sean! Good to see you."

"Hi. Small crowd today."

"Yeah, well. It's a weekday. Want to help hand out flyers?"

"Sure."

He accepted a stack of lime green flyers printed with the usual PRD spiel. A small box on the bottom of the page caught his eye. It announced a demonstration at Pena Blanca on the coming Saturday. Sean glanced up.

"I hadn't heard about Saturday. Is this at the development site?"

"Yeah." Pam nodded enthusiastically. "It just got scheduled. It's going to be a big deal, the TV people are coming. And since it's right there by Cochiti and Santo Domingo, the local Pueblo people should be out in force."

"But this weekend is Indian Market. Won't a lot of them be here in Santa Fe?"

Pam's brow creased with a surprised frown. "Well, I'm sure they won't all be here. There should still be plenty of them around."

Sean bit back a sarcastic comment. He thought it was poor timing, but the demonstration was scheduled and there wasn't much to be done about it now. He started handing out flyers to passersby.

Tom got up on the gazebo with his PA system. Somehow Sean felt the whole thing lacked energy. Maybe he was just comparing it to Sunday, when they'd had the music and roses, and there'd been a lot more people in the plaza. Five o'clock on a weeknight, people were heading home from work or on their way to dinner. It wasn't the best time to catch their attention.

Now and then folks stopped briefly to listen to Tom. Sean and Pam made sure all of them left with flyers in their hands.

Toward six o'clock things got slow, since most of the go-homes had already gone. Sean stood near the middle of the plaza and offered a flyer to anyone who passed. Pam drifted over to him.

"I missed your music today. Couldn't your friend make it?"

"No. He lives at Cochiti, and wasn't coming into town today. And anyway, Tom said the city won't let us play without a performance permit."

Pam looked surprised. "They won't?"

"He didn't tell you?"

"No." She glanced toward the gazebo. "He's got a lot going on."

"Have you known him long?"

"About a year. I signed up with PRD when it was first getting organized. I wanted to contribute, you know?"

Sean nodded. He'd met lots of Pams back in the Bay Area. True believers, devoted followers who sincerely wanted to make a difference. He'd felt that way himself, at first, but the years of watching good causes get defeated by political machinations had made him cynical.

"What got you interested?" he asked.

"Well, I was with a group called Waterwatch, that was keeping an eye on development and water issues all around the state. They kind of fell apart, though, around the time PRD was forming. The main organizer had some health issues and things just went by the wayside. It's too bad, it was a good group."

Sean nodded. People had limitations. Ideals were great, but making them real was hard work, and this kind of effort was almost always dependent on the energy and enthusiasm of volunteers.

"So PRD came along and you jumped aboard."

"Yeah. The focus isn't quite the same, but it's a good group. Tom's a great organizer."

"What do you think the focus should be?"

"Well, coming from where I came from, I think it should be the water, but I know there are other important issues too."

"Quality of life."

"Yeah, and that's important. Those folks in Cochiti and Santo Domingo could really see a decline."

"Harder to sell, though, than water running out for the

whole Rio Grande Valley."

"See, that's what I keep telling Tom, but he thinks water is too narrow a focus."

Pam looked up at him with earnest green eyes. Sean was glad to learn that she agreed with his point of view. More voices would have a better chance of swaying Tom.

Sean gazed thoughtfully at Tom, still doing his song and dance on the gazebo, even though the people listening were mostly the PRD crowd. "Maybe we could grab a cup of coffee."

"I'd like that."

Sean glanced at Pam. He'd been musing aloud, hadn't meant to invite her, but if she'd back him up on the importance of water it might be good to have her along.

By now the wind had kicked up enough to make standing outside unpleasant. Sean shut his eyes whenever a strong gust blew up dirt and sand from the plaza. It wasn't long before Tom wrapped his speech and started packing up.

Sean walked over to Tom, who glanced up at his greeting and paused to shake hands. "Good to see you," he said, smiling. "Thanks for your help."

Sean nodded. "I was wondering if you had time for a cup of coffee? Couple of things I'd like to talk about."

Tom glanced at his watch. "A quick one. Got a dinner meeting at seven."

"It shouldn't take long."

"Just let me get this stuff put away in the car. Why don't you grab us a table at that coffee place across the street?" Tom gestured to the south side of the plaza, where a chain espresso bar was tucked in between galleries and clothing stores.

"See you there in a few." Sean started toward the coffee place. Pam was coming toward him, and he paused to give her his leftover flyers.

"We're meeting for coffee over across the street."

"Let me put these in the box and I'll walk over with you." She retrieved a printer's box still half-full of flyers from under the gazebo.

"So, you going to come out on Saturday?"

Sean shrugged as they started toward the coffee place. "Don't see why not. Be good to get out of town during the

Market."

"Nobody seems to like Indian Market. I went last year, and I thought it was great."

"It is great. It brings in lots of tourist money. It's just the traffic that's a nightmare."

"Yeah, I guess. I'm so used to big city traffic that it doesn't seem that bad to me."

Sean opened the door of the coffee shop and held it for her. "How long have you lived here?"

"Three years. My folks wanted to retire here, and I helped them move. Fell in love with the place and followed them out."

The coffee place had only a few tables. They found a vacant one toward the back and put the box of flyers on it to stake it out, then went up to the counter to order. Sean bought an espresso, and Pam a tall iced mocha.

"How can you drink hot coffee when it's this warm?" she asked, laughing as they went back to the table.

Sean shrugged. "Habit, I guess."

She stirred her drink with her straw. "So those roses you had on Sunday came from your yard. You know the one that girl gave me—"

"Her name's Rosa."

"Rosa, right. Anyway, it's still fresh. I was worried it had been out of water too long, but I clipped the stem when I got home and it's fine."

"Good. Glad you like it."

"You must be an awesome gardener."

He shrugged. "Not really."

"Awesome musician, too. You're multitalented."

Sean took a swig of espresso, burning his tongue a little. He felt embarrassed at the compliments from Pam. Probably she was just making conversation, just trying to be nice. He gave her a brief smile and turned his attention to the front window, watching for Tom. When Tom finally came in, Sean stood and picked up his empty cup.

"I'm going to get some coffee. Want anything?"

Pam shook her head. Sean met Tom by the counter and refilled his cup from the urns of regular coffee by the sugar and cream and cinnamon and other fussy stuff available for doctoring. Sean added cream to his coffee, since the regular stuff served by this chain usually tasted burned to him. He waited for Tom to get his own cup, and they walked back to the table.

"Sorry it took me so long," Tom said. "Hi, Pam."

"Hi." She scooted her chair closer to Sean's to make room for him.

Tom sat down with a sigh and took a sip of coffee, then looked at Sean. "OK, what did you want to talk about?"

Sean glanced at Pam. He didn't want to alarm her, but she should probably know about the threat Rosa had received. He told them about the intruder and the email in undramatic terms, then added, "Rosa thought you should know. Whoever threatened her might try it on others."

"That's terrible!" Pam said. "Did she call the police?"

"Her brother's a cop. He checked it out, but didn't get anywhere."

Tom sat frowning, shaking his head. "This is very bad. We haven't had any threats before."

"Well, the news guys did a pretty big story on Sunday's rally. Did you see it?"

Tom met his gaze. "Yeah. She made a strong impression."

"Too strong, apparently," said Sean.

Pam shook her head. "I disagree. I mean, I'll understand if she doesn't want to go on camera any more, but actually, this means we're getting more effective."

Tom looked at her, still frowning. "I don't want anyone to get hurt."

"Sometimes you've got to take chances." Pam glanced at Sean. "If Rosa doesn't want to give another interview, I'll do it."

Sean looked at her, impressed by this show of gutsiness. "You said the media were coming to Pena Blanca on Saturday, right?"

"Yeah."

"Would you feel like being the spokesperson if the TV guys want an interview?"

"Sure!"

"Wait a second," Tom said. "I think we're rushing a little, here."

Sean faced Tom. "What have you got planned for Saturday?"

Tom drank some coffee. "It'll be something like the town hall meeting, without the speakers. We'll have the displays, and anyone who hasn't seen them yet can look at them and ask questions."

"You're bringing the PA?"

"No—there's no power to run it."

"No power?"

"We won't be in the village, we'll be a little south of there, right at the edge of the development site. We don't have permission to go onto the site, but we can look at it."

Sean took a swig of coffee. He'd been about to suggest that he and Angel could play, since they wouldn't need a permit, but without amplification the music wouldn't reach far.

"Are there going to be any talks at all? I mean, are you going to give your usual speech?"

"Yeah, I'll have a megaphone, and I'll do an abbreviated version."

"Have you thought about emphasizing the water angle? The Rio Grande?"

Tom raised an eyebrow. "We're not really about the Rio Grande. We're about stopping this specific development."

"But one of the major impacts of the development is the water use. You got my email, right?"

"I did. Haven't had a chance to look at the numbers yet."

Sean bit back impatience. "Well, when you do get a chance to look at them, I'd like to talk about it. I think if we can get the media to cover the water issue, we'll raise a lot more interest."

Tom folded his arms and rested his elbows on the table. "The thing is, your analysis isn't scientific."

"Sure it is."

"You haven't used real data."

"I used the data provided on Robbins Corp's brochures. I ran standard projections, and used data from comparable existing facilities in this area as the basis for my estimates on the golf course and so on."

"This sounds interesting," Pam said. "You ran an analysis on the development's water use?"

Sean glanced at her. "Yeah. It'll suck two percent of the river's volume, when all's said and done."

"Two percent!"

"Let's talk about this after I've had a chance to go over your numbers," said Tom. "Right now the most important thing is this Saturday's rally. It's our chance to really bring the issues to the people who live right by the development site, to raise awareness in Pena Blanca and Cochiti and Santo Domingo."

"Too bad a lot of them will be in Santa Fe for Indian Market," Sean said.

Tom shrugged. "So we'll miss a few. There'll be more at home."

Sean wasn't sure about that, but he didn't want to argue the point. "Have you notified the pueblos about this event?"

"We'll be distributing flyers." Tom nodded toward Pam's box of green flyers.

"That's my day tomorrow," Pam said. "Want to come?"

"Wish I could. Got to work. I'll be there Saturday for sure, though," he said.

Tom checked his watch, then drank the last of his coffee and stood up. "I've got to go. See you Saturday, and thanks again for helping today."

They shook hands, and Sean watched Tom make his way out of the espresso bar. He was disappointed that Tom hadn't looked at his analysis right away. They hadn't really discussed focus, either. He could understand Tom wanting to keep control of PRD's direction, since he'd organized the group, but there was such a thing as too narrow a focus.

"What does Tom do? Do you know?" He looked at Pam, who shrugged.

"As far as I know he spends all of his time on this."

Sean smiled slightly. "Like you?"

Pam tipped up her chin. "I'm an artist."

"Really? So's my mom."

"She is?"

"Yeah. Donna Carpenter. Paints tractors."

"Oh, of course! Solid and traditional. The gallery owners love that kind of stuff."

"Pays the bills. She put me through college."

Pam glanced up at him, looking a little concerned. "I didn't mean to be dismissive. I do admire her professionalism."

Sean smiled to reassure her. "I know what you mean. Her stuff isn't to my taste either. What sort of work do you do?"

"Abstract. I work in acrylic. Some sculpture, also. I haven't really found my place yet." She gave him a rueful look. "I'm going to have to find a job soon, to pay the rent. I usually look for part time."

Sean nodded. He'd seen more than a few friends struggle in arts careers. It was never as glamorous or as easy as people seemed to think. The ones who made it were the ones who never gave up.

"Rent's not cheap in Santa Fe."

"I've got one of those studios over by the railyard, so it's not too bad."

"Those are subsidized, right?"

"Yeah. You have to pass a jury to get in."

"So you've got talent. Just stick to it."

She smiled. "Thanks."

They walked out together, disposing of their cups on the way. Sean debated whether to offer to walk Pam to her car. She spared him the decision by turning to him, smiling, her arms wrapped around her box of flyers.

"Thanks for including me. It was nice chatting."

"Yeah." Sean nodded, smiled. "See you Saturday."

She turned and crossed the street, heading north. Sean crossed the plaza, thinking about what to do with his evening. Call Angel and see if he knew about Saturday. Send Rosa an email in case she wanted to come. He wouldn't be surprised if she didn't, after the threats, but down deep inside he hoped she would.

He hurried to his car and drove home, his stomach grumbling despite the coffee, or maybe because of it. He headed straight for the kitchen to make something fast for dinner, but was stopped by the view through the dining room window.

Half a dozen people were standing out in the alley beyond the wall of his back yard, looking at the rosebushes.

Sean went out the back door, and the people beyond the wall all looked up at him. Most were women, most Hispanic. There was one Anglo lady and one boy who looked about ten. Sean went over to the wall.

"Can I help you folks?"

"We heard this is where the miracle roses came from," said a young chicana, rather shyly. She gestured toward the rosebushes, which were growing level with the top of the wall.

Miracle roses. Oh, boy.

"Who told you that?"

The kid piped up. "My sister got one in the plaza on Sunday. She never put it in water, but it's still fresh."

"Really?" Sean was surprised, though he supposed he shouldn't be. "Wow, that's amazing."

"Please, may I buy one?" said the chicana. Her face was so earnest, for a moment she reminded Sean of Rosa.

"Uh...they're not for sale."

She looked crestfallen. Two of the other women murmured together.

"But I'll give you one, if ..."

Sean hesitated. What the hell? He kept hearing about the power of prayer.

"... if you promise to pray for the Rio Grande."

"The Rio Grande?" said the chicana.

"It's endangered. Did you know that?"

She shook her head, wide-eyed. "No."

Sean glanced at the others. They all shook their heads.

"It's one of the five most endangered rivers in the country. If you all promise to pray for the survival of the Rio Grande, I'll give you each a rose."

They all exclaimed. The chicana leaned forward against the wall, glanced eagerly down at the roses, then looked at Sean.

"Oh, yes! Yes, please," she said. "I'll pray for the river!"

"OK. Um, I'll be back in a minute."

Sean went inside for his scissors. He thought about getting some paper cups, but decided against it. If the roses were lasting without water, then the cups weren't necessary.

Amazing how practical you could get about a miracle.

He took out his scissors and went back out to the yard. Looked up at the chicana.

"What color do you want?"

"Red, please," she said with a shy smile.

He cut her a red one, then cut roses for the rest of the visitors. Most of them wanted red. One lady asked for pink, and the kid took a red and yellow one. They all thanked Sean and went away with their flowers, promising to pray for the Rio.

Sean stood for a moment staring at the bushes. He couldn't see any diminishment, as usual.

"Well, that was interesting."

He went inside, put away the scissors, and put a pot of water on the stove for pasta. While he waited for it to boil he called Ruby's cell phone. She answered on the fourth ring.

"Hi, Ruby, it's Sean. I wanted to ask if you and Angel knew about the rally out there near Pena Blanca on Saturday."

"No. This Saturday?"

"Yeah. Tom and the PRD folks are putting on a rally by the Valle del Sol site."

"I didn't hear anything about it. What time?"

"One o'clock. I'll be there. No PA, so it wouldn't work for me and Angel to play, but I was hoping I'd see you guys anyway."

"Yeah, we'll go! Well, I will anyway. I'll tell Angel too, and I'll call people. How come they didn't publicize this?"

"I think they're just getting a late start."

"You going to bring some more roses?"

Sean glanced at the back yard and stifled a sigh. "Sure, why not?"

"Good! I wanted one for me, but we gave them all out last time."

"Funny thing about the roses. I've had some people over here asking for them."

"At your house?"

"Yeah, my neighbor saw the news story and guessed that they came from my bushes. I just gave out half a dozen more of them. One kid said a rose from last Sunday stayed fresh out of water."

"Oh, yeah?"

"Yeah. Weird, huh?"

"No weirder than dead bushes blooming."

"They weren't *completely* dead."

The water was starting to simmer around the edges of the pot. Sean opened a cupboard and took out a bag of macaroni.

"Is Angel around?"

"No, he's out with some friends. I'll tell him you called."

"OK. Tell him I hope to see him on Saturday."

"I will. Thanks for letting me know about that rally. I'm going to tell my neighbors. Of course, a bunch of them will be in Santa Fe for the Market."

"Yeah, I know. Not the best timing, but we'll see if we can draw some of the stay-at-homes."

"I'll call around, let everybody know."

"Great. See you Saturday."

Sean put the phone down and added macaroni and some oil to the boiling water. He got a jar of spaghetti sauce out of the fridge, along with a plastic container of grated Romano cheese and a package of bag salad. Bachelor meal, quick and easy. In five minutes he was sitting at the dining table, chowing down.

Halfway through his meal he noticed someone out in the alley, a middle-aged Hispanic woman, standing by the pink-and-white rosebush. She looked like she was praying.

Sean looked away and finished his meal. He didn't think she was one of the ones he'd just given flowers to. He sure hadn't meant for anyone to pray in his back yard.

When he'd finished his supper he took the dishes to the kitchen, then went out back. The lady was gone. The smell of roses was heavy in the air, and he thought it had a slightly different scent. Sean went over to the rosebushes, and looked at both closely, but couldn't see any changes. Finally he leaned over the wall between them and looked in the alley.

A Guadalupe candle sat at the foot of the wall, just opposite the pink and white rose bush. One of those tall candles in a glass, this one had a picture of *La Guadalupana* surrounded by roses. The wax was pink, and was giving off the rose perfume he'd smelled.

Sean frowned down at the candle. He wished it wasn't there, but he was reluctant to move it because he knew it represented a prayer from the person who'd left it. It was sitting on the dirt, and there weren't any weeds or dry grass nearby, so if it fell over it probably wouldn't start a fire. He left it alone and went back in the house.

After cleaning up his supper dishes he sat in the living room, working up the courage to call Rosa. He could email, but he wanted to talk to her about the roses. About anything, actually. He just wanted talk to her.

Finally he grabbed the phone and dialed her number. After a couple of rings she answered. Just the sound of her voice gave him a thrill.

"Rosa, hi! It's Sean."

"Hi, Sean."

"You won't believe what's been happening in my yard."

He launched into a description of his neighbor that morning, and the others that had come asking for roses, and the woman who'd left the candle. He was afraid he was babbling, but now that he'd reached Rosa he was blurting out the stuff about the roses to keep from saying other things he was worried she wouldn't like.

"One of them said a rose from Sunday had stayed fresh out of water."

"Oh, yes!" Rosa said. "The same thing happened to one of my roses. I've been meaning to send you an email about it."

"I put yours in water, though."

"Yes, and I moved them to a vase, but I took one out of it and laid it on the altar. It stayed fresh even though it was lying there all night.

"Wow."

"So they really are a miracle."

Sean looked out the window. The sun was starting to set, and the last wash of golden light was climbing up the rosebushes. Miracle roses.

"Um, there's another rally Saturday. We're thinking of handing some more roses out."

"On the plaza?"

"No, this one's in Pena Blanca. Out by the Valle del Sol site. Can you come?"

Rosa didn't answer for a moment, and Sean bit his lip. That had sounded too hopeful, he guessed.

"I don't know. I would like to see the site."

"There'll be TV people there, but you wouldn't have to give an interview."

Rosa was silent again for a long moment. Maybe he shouldn't have mentioned the media.

"I'll be there," she said at last.

Sean's heart gave a couple of intense thumps. He really shouldn't be taking this so seriously.

"Maybe we can have dinner again, after," he said.

"Are there places to eat in Pena Blanca?"

"I don't know." He laughed nervously. "I'll find out."

"Why don't we just play it by ear. See how long the rally goes."

"Yeah, OK."

Silence stretched again. Sean stared at the kiva fireplace in the corner of his living room. Empty this time of year, all the ashes cleared out.

"Is everything all right?" he asked.

"Oh. Yeah, I guess. Things are a little weird at work."

"Weird? More *koshare*?"

"No, but I saw Kyle Robbins again. I just missed getting asked to lunch with him, apparently."

Fear welled in Sean's heart. "Do *not* go to lunch with him."

"Don't worry, I didn't."

"He could be trying to threaten you again, or trying to get control of you. Don't get in a car with him, don't accept a drink from him—"

"Hey, relax! It didn't happen."

"He might try again."

A pause. "Yeah, he might. Don't worry, I'll say no."

Sean closed his eyes. "Sorry. I shouldn't be telling you what to do."

"That's OK. Thanks for caring."

I do care. He wanted to shout it, wanted to follow it with a lot more that he was sure Rosa wasn't ready to hear.

"And thanks for the call," Rosa added. "I'll be there on Saturday. Maybe I'll bring a friend from Sandia. I think he might be interested."

Sean made himself answer politely. "That'd be good. The more the merrier."

"See you then."

He listened until he heard the click of a disconnect, then turned off the phone. He sat wondering why he'd reacted so strongly to her mentioning Robbins, and decided it was because he believed Robbins was behind the threats she'd received. Who else would have an interest in discouraging Rosa from talking to the media? Who else had a motive for squashing "Roses for the Rio?" No one he could think of.

He hadn't mentioned the threats to Ruby, he realized. Well, he'd tell her when he saw her on Saturday, and she could decide for herself if she was worried about it. She was probably in no danger. It was Rosa who'd caught Robbins's attention.

Rosa wanted to bring a friend on Saturday. That was a big negative signal. No intimate dinner if she had a friend along.

Sean got up to put away the phone, shaking his head slightly. He needed to chill about Rosa. He was getting his priorities confused. The river was important—the river was what Saturday was about. Saving the river was what he and Rosa had in common. If there was ever going to be more between them, he had to maintain that common ground.

He gazed out the back door at the yard, now nearly dark. Shadows of blue dusk hovered in the corners of the walls. Pale blooms glowed softly on the rosebushes, blobs of lightness against the dark leaves. On impulse he took his flute out back and played. No rain chant this time. He was playing for Rosa, playing out his feelings, making up a wordless prayer for her safety.

He played himself out eventually and just stood in the darkening yard, listening to the quiet sounds of the neighborhood. A dog barking, a car going by, somebody's TV blaring a sports program. A flicker of light in the alley reminded him of the candle sitting there, like a silent watcher, standing vigil over the miracle roses.

If he cut every single flower—assuming that he even could—

would they all grow back by morning? Silly idle thought.

Sean went back in the house and closed the blinds on the dining room window. He put away his flute and went to his office, also known as the spare bedroom. He'd intended to surf the web for a while before crashing, but as he sat there he kept thinking of the candle the woman had left out back. The roses seemed to have considerable power to inspire. Maybe they could use that.

"Roses for the Rio."

He did a quick search. As he thought, it was unique enough that no one had registered it. Sean went to his favorite domain registry, and after five minutes and the expense of a few electronic bucks, he was the official owner of rosesfortherio.org.

He smiled at the screen, then out to the kitchen to put on some more coffee. He was too wired to sleep anyway, so he might as well get the website up and running.

It wasn't the doorbell, but voices that woke him the next morning. He looked at the clock.

"Oh, good. Made it to six-thirty today."

Considering that he'd gone to bed at one-thirty, it wasn't that much of a luxury. He got up and pulled on his robe, then went down the hall. Before going into the kitchen he stuck his head in the living room to glance out the back door.

"Holy crap!"

The back wall of the yard was crowded with people, maybe two or three deep. They hadn't invaded his yard, but it looked like it was only a matter of time.

Sean ducked back into the hall. How should he handle this? Word had gotten around, apparently. Maybe he should have told Mrs. Trujillo to go to hell.

No, that wasn't fair. And anyway, he liked Mrs. Trujillo.

"Coffee. Coffee first."

He got the pot going and went back to his bedroom to get dressed. The coffee had brewed by the time he returned, and he stood in the kitchen nursing a mug.

How to deal with a bunch of pilgrims in the alley. Telling

them to go away would probably have zero impact. He wondered if they were taking roses. Maybe. Hard to tell, with those bushes. He could chop the bushes down to the ground, but he had a suspicion they'd just grow right back.

OK, so he couldn't just get rid of the pilgrims, they'd keep coming as long as the roses were here. What could he do to make them go away voluntarily?

Give them roses.

Grimacing, he opened the drawer where he kept the kitchen scissors. There was a roll of twine in there, too, and he grabbed it. He finished his coffee, set the mug down on the counter with a sharp clack, and went out to face the horde.

It wasn't that huge a horde, when he got out in the yard. Fifteen or twenty people, clustered around the wall by the rosebushes. They raised an excited chatter when Sean appeared.

"OK, all right." He gestured for quiet. "You can each have one rose if you promise to pray for the Rio Grande, OK? That's the deal."

A couple of them were already praying, it looked like, with their elbows on the wall and their heads bowed. He doubted they were praying for the river, but oh well. He started cutting roses, handing them across the wall to eager waiting hands.

"Thank you," the pilgrims told him, and "Bless you."

Sean just nodded and kept cutting roses until everyone had one. Some of the pilgrims drifted away with their flowers, others seemed inclined to hang around, gazing at the rosebushes or praying.

Sean cut a ten-foot length of twine and used it to tie his kitchen scissors to an old, disabled sprinkler head near the foot of the rosebushes. He set the scissors on top of the wall between the roses, then went in the house and used his computer to print out a sign that said "YOU MAY HAVE ONE ROSE IF YOU PRAY FOR THE RIO GRANDE." He brought this back outside along with a couple of thumbtacks which he used to post the sign on the trunk of the elm tree nearest to the rosebushes. By then it was time to go to work.

He went back in the house, pursued by the thanks of the pilgrims. He gave them a nod and a wave as he shut the door, then made sure it was locked and pulled the vertical blinds he seldom used across it.

"Wow."

Breakfast. Hadn't had breakfast. He grabbed a couple of granola bars from the cupboard and poured the rest of his coffee into the travel mug he'd loaned to Rosa. Stuffed his pockets with wallet and such, then went out, half-worried he'd find more pilgrims outside the front door. He didn't, and he hurried to get in his car, glad to get away from the house and the infestation of the faithful in his back yard.

15

Halfway through the morning, Arturo called Rosa into his office. With a sense of foreboding, she locked her desk and told Frank to keep an eye on things. Wednesdays were usually slow, unless it was the end of the month. Telling herself not to be so nervous, Rosa left the teller line and crossed the lobby to Arturo's office.

The blinds were drawn, as usual. Sunlight snuck in along their edges, creating a bright backlighting that made it hard to see Arturo's face as he sat with his back to the window.

"Come in, Rosa. Have a seat."

Arturo got up as she came in, and moved to close the door behind her. Rosa sat in one of the visitor chairs.

She wasn't comfortable in Arturo's office. Practically the only time she came in here was for her annual performance review, or to discuss hiring new tellers, but they weren't hiring at the moment and her review was still a couple of months away.

Arturo returned to his chair behind the desk and sat down with an exaggerated sigh. "Mr. Robbins was here the other day," he said.

"Yeah, I saw him in the lobby."

Arturo picked up a pen and started tapping it against the blotter on his desk. "He'd like to take you to lunch."

"Gerry mentioned that. Isn't he married?"

"This would be a business lunch."

"Oh."

Rosa's confidence faltered. She sat silent, feeling the arguments she'd prepared disintegrating, slipping through her fingers like faded flower petals. It hadn't occurred to her that Robbins wanted to talk business.

Yeah, right. Like the guy in her yard had wanted to talk business.

"I don't have to tell you that Mr. Robbins is an important client," Arturo said. "He represents a significant potential income for the bank."

"I don't see how I can make a difference there. I'm just a

teller. Shouldn't you be the one going to lunch?"

"Mr. Robbins has taken an interest in you. It would be a good idea for you to go and listen to what he has to say. It would be good for your career."

Rosa sat up stiffly and frowned at Arturo's shadowed face. "Are you threatening my job?"

"No, no, no! Jeez, Rosa, you watch too much television!" Arturo laughed, but it sounded slightly forced. "All I'm asking is that you go to lunch, hear him out. He's got some interesting ideas and he wants to talk about them with you."

"Gotta keep the big honcho client happy," Rosa said.

Arturo ignored her tone. "Just do this as a favor for me, OK? One lunch. Costs you nothing. You can even count it as work on your timesheet."

Rosa shifted in her chair, uncomfortable. She wanted to say no, but she couldn't think of a good reason to. Not a reason she could talk to Arturo about, anyway. If she suggested Robbins was responsible for the intruder in her yard, he'd say prove it, and she couldn't. She'd sound totally paranoid.

"I've already got lunch plans," she said in desperation.

"Mr. Robbins was hoping you'd be free tomorrow."

"I ..."

"You don't have plans for tomorrow, do you?"

"No, but—"

"Good, I'll tell him you can make it. He'll pick you up at a quarter to twelve."

Rosa felt panic rising in her chest. She remembered Sean's concern on the phone.

"I'd rather drive my own car."

Arturo leaned back in his chair, swiveling slightly. "Really, Rosa. You're acting foolish."

"I might have an errand to run."

"Can't you take care of your errands after work?"

Rosa tipped up her chin. "I'll drive myself, or I'm not going."

Arturo was silent for a long, agonizing moment. "OK, fine," he said at last. "I'll find out what restaurant, and I'll tell Mr. Robbins you'll meet him there."

Rosa stood. "Can I go now?"

"Yes. But Rosa—"

She paused at the door and looked back. She couldn't see Arturo's eyes, but she could feel them.

"Don't fail me on this. It's important to *my* job, OK? Never mind yours. Understand?"

"I understand."

She fled from his office, feeling as if she couldn't breathe, and made a beeline for the restroom. Once inside she stood at the sink and splashed water on her face, then dabbed at it with a paper towel, hoping to keep from crying.

It shouldn't be so frightening. Like Arturo said, it was just one lunch, right? Lunch in a public place, with a man who would be recognized and remembered by the people around them. It wasn't as if he could get away with doing anything to her under those circumstances.

Maybe all he really wanted was to talk. She could guess what he'd say—another warning, more subtly phrased, perhaps. A warning to stay away from the Valle del Sol protests.

Rosa straightened and looked at herself in the mirror, dabbed at her makeup where she'd rubbed some mascara at the corner of one eye. She would listen, but she would make her own decisions. If Robbins threatened her at all, she'd call Miguel and raise hell.

Maybe she'd call him beforehand. Call him tonight and get some advice. Maybe Miguel could get her one of those tape recorders you wore hidden under your clothes, and she could record what Robbins said at the lunch.

A tingle went through her. If Robbins threatened her, or implied anything illegal, she'd have a record of it on tape. Wasn't it legal to record a conversation you were having without telling the other person? She'd have to ask Miguel for sure, but she thought it was.

Feeling better, she smoothed her hair and went back to the teller line. There were no customers in the lobby. Frank and Margo were gossiping about the Lobo football team. In the drive-up, Rosa saw Sandy working on a deposit, the pneumatic carrier sitting open on the counter beside her. Everything normal, not very busy.

Rosa unlocked her desk and took out some paperwork, trying to relax. After a few minutes, she called Miguel's cell phone. To her surprise, he answered.

"Hi, bro. I expected to leave you a message."

"Slow day. Everything OK?"

"Yeah, I just wanted to ask you a couple of questions. Could I come over to your place after work?"

"How about lunch instead? Like I said, it's slow."

Rosa glanced toward Arturo's office. The door was closed, and Gerry was on the phone at her desk.

"That would be great. Where?"

"Garcia's OK?"

"Fine. Meet you there at noon."

Rosa hung up and busied herself with paperwork until a little before noon. Just as she was locking her desk, she saw Arturo leave his office and head out the front doors. He didn't look her way. She felt relieved.

No *koshare*, she realized. She hadn't seen one since Sunday night. Maybe that meant this lunch with Robbins would be OK.

She drove to Garcia's, a little hole-in-the wall New Mexican restaurant. There were other locations around town, but Miguel preferred this one with its vinyl booths and the feel of an old diner.

He was sitting in a booth halfway back, facing the door and eating chips and salsa. In his uniform he always looked younger to Rosa, like a kid just out of training even though he'd been a cop for five years now. She joined him, smiling as she slid into the opposite seat.

"So what's up?" Miguel asked. "You haven't had any more intruders have you?"

"No. All quiet at home. I've had an unusual invitation, though."

Leaning close and talking in a low voice under the clatter from the kitchen, she explained about Robbins wanting to go to lunch with her, and that she suspected he might be behind the threat she'd received. Miguel's frown deepened as she asked about recording Robbins at lunch.

"That's dangerous, sis. People who find out they're being recorded tend to get angry."

"Well, he wouldn't find out, right? This is just lunch. It's not like he's a drug dealer or something."

"How do you know?"

Rosa stared at him in surprise. Sometimes Miguel's cynicism astonished her. Part of being a cop, she supposed, but it made her sad to think that he saw the world that way. She often thought that he must have terrible *Susto*, wounding of the soul, from the work that he did. She hadn't ever got up the nerve to ask him about it.

She leaned her elbows on the table and lowered her voice. "If he threatens me or refers to the threat, then I'll have proof. I could use it to keep him from bothering me any more."

"Use it how?"

"I don't know. Maybe get a restraining order."

"Women who get restraining orders end up dead, half the time. If you got any information to use against him, you'd better use it to put him in jail."

Rosa blinked. "I don't know if I could do that."

"Let me put it this way. If you got something incriminating, something he could be prosecuted for, the best thing you could do is hand it over to me. I could get it into the right hands. You shouldn't go trying to blackmail him into leaving you alone."

Rosa was silent. She hadn't had a very clear plan about what to do with the recording, if she caught anything useful.

"He's powerful, Rosa. It would be better if you didn't go to lunch with him at all."

"Well, I have to go. I agreed to."

"What if you called in sick tomorrow?"

"That would only postpone it. I have a feeling Robbins isn't going to let this slide. I might as well get it over with."

Miguel grimaced and ate another tortilla chip. A waitress came to take their order, and brought them large glasses of iced tea. Rosa didn't say anything more about the recorder. She knew Miguel had to think about it before he decided anything. She ate a couple of chips, dipping a corner of each in the salsa.

"You going to any more of those protests?" Miguel asked after their lunch arrived.

"There's a rally on Saturday, at the development site."

"Don't talk to any reporters."

"I'm not going to."

He stabbed his fork into his *carne adovada*. Rosa ate a couple of bites of her *rellenos*, enjoying the cheese and green chile. Salt and fire, she thought, savoring the flavors. She drank some tea to cool her mouth.

Miguel took a long swig of his own tea, then took a *sopaipilla* from the basket between them and tore it in half. "OK, look. I can help you, but you'll have to be certified as a confidential informant. Otherwise anything you record won't be admissible in court."

Rosa frowned. "Will that take a long time?"

"There's some paperwork to fill out. I can set up a meeting with my supervisor this afternoon. Can you get off work a little early?"

"If I can get Frank to close. I'll try."

"Where's this lunch going to be?"

"I don't know yet. I said I'd drive myself there, so as soon as I find out where I'll let you know."

"Good. I'll be in the area. Park in a visible place, like right by the front door."

"OK."

"I'll bring the phone over tonight and show you how to put run the app."

"App? I thought it would be a tape recorder..."

Miguel grinned. "You've been watching old movies, sis."

"If it's an app, can't I just put it on my phone?"

"Nope. Restricted to police use. That's why you have to be an official informant."

"OK. Thanks, I really appreciate this."

Miguel met her gaze, still frowning slightly, dark eyes worried. "You want to show your appreciation, be careful. Don't piss this guy off. He's got a long arm, you know?"

Rosa nodded. "I'll be careful."

Miguel wiped chile off his plate with a piece of *sopaipilla* and ate it. "You going to be at Mama's for dinner on Sunday?"

Rosa laughed. "Have to. I can't miss two in a row."

They talked family for the rest of their meal, and parted with a hug in the parking lot. Miguel's watchful eyes glanced all around as they headed for their cars.

"Take care, Rosa. I'll text you about getting certified."

She blew him a kiss, then drove back to the bank, arriving a couple of minutes late. Gerry intercepted her as she crossed the lobby, holding out a pre-printed message slip.

"Arturo said to give you this."

Rosa took the slip and glanced at it. Arturo's dark scrawl, saying, "McGrath's, 12:30."

"Thanks," she said.

"Not the Rancher's Club, but still pretty nice." Gerry smiled slyly. "So you decided to go after all, hm? Have fun."

"It's a business lunch."

"Right."

Gerry sidled off toward her desk. Rosa stuffed the message slip in her pocket and headed for the teller line.

McGrath's was downtown, in a big hotel. A comfortingly public place, but there was no parking right outside. She'd have to park in the big underground lot across the street, or on a side street, and she didn't know where Miguel could sit in his car. A squad car in the valet parking drop-off might be a bit obvious.

She texted the time and place to Miguel, then arranged for Frank to close up at 5:00 so she could leave early. While she waited to hear back from her brother, she dove into work to keep herself from worrying. To her relief, she didn't see Arturo again.

Halfway through the afternoon her phone buzzed with a text:

meet 4:30 main station downtown

A tingle went down Rosa's arms. She answered that she'd be there and spent the rest of the afternoon watching the clock. At 4:15 she put Frank in charge of the teller line and the vault, and headed downtown.

Miguel was waiting at the door of the police station. He led her down a couple of hallways to a small office with two desks, one of which was occupied by an Anglo man in uniform with dark hair going grey.

"Rosa, this is Captain Wilson, my boss. Cap, this is my sister, Rosa."

The captain stood and shook hands, watching her all the while with intense, green eyes. "Nice to meet you. Miguel's been telling me about your harassment."

"Harass?—Oh, yes." She glanced at her brother. He had his

stone face on.

The captain gestured to a chair and sat in his own, leaning back and folding his hands across his stomach. "What do you expect to gain by recording your meeting with Kyle Robbins?"

Rosa swallowed as she sat. Maybe this was a dumb idea after all.

"I think he's behind the threats," she said. "The harassment. I thought maybe I could get him to say something that will prove it."

"Don't try to lead him to it. That'll just make him suspicious."

She nodded. Sounded like she was going to get to do this.

He asked her some more questions and made her fill out a form. While he looked over what she'd written, Rosa snuck a glance at her brother, who smiled and gave her a small thumbs-up.

Captain Wilson scrawled his signature on the form and set it aside, then stood and took a backpack and a cell phone off a shelf behind his desk.

"Here's the gear." He handed the backpack to Miguel and the phone to Rosa. "Miguel will show you how to use the app. Be careful, and good luck."

"Thank you."

Rosa's heart was beating hard as Miguel walked her to her car. Somehow, the whole thing felt more real now, and more dangerous.

"I'll follow you home and show you the app," Miguel said.

"Thank you. I never realized this would be so complicated. I'll make it up to you."

"Cook me dinner, then."

"I'll cook you three dinners."

"Not all at once, OK?"

At her house, Rosa hurried out back to cut some herbs to throw in a pan with some chicken. Fresh rosemary, thyme, and oregano—their fragrance eased her tension. She paused to glance at her statue of *La Guadalupana*. The rose bush beside it bore no flowers—it was dormant. In September and October it would bloom again, but right now it was waiting, patiently enduring the summer heat.

Rosa could sympathize. She felt a little that way herself, like she was enduring the attention from Robbins and the threats. Soon, she hoped, it would all end.

Miguel had put the backpack on her dining table and opened it up, revealing a black box a little smaller than a motorcycle battery. Rosa started the chicken and some rice cooking, then joined him.

"This is the remote unit. It records whatever the app picks up, and I can also listen in real-time. I'll be in the hotel lobby with this. That way I can keep an eye on the entrance, too. If Robbins tries to hustle you out, I'll see it."

"I don't think he would try that."

"You never know." Miguel zipped the backpack shut. "There's a side door, but I doubt he'd try to use that. It opens to the outside, and it might have an alarm. I'll check it out ahead of time."

"I didn't realize this would be so complicated."

"The idea is to be prepared for anything, OK? So if something strange happens and you need help, you say 'Santa Maria' into the phone. Got it?"

"OK."

"Now get out the phone, and I'll show you the app."

Rosa fetched the phone from her purse and listened intently to Miguel's instructions. He had her practice turning on the app a few times.

"Turn it on as soon as you get out of your car."

"I will. Thank you, Miguel."

"Don't try to get him to incriminate himself. Don't ask him any leading questions, understand? This isn't TV."

Rosa nodded. "OK."

"Just let him talk. If he makes a threat, excuse yourself and leave. Don't stick around trying to get more dirt, right?"

"Right."

"And if anything goes wrong, or even if you just get a bad feeling, get out of there. Say you have to go to the restroom, then come out to the lobby and find me."

"OK." Rosa managed a smile as she walked with him to the door. "It'll be an adventure."

"I'm hoping it'll be boring as hell." He folded her into a tight hug. "Be careful, sis."

"I will. Thanks for helping me. I'm glad you'll be there."

Miguel smiled and kissed her cheek. "Remember, 'Santa Maria' if you need help."

"I'll remember."

She turned off the phone and put it back in her purse, then finished fixing supper. They talked about family stuff, football, anything but tomorrow, though Rosa never stopped thinking about it.

When Miguel said good night after supper, she watched him walk down the path to the street, his head turning right and left, always watching, always looking for trouble. The sun was just down, and the few scraps of cloud were flaming orange. She stood watching the sky long after Miguel had driven away, grateful for the beauty of that sunset, for the reminder that the world was a wondrous place.

16

Sean sat watching the late news with the blinds drawn and the TV up loud, feeling trapped. He'd come home to find a steady stream of visitors at the back garden wall, some clipping roses with his kitchen scissors, others standing in a semicircle in the alley with roses in their hands, praying. The front doorbell rang twice while he was eating dinner—people looking for the miracle roses. Sean had directed them to the back yard, then printed out a sign to put on the door so the doorbell wouldn't drive him crazy all night.

He'd gone out back once, out of curiosity to see if the rosebushes looked any less robust. They didn't. He'd said hello to the people in the alley, and glanced over the wall to see at least two dozen glass votive candles burning on the ground, the reason the pilgrims were in a semicircle instead of crammed up against the wall.

"Will you lead us in a prayer?" someone had called to him.

"Ah—no. I think you should all say your own prayers. Silently," he added, glancing toward the neighboring house. "Remember to pray for the Rio Grande."

After that he'd retreated into the house, and stayed inside all evening. He was a little annoyed at not being able to go out and play the flute in his yard if he wanted to. Maybe he shouldn't have started giving the roses away, but it was too late now. Word had spread.

The phone rang. Sean muted the television and answered it.

"Hi, Sean, it's Tom. I wanted to talk to you about your water analysis."

"Yeah?"

"I called Ben Lucero and asked about the status on the EIS. He forwarded the preliminary results to me. It doesn't match yours at all, I've got to say. I think there must be something wrong with your numbers."

Sean frowned in annoyance. "They came straight off the Valle del Sol brochure."

"Then there's something wrong with the calculations. You're showing three times what the EIS shows."

"They're probably only covering the first phase of the development. Take another look, you'll see how I've broken it down."

"The point is, this is the State Engineer's Office. We've pretty much got to accept their conclusions."

"I don't agree."

"State's where we're going to get the project blocked, if we manage to block it. We can't just blow off their analysis."

"I'm not saying to blow it off, I'm saying—"

"And their analysis says the impact to the river will be less than two percent."

"It's five percent, for the full development. Five *percent* of the river!"

"Even if that were true, it's not enough to really justify complaining about. I've thought about it, and I'm going to stick with the focus we have."

Sean stood up and started pacing, struggling to keep his tone level. "If you stick with 'quality of life' as your main focus, you'll get mostly the two nearest pueblos and a few environmentalists on board. If you go with saving the river, you could get every landowner in the Middle Rio Grande Valley. That's hundreds of people! Thousands!"

"It isn't realistic, Sean."

"Yes it *is*! We can set a general stream adjudication in motion. In fact, I think we should do that. It would tie up the water issues in court for years, and that alone could stall Valle del Sol."

Tom was silent for a long moment. Sean could hear voices from his back yard—someone had started singing "Amazing Grace." He stopped pacing and glared at the blinds covering the glass door.

"I think that would do more harm than good," Tom said slowly. "It would cause trouble for everyone along the river."

"Well, maybe it's time to cause trouble! Maybe everyone on the river should wake up to the fact that it's not an infinite resource."

"I'll think about it. It's not a step to be taken lightly."

"I know."

"We've got a couple of lawyers in the group I can talk to. I'll let you know what they say."

"OK." Sean felt himself calming down, though he was still annoyed and frustrated.

"You're coming to the rally on Saturday, right?"

"Right. I'll be there at one, or a little before."

"See you then."

Sean put the phone back on its charging station and ventured to peek out through the blinds in the dining room window. The glow from the candles lit the faces of the pilgrims out in the alley. He wondered if they were going to stand there all night. Some of them had been around since he'd come home that evening.

Disgusted, he shut off the TV and went to bed. He couldn't get to sleep right away, lying there thinking about the pilgrims and wondering if he should put up another sign. "NO SINGING. PRAY QUIETLY. DON'T DISTURB THE NEIGHBORS."

Shit, it shouldn't be his job to tell strangers how to behave. *Guadalupana* hadn't done him any favors.

In the morning Sean got up and got ready for work without looking out back. He didn't want to know what was going on out there. He was just about to head out when the doorbell rang.

"Damn. Didn't they see the sign?"

Maybe it had fallen down. Sean looked out the peephole and his heart skipped when he saw two cops standing outside, a man and a woman. He took a couple of deep breaths, then opened the door.

"Hi. What can I do for you?"

"You the homeowner?" said the male cop.

"That's right."

"We're going to have to ask you to keep the alley clear behind your house. We've had some complaints."

"I didn't invite any of those people to stand in the alley. You want to tell them to go away? Go right ahead."

"There's also the candles. They're a fire hazard."

Sean raised his hands in a gesture of helplessness. "I didn't put them there. And the alley isn't my property anyway. Look, I'm not trying to be obstructive, but I didn't ask these people to come. They just came."

The female cop, a Latina built on more butch lines than Rosa, gave him a skeptical look. "They're saying your roses are a miracle."

Sean shrugged. "They're just roses."

"People are saying they stay fresh without water."

"I haven't tried that, so I don't know if it's true."

"Mind if we try?"

Sean sighed. "Be my guest."

Her partner took a step forward. "OK if we come through the house?"

"Sure, fine."

Sean swung open the door and led the cops through the living room. He noticed the guy giving the room a look-over.

Tough luck, dude. No illegal substances here.

He pulled the vertical blinds and opened the back door. What he saw rocked him back for a second. The alley was packed with people. Jam packed, completely blocking the way. No wonder the cops had come.

"W-wow. There weren't that many yesterday."

The male cop gave him a skeptical look. Sean led the way out into the yard, and the guy paced around its edges while the woman went up to the rosebushes. Sean slid the glass door closed and followed her.

The scissors had fallen off the wall. Sean picked them up, brushed dirt off them, and looked at the cop.

"Take your pick."

She glanced at him, then reached for a red rose down on the side of the bush. Sean clipped the stem.

"Thanks," she said.

"Please, may I have a rose?" called a woman in the alley.

Sean looked at the cop, who was smelling her rose. Her partner came up, glanced at Sean's sign on the tree, then gave him a resigned nod.

"I'm going to have to ask you to go home," Sean said as he started clipping roses and handing them across the wall. "I'm getting in trouble with my neighbors, see? So please, you can have a rose, and then I need you to take your candles and go."

"But we want to pray before the miracle!"

"You can pray at home," said the male cop. "Come on, folks, clear it out. You're creating a nuisance. Don't make me write tickets."

Grumbling, the pilgrims gradually dispersed, clutching the roses Sean gave them. A couple had to be roused from their prayers, which the woman cop did, gently. When the alley was clear most of the candles remained, along with a litter of slips of paper scrawled with prayers, letters, and photographs, a couple of them even in frames. The candles generated an amazing amount of heat, and enough of them were scented to make a cloud of heavy rose perfume. With all that paper scattered around them, it was no wonder the cops were nervous.

Sean got a cardboard box from the house and went out through the back gate into the alley, collecting up all the paper and the photos. He had no idea what to do with the stuff. He couldn't just throw it away.

The female cop came out to help him. The male watched for a while, then came into the alley and picked up two of the candles and started to blow them out.

"Don't—those are prayers!" said the woman.

"We can't leave them here," said her partner. "They're a hazard!"

She glanced at Sean, then stood up and looked over the wall. "We could put them on the patio. That OK with you?"

"I guess," Sean said. "Won't it encourage people to bring more, though?"

"Post a 'no trespassing' sign," said the male cop. "You're good at signs."

Sean ignored the jibe and took the box of prayers into the house, then came back and started carrying candles to the small cement slab just outside his back door. Both cops helped. There had to be at least fifty candles. Before they were done moving them three more people had come to the wall. Sean cut roses for the visitors and sent them on their way.

"OK, this is all right for now," said the male cop. "You can't let people stand in the alley, though. If we get more complaints we'll have to come back."

"I'll do what I can to discourage them," Sean said.

"What's the deal with praying for the Rio?"

Sean gave a helpless shrug. "When people first started coming, I offered them a rose if they'd say a prayer for the river. I had no idea it was going to get this crazy."

The cop looked at the rosebushes. They looked gorgeous as always, even though Sean had just cut two or three dozen flowers.

"You might want to take down that sign."

Sean didn't think it would do any good, but he went to the tree and pulled off the sign. He resisted the temptation to voice his opinion. Instead he glanced at his watch.

"Oh, sh—shoot! I'm late for work!"

"We'll get out of your way, then. Thanks for your cooperation," said the male cop, heading for the house.

Sean and the other cop followed him in, through the living room to the front door. The woman glanced back at him.

"Thanks for the rose."

"You're welcome."

A slight frown creased her brow. "How many of them have you given away?"

Dozens. Hundreds.

"I have no idea," Sean said, crumpling the paper sign in his hands into a ball.

She turned and followed her partner to a squad car parked at the curb. Sean closed the door and went into the kitchen to call the office. The receptionist answered.

"Hi, Renée, it's Sean. I'll be in soon—had to take care of an unexpected problem at the house."

"Is it the roses? I heard about them from a friend."

"Ah...yeah."

"They're still all right, I hope?"

"They're fine. They're just attracting too much attention. I just had a visit from the cops."

"Oh!"

Sean noticed the coffee maker was still on. He shut it off and took out the carafe, looking around for his mug from breakfast. He spotted it on the dining table.

"So tell Nick I'll be there soon, OK?"

"OK. Could you bring one for me?"

"What?" Sean paused in pouring the leftover coffee into his mug.

"A rose. Sheila said you were giving them away."

Sean closed his eyes and counted to five. "Sure. What's your favorite color?"

"Pink."

"You got it. See you in a few."

He hung up, chugged the lukewarm coffee, and went to his office to print out a new sign. "NO TRESPASSING. NO LOITERING." At the bottom in smaller letters he added, "You may take one rose home. Please do not leave any candles or prayers, and please pray for the Rio Grande."

It seemed ironic that he was telling people how to pray. He had prayers in a box in his living room and prayer candles turning his patio into a rose-scented sweat lodge. He was becoming a prayer manager.

He went outside and tacked the sign to the elm tree. Two Hispanic women were standing in the alley, looking at the roses. One of them held another Guadalupe candle, one of the pink smelly ones, unlit.

"Sorry, but you can't leave that here," Sean told her. "The cops don't want any candles in the alley. It's a fire hazard."

"What about those?" She gestured to his patio.

"Those are left over from before the cops came."

"Could I put mine with them?"

He should say no, but he didn't have the heart. "Yeah, OK, but don't tell your friends. From now on everyone needs to burn their candles at home."

Sean went to the gate and opened it, letting the two women into the yard. The second one smiled shyly at him as he closed the gate behind them. The women went to stand by the rosebushes, gazing at them in awe. The one without the candle started moving her lips in silent prayer.

Sean clipped a rose for each of them, then a pink one for Renée. He was about to put the scissors back on the wall, then muttered a mild curse and cut another dozen roses of mixed colors. That should take care of everyone at the office.

While he was doing this, the two women went over to the

candles and knelt down before them. It made Sean feel funny to see them worshiping at his patio. Finally the one woman lit her candle and they both stood up. Sean let them out the gate, accepted their thanks, and shooed them away, then went back in the house and locked up before driving to work.

Renée gave a little squeal of delight when Sean handed her a pink rose as he came in. His boss, Nick, an energetic middle-aged geek with a skier's lean physique, came out of his office and accepted Sean's apology along with a rose.

"I heard about these. They're all the rage."

"Huh?"

"Yeah, everyone in town is talking about them. Miracle roses. Someone's selling one on Ebay."

"Oh, crap!" Sean said.

Nick twirled his rose in his hand and took a sniff. "So what's the gimmick?"

"Gimmick?"

"Yeah, how do they stay fresh?"

Sean shrugged. "Search me. I'm just the caretaker. I didn't even plant them."

"So they're really a miracle?" Renée asked.

"It does sort of look that way. I honestly don't know." Sean glanced at Nick. "And I'd better get to work."

He got a tall glass from the break room, put some water in it just for show, stuck the roses in it and set it on his desk, ready to give the flowers away to curious coworkers. He had a feeling it was going to be a long day.

Rosa spent the morning at her desk, trying to look calm while she sorted through Margo's transactions from the previous day to chase down an imbalance. She had to resist the impulse to keep checking that the police phone was still in her purse.

At noon she locked up her desk and went to the ladies room to check her hair and makeup. She'd dressed in a heather-colored tweedy jacket, cotton slacks a darker shade of heather, and a purple silk blouse. The little Kokopelli pendant Sean had given her hung at the base of her neck. She'd spotted it in her jewelry box that morning and remembered his concern for her, and had put it on for good luck. Now she gazed at it in the mirror, thinking over the whole strange journey of the last few days, the journey that had started with Kokopelli.

Coming out of the restroom, she saw Arturo in the lobby. He cast an appraising glance at her.

"You look nice," he said grudgingly.

"Thanks," Rosa said, though she had the feeling he would rather have seen her in a sexy dress. Well, that was too bad. Business lunches, real ones anyway, weren't sexy.

"Don't be late," Arturo told her, then strolled off toward the bookkeeper's office.

Rosa drove downtown and parked in the public underground lot rather than the hotel's parking lot, even though it meant she'd have to pay instead of getting validated parking. Between Sean and Miguel, she was feeling paranoid about this meeting. She wished she hadn't let herself get bullied into it.

That was not the right attitude, she thought as she got out of the car. She was not a submissive, cowed woman. She was a woman of vision, a woman of power, and she was coming to this lunch to try for more power. Power over a powerful man. Power to save the river.

She turned on the phone app, slipped the phone into her pocket, and went up the spiral stairs to the Civic Plaza. Bright sunshine reflecting from vast expanses of concrete made her blink. Across the street loomed the glass towers of the Hyatt and its matching office building, with McGrath's on the corner of the ground floor.

She crossed the street and went into the hotel, glancing at the cushy sofas and chairs in the lobby. Miguel was slouched in an armchair, dressed in jeans and a leather jacket over a dark shirt, reading a newspaper. The backpack sat at his feet. He didn't look up at her.

"Here I go," she said softly, and saw him give a slight nod.

She turned right and passed through a small waiting area just outside the restaurant. A hostess smiled at her from a podium by the entrance and ask if she had a reservation.

"I think so. I'm meeting someone."

"What's the name?"

"Robbins."

"Oh, yes. He's already here. Right this way."

Rosa followed her into the restaurant, which was filled with light coming in through walls of tinted windows. Nervous that she was late, she glanced at her watch, and was glad to see that she was actually early. Just not as early as Mr. Robbins.

There he was. She recognized his face from his website and countless news stories on TV, a handsome Anglo man with flecks of silver in his brown hair. He was dressed in a light gray suit—probably silk—and a blue and yellow striped tie. Rosa managed a polite smile as he stood up and pulled out a chair for her. She sat down, careful not to crush the box at her waist, and picked up the menu in front of her.

"Thank you for joining me, Ms Marquez," said Robbins. His teeth flashed white in his tanned face as he smiled.

"I hardly had a choice," she said, watching his face. "Mr. Gonzales is pretty anxious to please you."

"Did he pressure you? I certainly didn't mean for him to."

Yeah, right. Rosa looked at her menu, ignoring the question.

A waiter came to take their drink orders. Rosa glanced at the glass of ice water already sitting at her place and remembered Sean's concern that she not drink anything offered by Robbins. Paranoid? Maybe, but she resolved not to taste that water.

"Iced tea, please," she said, smiling at the waiter.

"I'll have the same," said Robbins.

The waiter went away. Rosa looked back at the menu, feeling nervous. She scanned the various offerings without seeing them. Robbins didn't say anything. He was waiting for her attention. Finally she put the menu down, folded her hands on top of it, and waited for Robbins to speak. He smiled slowly.

"I saw you on television Sunday night."

Her heart gave a small lurch. "Did you?"

"You're very photogenic."

"Thanks."

"You couldn't have planned it better, that blue dress to set off the roses."

"I didn't plan anything. I didn't even know the cameras would be there."

Robbins raised an eyebrow. He didn't believe her. Rosa felt annoyed, but she didn't say anything.

Wait for him to talk. Just listen. She was good at that—listening was part of *curanderismo*.

"Well, you made a strong impression," he said finally. "I'm not the only one who noticed. My marketing manager called me the next morning to ask who you were, and when PRD had hired you."

Rosa blinked in surprise. "Hired me? They didn't hire me. I heard about the rally and I was interested, so I went."

"You drove all the way to Santa Fe for a rally about a scrap of land near Pena Blanca? Why?"

"Because I care about the Rio Grande."

The waiter returned with their glasses of tea, and proceeded to rattle off the specials of the day. Rosa squeezed lemon into her tea, dropped the slice into the glass and stirred it. She could feel Robbins watching her.

"Do you need a minute to decide?" the waiter asked.

"I'll have that salad special," Rosa said.

"I'll have the salmon," said Robbins.

The waiter collected their menus and left. Rosa sipped her tea.

"I care about the Rio Grande too," Robbins said.

Rosa put down her glass and looked at him, amazed that he could say this. He was smiling, but his eyes were calculating. She returned his gaze, waiting for him to lie some more.

"I have to care." He laughed a little. "It's where our water's coming from. We're very concerned about maintaining water quality and availability. I know we haven't done a very good job so far at conveying that to the public. That's why I asked to meet with you, Ms Marquez. I think you'd be a wonderful spokesperson."

Rosa frowned. Was he offering her a job?

"I don't understand," she said.

"We need someone to present our position on the water issue. Someone with passion and conviction, who can express our concerns in a way people will understand. Someone who can talk to the media like you did on Sunday."

"I'm not a PR person, Mr. Robbins. I'm a teller. I know about banking, not about marketing."

He waved a hand. "I'm not looking for experience, I'm looking for presence. You've shown that you care passionately about water issues. That's what I need, someone who cares. I can talk about acreage allowances all day, but a lot of people won't care what I say. Someone bright and enthusiastic like you will make a stronger impression."

Rosa tried to imagine being enthusiastic about anything to do with Valle del Sol. The idea was ridiculous. She saw what Robbins was trying to do—he was trying to buy her off. Something Sean had said at that first meeting, the town hall meeting, flitted to mind.

Robbins picked up his glass. "I'd like to offer you a retainer of fifty thousand dollars for one year. We'll cover any travel expenses you might have, and pay you a thousand dollar bonus for each television appearance or print interview."

Rosa drew in a sharp breath. She was stunned by the amount he was offering, and furious that he thought she could be bought. It was shut-up money. Shut up and keep quiet. Smile for the camera while we strangle the river to death. She wanted to stand up and fling his offer in his face, but instead she made herself stay in her seat. She took another sip of tea to moisten her suddenly dry throat.

"You're asking me to quit my job? What do I do when your development is finished?"

"Not to quit. You can take a leave of absence. I've already

discussed it with Mr. Gonzales. Your job would be waiting for you when Valle del Sol opens—excuse me," he said as his cell phone rang. He took it out, glanced at the number, and answered.

"I'm in a meeting. Call back later. No, not him. Get Guzman. Yeah, Emilio. OK."

He closed the phone and put it back in his pocket, then smiled at Rosa. "My apologies. As I was saying, you'd still have your job at the bank...if you still want it." Robbins smiled. "You might prefer to stay on as our spokesperson for other projects."

She gazed at him, wondering how much he'd bribed Arturo to give her a leave of absence. Maybe nothing. Maybe the prospect of a huge finance deal was enough to make Arturo agree to anything Robbins wanted.

"It's an interesting idea," she said slowly. "I'll have to think about it."

Robbins's smile broadened. He thought he had her. Rosa looked out the window at the people walking along the pedestrian mall outside. She wished she was out there, in the sunshine, instead of the refined, industrial cool of this restaurant. She was sorry she'd agreed to this meeting, sorry she had wasted Miguel's day.

Their lunches arrived, and Robbins changed the subject. "Do you like football, Ms Marquez?"

She shrugged. "I watch the Lobos sometimes."

"You know about the new stadium, of course. It'll be close to here." He gestured toward the windows to the north.

Rosa stirred her salad around with her fork and stabbed a green bean. "I heard about it. Wasn't it voted down?"

"That was the first plan. There's a new one now."

Rosa listened while he talked about the new sports stadium and how he was sure his company would win the bid. He dropped hints about her being an ideal spokesperson for the stadium, and how there'd be a luxury private box available "for promotional purposes." He smiled all the while and spoke pleasantly, but all she could think about was his arrogance.

She tried to eat her lunch, though she wasn't very hungry. Her stomach felt like a big knot of anger and indignation. At least she no longer felt afraid, though she wasn't sure that was wise. Having lunch with Robbins hadn't changed her opinion of him. He was dangerous, and perfectly capable of sending an armed thug to warn her off.

That had been the stick. This was the carrot. Rosa put down her fork and drank some more tea, then looked at her watch. Quarter after one.

"I should probably be getting back to work," she said.

"You've got plenty of time. Mr. Gonzales knows this is a business lunch. Wouldn't you like some dessert or coffee?"

Rosa looked at her salad. She hadn't even eaten half of it.

"I'm pretty full." She met his gaze and decided to stop making excuses. "And I need some time to think about your offer."

"Of course." Robbins took an envelope out of his coat pocket and slid it across the table toward her. "These are the full terms, including benefits. Look it over, think about it for a day or two. But don't take too long," he added smiling in his calculating way. "We break ground in a week."

"I thought the groundbreaking was in September?"

"It was, but we've moved it up. We managed to deal with some obstacles." He smiled. "The groundbreaking is a week from Friday. I'd sure like to have you on board before then."

I bet you would, Rosa thought. She smiled briefly and picked up the envelope, glanced inside to make sure he wasn't handing her any cash as a bribe. Just letterhead. She tucked it into her purse, took a last sip of tea, and stood up.

"I'll think about it. Thanks for the lunch, Mr. Robbins."

"My pleasure. Thank you for joining me."

He stood up as she left. She had to force herself to keep to a walk, when all she wanted to do was run to get out of there.

Miguel was still sitting in the lobby, though he'd moved to a different chair. He glanced at her as she came out of the restaurant, then went back to staring at his newspaper. Rosa went out, glad for the wave of heat that hit her as she left the air-conditioned lobby. When she was back in her car with the doors locked, she took out her own phone and called Miguel's cell.

"Marquez," he answered.

"It's me," Rosa said. "I'm sorry I wasted your time."

"You didn't waste it. Now that you're going to be rich and

famous, I expect you to take care of me."

"Shh! What if he hears you?"

"He left a few minutes after you did, and I'm on my way to the station. Now how about those Lobo tickets your friend hinted at?"

"You can't be serious."

He laughed. "I'm not. I'm glad it was just a job offer."

"An insulting job offer."

"Yeah, he's got *cojones*. You must have made a big impression."

"I wish he'd never heard of me."

"Too late for that. Listen, Rosa. Be careful how you turn this offer down, OK? I assume you're going to turn it down."

"You assume right."

"So just be careful how you phrase it. He's still a dangerous man, you were right about that."

"He's a scumbag!"

"A scumbag with a lot of money and influence. They're the worst kind."

Rosa took a deep breath and let it out slowly. "I'd better get back to work. When can I get the phone back to you?"

"Turn it off now, or I'll be listening to everything you do all afternoon. I'll come pick it up at your house after work."

She took the phone out, shut it down, and put it in her purse. "Shall I make you dinner again?"

"You don't have to tonight. I don't want you to be in a hurry. I want you to have time to plan something real nice."

Rosa laughed in exasperation. "I'll see you later. Thanks again."

"You're welcome."

Rosa hung up, smiling, thinking she was lucky to have Miguel for a brother. The thought kept her smiling all the way back to the bank, where what was left of the afternoon passed quickly enough. She saw Arturo in the lobby a couple of times but avoided his gaze, and managed to leave for home while he was on the phone.

Miguel's squad was parked out in front of Rosa's house when she got home from work. He met her on the way to the door.

"How's my secret agent?"

"Embarrassed. It was a stupid idea."

"Not really. You learned something, no?"

Rosa shot him a glance as she opened the door. Bruja hopped down from the windowsill and came to dance around Rosa's ankles, mewing. Rosa reached down and scooped up the cat, needing to hug something.

Miguel closed the door and threw the deadbolt. Rosa sat on the couch, letting her purse slide to the floor. She cuddled Bruja until the cat escaped, then took the police phone out and handed it to Miguel.

"Now you know what it's like to be an investigator," Miguel said.

"Ha, ha."

"No, it's true. Most of the time it's like that. Dull, boring work that doesn't turn up a thing. Same for cops, ninety-five percent of the time."

Rosa grimaced. "And the other five percent?"

"The other five percent will give you a heart attack."

She looked up at him. She knew he'd had a couple of close calls. He didn't talk about such things much, or brushed them off with a joke if he mentioned them at all.

"I worry about you, Miguel."

"I know," he said quietly. "Thanks."

"I pray for you every day."

"*Muchas gracias.* I need all the help I can get."

"If you ever want to just talk—"

"I'll let you know."

Rosa sighed. He wouldn't talk. Maybe he was worried that if he let himself think about the worst things, talk through them, he might not have the guts to go back to the job.

She got up and went to the kitchen, put some food in Bruja's bowl, then opened the refrigerator, trying to decide what to fix for dinner. Something fast, because she was hungry. She had some leftover chicken. Maybe a *quesadilla*?

Miguel came into the kitchen as she was pulling out tortillas, cheese, and sour cream. "Whatever that's going to turn into, I want some."

"Just some *quesadillas*. You want to stay for supper after

all?"

"You got salsa? Got beer?"

Rosa piled everything on the counter and grinned. "Am I Mama's daughter?"

"OK, you talked me into it. But you owe me two more dinners, and one of them better be steak."

He took a beer out of the fridge and wandered off to the living room to watch the news while Rosa fixed supper. Cooking made her feel better. When the smell of grilled onions went up from the skillet, she knew the world was all right.

They ate in the living room, watching a sitcom. Rosa sipped her beer and tried to forget about Robbins, but when the show ended Miguel brought it up again.

"That was quite an offer he made you. Sure you don't want to take it?"

"He's trying to buy me off. I would never work for that scumbag."

Miguel gave an exaggerated sigh. "OK. Just thought I'd check."

"And you wouldn't respect me if I did accept it."

"I'd kick your butt. All the way down to that new stadium."

Rosa laughed, then remembered the envelope Robbins had given her. She dug it out of her purse, where it had gotten crumpled when she'd crammed the wire on top of it. She smoothed it and took out the letter inside.

It was a formal offer of employment, covering the same terms Robbins had mentioned in greater detail. Fifty grand for a year, plus travel, bonuses, and benefits. Full medical was one of them, and a company car was another.

"Lemme see," Miguel said. Rosa handed him the page, and he glanced down it, then whistled. "He really wants to shut you up."

"Yeah."

"You know, I don't like thinking about how he'll react when you turn him down."

"Maybe I should call him from Florida."

"That's not a bad idea."

"I was joking."

Miguel dropped the letter on the coffee table and tipped up

his beer bottle, draining it. Rosa picked up their supper plates and the empty bottles.

"You want another beer?"

"No, I'd better get going. Thanks for the supper, it was *primo*."

She took the plates out to the kitchen and came back to give him a hug. "Thanks again, Miguel."

"You're welcome, sis. Lock up, and sleep tight."

"I will."

When Miguel had driven away, Rosa went back inside and cleaned up the kitchen. Twilight glowed through the window, drawing her out to the garden. The evening star hung bright in the west. Venus, a planet not a star, but still the evening star.

Rosa turned to face the east, where the mountains had already darkened. Her statue of the Virgin glowed pale in the twilight. Rosa went over to it and touched the rosemary bush growing to one side, opposite the dormant rose. She broke off a small sprig and held it to her nose, breathing in the cleansing, evergreen scent.

She needed a *limpia*, after all the worry and excitement of the day. She went inside, taking the rosemary sprig with her, and went to her work room.

The vase of roses Sean had cut for her—almost a week ago now—were all still perfect. They had been open when they were cut, and the blooms were still firm, no faded or drooping petals. She selected a pink rose, drawing it out of the vase and laying it on the altar while she prayed and lit a candle.

With the rosemary in one hand and the rose in the other, she gave herself a *limpia*, closing her eyes and enjoying the mingled fragrances as she brushed her whole body, cleansing it of unwanted energy. She took her time, luxuriating in the velvet touch of the rose, the tickling whisper of the rosemary. *Romero*, its Spanish name. She smiled, remembering a boy she'd known in mid school named Rudy Romero. She'd liked him, though she'd never got up the nerve to let him know.

When she was finished with the *limpia* she opened her eyes and let out a long sigh. Leaving the rosemary on the altar, she took the rose outside to the Virgin's statue. The garden was still, now, and darker, though she could still see the statue glowing.

"Santa Maria, Blessed Mother of Christ, watch over me. Lend me your protection and your grace."

She stuck the rose in the flower bed in front of the Lady's pedestal, shoving the stem into the soil moistened by her watering the day before. At least the Lady would have one rose in this dry season.

Stars were coming out now. Only the brightest ones could be seen in Albuquerque, the city sent up so much light. Rosa counted a dozen stars scattered through the sky. Too few to identify constellations, and she didn't know any really, except for the big dipper. Turning north, she was able to make out the four stars of the cup and the fainter stars of the handle. She followed the line of the cup's two outside stars up to the north star, as Miguel had taught her when they were kids.

Looking north made her think of her new friends: Angel, Ruby, Sean. She ought to tell Sean about her lunch with Robbins. She was a little embarrassed that nothing had come of it.

There was the new date for the ground-breaking, though. Maybe Sean didn't know about that. With a last glance at the sky, she went inside to write him an email.

All day Thursday Sean had been interrupted by co-workers coming to talk about the roses and get some for themselves. By Friday they mostly left him alone, though a few came to get extra roses for friends and family members. Sean had cut another handful in the morning when he went out to chase the pilgrims out of the alley again. He'd also picked up a few candles people had left in spite of his sign, and put them with the rest on the patio. That kind of candle burned for days. The sweat lodge would be there a while.

Despite his best efforts, he didn't get much work done on Friday, and by the end of the day he was in a rotten mood. His boss came into his office a little before five, took one look at him, and told him to go home.

"I didn't finish the Vacadero analysis," Sean said.

"Finish it Monday. There's no rush."

Sean glanced up at Nick. "Sorry I've been such a waste. It's those damn roses." He poked an accusing finger at the glass on his desk, which still held three flowers, two whites and a yellow-and-red.

"Don't worry about it. It's a fad, it'll blow over soon."

"Yeah, right," Sean said. "How long did it take for the Jesus tortilla to blow over?"

"Hey, that tortilla's an institution. I think it's been enshrined by now."

"Ha, ha."

"Go home and have a beer. You'll feel better in the morning."

"Yeah, OK. Thanks, Nick."

"Don't thank me. Give me a rose for my wife."

Sean stood up and waved toward the roses. "Take 'em all. Just don't sell 'em on Ebay."

Sean drove home. Getting out of his car, he paused in the driveway to listen, thinking he heard voices out back. He went into the house and peeked out the dining room blinds. There was a news van parked in the alley, and a reporter and cameraman setting up right outside the wall.

"Great. Just great."

He went to the phone and checked his voicemail. Multiple messages from all the local TV stations, the papers, radio stations. In amidst them, a message from his mother asking him to call. No doubt she'd heard about the roses, and wanted to know what the hell was going on. He dialed her number, but got a busy signal. The phone rang the minute he hung it up. He unplugged it.

At least they hadn't got hold of his cell number.

Feeling annoyed, Sean went out in the back yard to confront the news crew. He walked up to the wall and folded his arms.

"I'm sorry, but you're going to have to move. The police want this alley kept clear."

"Mr. Carpenter, I'm Dale Washington, channel seven." The reporter smiled and offered to shake hands while the cameraman shouldered his camera.

"Put that away, please," Sean said to the cameraman. "I'm not giving interviews."

"Just a couple of questions?" said Washington.

"No."

"We'd just like to know about the miracle roses."

"No. Just, please leave. And don't show my picture on television."

Sean turned and went back in the house, ignoring the questions Washington called after him. The news crew showed no sign of leaving. Maybe he should call his friends the cops and get them to evict the press, except he had a feeling that would just make things worse.

He started to fix some soup and a sandwich for dinner, but was interrupted by the doorbell halfway through making the sandwich. He looked out the peephole, saw another TV crew on his doorstep, and went back to the kitchen. The doorbell rang again, then a few moments later a floodlight seeped through the edges of the frame. They were doing a news story on his front porch. One of those, "here's the door, they're not answering" stories.

Sean carried his supper and a beer into the living room and ate in front of the TV with the volume down low, switching from channel to channel to see how much news coverage the roses were getting. Channel four played a story that had been taped earlier in the day, a shot of the rosebushes with a couple of pilgrims cutting flowers for themselves, a shot of the candles burning on the patio, and one of the "NO TRESPASSING" sign.

Channel seven ran a live broadcast with Washington saying snidely that the owner of the miracle roses had refused to talk to him. The reporter had cut a red-and-yellow rose from the bush and displayed it for the camera, describing its reputed non-fading qualities.

"Are these roses really miraculous? No one knows for sure, and Mr. Carpenter isn't telling." The reporter gestured to the sign on the elm tree, and the camera zoomed in on it. "You can come and see for yourself, and even take a rose home with you. Oh, and don't forget to say a prayer for the Rio Grande."

Sean grimaced. Trying to make him out as a whack job, but it could have been worse, and the bit about praying for the river might actually help. The reporter had said it sarcastically, but not everyone would take it that way.

When the news was over Sean dared to hope that the press would go away. The crew out front did pack up, but the channel seven guys in the alley showed no sign of leaving. They must be waiting to do another broadcast on the ten o'clock news. Sean peeked out and saw them interviewing someone in the alley—some pilgrim who had come for a look at the roses. The TV coverage would bring them out in droves again, no doubt.

He paced the living room, feeling caged. He couldn't leave his house. He was trapped.

He could use the Internet, though. He could send email. "Help, I'm trapped, bring lots of beer!" He smiled, feeling a little better as he went into the office and booted up his computer. Thank god for DSL!

He popped his email and was relieved to see that the press hadn't got hold of his address yet. There was a message from Forrest and a couple from other friends, and one from Rosa. He saved that one for last, first answering the others and sending a quick note to his mother explaining briefly about the roses without going into the miracle stuff.

Finally he read Rosa's message, which she'd written last

night, telling him she'd gone to lunch with Robbins and he'd made her a job offer. She hadn't given Robbins an answer yet. She said she intended to turn the offer down, but Sean had a bad feeling about the whole thing.

At the end of her message, she mentioned that the date of the ground-breaking had been moved up. His stomach sank as he read it. A week! Robbins was trying to push his project through before the opposition could organize more protests.

What could he do?

He wrote a brief reply to Rosa, trying to sound supportive, and added a joke about the roses. Then he emailed Tom about the new date for the groundbreaking. They'd need to ramp up their efforts, fast.

By the time he sent the email off, another half dozen inquiries had come in from friends and coworkers. He opened the first one, then the doorbell rang.

Sean glanced at the time. Eight fifteen, too early for news crews, or maybe not. He thought about ignoring it, then thought that it might be the cops, so he'd better at least go and look.

Through the peephole he saw a familiar face outside, a silver-haired man. It took him a moment to place it, then the priest's collar clicked the memory. Father Mahan.

"Now you believe me," Sean muttered. He unlocked the door and opened it.

The priest gave a deferential nod, almost a bow. "Mr. Carpenter."

"Come in, before the cameras show up."

Mahan stepped into the house, looking around as if expecting to see a choir of angels, maybe a glimpse of *La Guadalupana*, or at least a glow of holy radiance. Sean invited him into the living room.

"Would you like some coffee?"

"No, thank you. What I'd like is to see the roses."

"You know, they're just roses. They don't look like anything special."

Sean glanced toward the back door. The glow from all the candles gleamed through the blinds, lighting them up with a golden, flickering haze.

"The press is out there," he added. "I'd rather not go out, and if you do they'll try to interview you."

Mahan frowned slightly, gazing at the door. "I saw it on the news. When they said your name I remembered you coming to me. Why didn't you mention the roses?"

"I didn't notice they were blooming until after I talked to you."

"I see." Mahan glanced around the living room as if looking for a lost set of keys, then met Sean's gaze. "Actually, coffee sounds good. I think I'd like some after all."

Sean put a pot on and came back to sit in the living room with Mahan while it brewed. They didn't say anything for a couple of minutes. Finally Mahan leaned forward in his chair, elbows on his knees and his hands loosely clasped before him. Not quite a gesture of supplication, but close.

"I'm afraid I owe you an apology," Mahan said. "I didn't take your claim seriously. We get so many, you see. People hoping, desperately wishing for a miracle."

"Not me. At this point I'm wishing the miracle would go the hell away."

Mahan nodded. He didn't protest the language. Sean regretted it; he'd said it partly to annoy the priest, largely because of his own annoyance.

"Tell me again, if you would," Mahan said gently.

"On one condition. You don't share any of this with the press."

The priest frowned slightly, but nodded. "In confidence."

Sean went through the story again. It had been a while since he'd actually thought about *La Guadalupana*. He'd been distracted by the roses and the whole Valle del Sol thing. He told Mahan all about that, too—how he'd gone to the meeting and met Rosa, how she'd had visions too, and how they'd agreed to work together to fight the development.

"I'd like to meet this Rosa," Mahan said.

"She lives in Albuquerque. I can tell her you want to meet her, and she'll contact you if she's interested."

"Thank you."

Sean stood up. "How do you take your coffee?"

"Sugar, no cream."

Sean fixed mugs for both of them and came back to the living room. Mahan was standing by the back door, peeking out between the blinds.

"There are quite a few people out there."

Sean handed him a mug. "I'm sure there are. This'll probably make the neighbors call the cops again."

"I can see how you must find it frustrating."

"That's putting it mildly."

"But in a way it's also wonderful." Mahan sipped his coffee, then looked seriously at Sean. "It looks like you do have a miracle."

"What brought you to that conclusion?"

Mahan glanced toward the blinds. "Because your bushes are still covered with flowers. How many have you given away?"

"Uh, I haven't kept count."

"But it's more than you'd expect from a normal rosebush."

Sean gave a cough of laughter. "Oh, yeah. Way more."

Mahan smiled, looking immensely pleased. He strolled back to his chair and sat down. Sean's glance fell on the cardboard box sitting in the corner by the fireplace.

"Oh, hey, I could use your help on something." He put down his mug and carried the box over to the coffee table, setting it in front of Mahan. "People left this stuff in the alley. The cops made me clean it up, but I don't want to throw it away. It's people's prayers."

Mahan glanced in the box. "Oh, yes. I can take them, if you like. We get them all the time at the cathedral."

"What do you do with them?"

"We burn them, mostly. Everything that can be burned. The prayers rise up to heaven that way."

"Oh. I see."

"Maybe you'd like to add a prayer of your own."

Sean glanced at him, biting back a sarcastic response. "Look, I'm not religious. Don't try to recruit me, OK?"

"'Recruit'? I'd say you've already been recruited. I won't try to convert you, though. If the Holy Virgin couldn't persuade you, I doubt that I could."

Sean retrieved his coffee, hiding annoyance. He had a short fuse just now, and he didn't want to blow up at Mahan, who was only trying to help.

"Tell me more about the roses," Mahan said. "Do they really stay fresh out of water?"

"I haven't tried that, but I've heard it from several people, one of whom I trust."

"Marvelous." Mahan smiled over his mug. "And you began giving them away a week ago?"

"Last Sunday."

Mahan leaned forward. "What made you decide to ask for prayers in return?"

"That was Rosa's idea. Well, not the prayer part, but the 'Roses for the Rio.' She came up with it on the spur of the moment at the rally on Sunday."

"Catchy."

"Yeah, no—no kidding."

"So you added the prayer part."

Sean looked at the priest, sensing an imminent trap. "People came asking to buy roses. I didn't feel right selling them, so I gave them the roses and asked them to pray for the river in return. I thought that would be what she wanted."

"She...*La Guadalupana*."

"Yeah."

Mahan nodded. "I think that was a good choice."

Sean looked toward the window and stifled a sigh. The doorbell rang, and he excused himself to go check it. He saw TV people outside, a different crew from a different channel. He made sure the door was locked and came back to the living room.

"It's a news crew. I think you're stuck here until after ten-thirty."

"That's all right with me, if you don't mind my company."

Sean shrugged. "Beats twiddling my thumbs. Want some more coffee?"

"Yes, please."

They refilled their mugs and took another peek out back. The news crew was still there, and a big crowd had assembled in the alley. Several of them were holding lighted candles, and a couple more candles stood on top of the wall. Sean chewed his lip, dreading a possible fire.

"May I ask a favor, Mr. Carpenter?"

"Call me Sean, OK?"

"In that case I'm Robert."

"What's the favor?"

Mahan sipped his coffee. "Would you show me your flute? The one you were playing when the Holy Virgin appeared to you?"

Sean hesitated. The flute was personal, his music private. He remembered Angel's protectiveness about music and almost said no, but he thought maybe Mahan was just trying to understand the whole phenomenon.

"Yeah, OK. It's right here."

He took the flute down from the mantel and brought it over to the couch. Mahan put down his mug and accepted it gingerly, holding it on the palms of his hands.

"A Native American flute."

"Yeah. My teacher made it. He's from Cochiti."

Mahan ran his fingers over the flute, touched the little carved fetish tied near the airhole. "What's this?"

"A wolf. Angel says the wolf's my totem animal."

"Angel?"

"My teacher."

"Interesting name."

"I think his mom's a romantic."

"Well, it's not that uncommon a name. There are several men named 'Angel' in our parish. All Hispanic, though, and they mostly use the Spanish pronunciation."

Sean nodded. "'Anhel.' That's how his mom says it. Angel says it's just easier to use the Anglo pronunciation than to explain."

Mahan handed the flute back carefully. "I'd love to hear you play."

His voice was gentle, undemanding, slightly wistful. He must be very good at his work, Sean decided. Again he considered refusing, but the truth was that he hadn't played in a couple of days, and he wanted to.

He stood up, blew a few long notes and wandered over to the fireplace, getting a little distance. Glancing at Mahan he saw that the priest had closed his eyes, though he sat upright, listening intently. Sean improvised a bit, then slid into the rain chant.

The music lifted him up, and he felt his tension dropping away. He closed his eyes and poured his heart into the melody, not caring that Mahan was listening, just wanting to play, to be free. He played the chant twice through, then lowered the flute and opened his eyes.

Mahan was still sitting with eyes closed, looking as if he was in a trance. A slight smile hovered on the priest's lips. Finally he opened his eyes and looked at Sean.

"Remarkable," he said reverently.

"See anything?" Sean asked, half joking.

"No. No, but I certainly felt something."

"Hm. Well, thanks."

Sean put the flute back on the mantel, suddenly feeling shy. Mahan *was* good at his work. He'd gotten Sean to tell him pretty much everything about himself, and to show him the things he cared most about. Except Rosa. He hadn't mentioned how he felt about her. He'd only spoken of her in context with the Valle del Sol rallies.

Sean returned to the couch and picked up his coffee. It was no longer hot, but he took a swig anyway.

"So, have you decided?" Mahan asked.

"Decided what?"

"What to do about the roses."

Sean gave a helpless shrug. "I don't know what I *can* do about them. I can't stop people from coming."

"No, probably not."

"I take it you have something in mind."

Mahan smiled and leaned forward. "I have a couple of suggestions."

"OK. Shoot."

"Get some help. You can't spend all your time monitoring the alley. It's more than one person can handle."

"You've got that right." Sean glanced toward the back door. "What are you suggesting, I hire a security guard?"

"No, I was thinking you might get some volunteer help. I could probably find plenty of volunteers among the members of our congregation. I'd be happy to arrange it."

Sean frowned. "I don't know. I don't think I'd like to have

anyone proselytizing on my property."

"No proselytizing, I promise. We have plenty of other opportunities for that. I just meant that one or two people could be available during the day to make sure people don't loiter, make sure no one takes more than one rose, no one leaves candles in the alley, that sort of thing."

"That sounds good. That would be helpful, actually. But what would they want in return?"

Mahan smiled. "I think they'd consider being in the presence of a miracle reward enough. Along with a rose for each volunteer, perhaps."

Sean finished his coffee and put down the mug. "Yeah, sure. I don't seem to be in danger of running out."

"I have another suggestion. You're not going to like this one."

Sean gritted his teeth. "OK."

Mahan leaned forward in his chair. "Let people know about your vision."

"About Our Lady? No way! The cops and the media already think I'm a nut case!"

"It would place this miracle in context." Mahan gestured with his hands as if shaping something round, like a ball that was precious and fragile. "It would make sense of it for everyone."

"I didn't see her *here*."

"But you believe she's responsible for the roses."

Sean grimaced. "Yeah."

"Then it makes sense to let people know that. You wouldn't even have to explain about the vision if you don't want to. You could just say that these roses have been blessed by the Virgin."

"I don't know. Seems like that would be opening a can of worms."

"I think the can is already open, my friend. I think you've been trying to deal with the tangle."

Sean gazed at Mahan. "What would the archbishop have to say about all this?"

"I'll have to ask him. He'd probably like to meet you."

"Oh, man." Sean shook his head. "This is too much. It's just nuts."

He got up and paced around a bit, until he realized he was acting like a caged animal. Feeling like one again, too. The peace that playing the flute had brought him was gone. He stopped, looked at Mahan, then glanced at his watch and sighed.

"Want to watch the news?"

"Sure."

Sean turned on the television, then went to the kitchen to start another pot of coffee. When the headlines came on he came back to the living room.

The top story was a bank robbery, but the roses had climbed to the number two story on channel seven. Dale Washington was doing his shtick in the alley again. He talked to a couple of the people out there, then the studio played a tape of some earlier interviews. Sean listened in silence. All the people on camera seemed happy and excited. He wished he could feel that way, instead of being worried.

He switched channels when Washington signed off. Channel four was playing the same tape they'd run at six. Channel thirteen had some other story on. Sean poured himself a fresh cup of coffee and offered more to Father Mahan, who shook his head.

"Not this late. It'll keep me awake."

Sean didn't care if it kept him up. He doubted he'd sleep much tonight, anyway. He'd have to go out in the yard at some point and make sure things were OK out there. He needed to cut roses for the rally tomorrow, too. He'd promised Ruby he'd bring some. Three a.m. might be a good time.

The rally. He could have used the media attention to publicize the rally! Crap!

He went to the back door and pushed aside the blinds, just in time to see channel seven's van pull away. Muttering a curse under his breath, he let the blinds go. They swung back and forth, clattering softly together.

"What is it?" Mahan asked.

"Nothing. The TV crew's gone. Want to have a look at the roses now?"

"Yes, please."

Sean pulled the blinds and opened the door. A wave of rose perfume hit him as he stepped onto the patio and past the candles. Passing out into the yard, he saw that the alley was still crowded. He walked over to the wall with Father Mahan following him.

"Hey, folks," Sean said, "I'm sorry but you're going to have to leave. The police want this alley kept clear, OK? Thanks. Yes, you can have a rose if you haven't already got one. Here."

He found his scissors and started cutting roses. Eager hands reached across the wall.

"OK, there you go. Go on home, now. And take your candles with you, please."

A camera flash went off. Sean glanced up, startled, and another flash blinded him. He turned his back, stifling a curse.

"No pictures, please," said Father Mahan, stepping up to the wall. "Please honor Mr. Carpenter's request and go home, all right?"

"Father, is it true that it's a miracle?"

Mahan turned his head toward Sean. Still seeing blue blobs, Sean couldn't see his face.

"I believe that it's true," Mahan said.

"Does the Church say so?"

"That's my personal opinion. The Church hasn't made a ruling."

"Who created the miracle?"

"I believe it can be attributed to the Holy Virgin."

"To *La Guadalupana*," corrected Sean. Might as well be accurate.

"Ahh, Santa Maria!" cried a woman's voice.

Sean went back to cutting roses, keeping his face turned away from the alley. No more camera flashes went off. He handed the roses to Mahan, who passed them across the wall to the pilgrims and acknowledged their thanks and their blessings. The priest clasped the hands that stretched toward him and smiled at the faithful.

"We ask that you pray for the Rio Grande," he added now and then as he handed out roses.

After a while the stream of pilgrims slowed to a trickle. Sean fetched the two buckets he'd used for the roses at the rally, and began filling them again. Father Mahan stayed by the wall talking to people as they came, giving them roses, gently sending them home.

When the buckets were full Sean stood up, set the scissors on the wall, and carried the roses into the house, with Father Mahan trailing behind. Mahan paused on the patio, gazing back toward the rosebushes.

"You must have cut over a hundred roses just now."

Sean set the buckets inside the door. "Yep."

"Amazing. No wonder you're not worried about leaving the bushes unattended."

"I am worried about it, but only because I don't want people starting fires in the alley. I'm not worried about them hurting the bushes. If I cut those bushes down to the ground, they'd probably grow right back."

Mahan nodded as he stepped inside. "And fast."

Sean slid the door closed. "By the way, I haven't watered those bushes all year. I was letting the yard die back."

"I suppose I shouldn't be surprised."

"The day I came to the cathedral there weren't any flowers on them. Hardly any leaves."

"And...the next day?"

"The next day they were like this. Well, not quite as big. They've grown a little, and I think they've been spreading."

Mahan crouched down to admire the roses in the buckets. "Why did you cut these?"

"There's another rally tomorrow. I promised to hand them out."

"Not in the plaza—"

"No, it's out at the Valle del Sol site."

Mahan looked up. "Would you like someone to help here while you're gone?"

Sean stared down at him, debating. "Maybe."

"I'd be happy to come back, and I'm sure I could get some of our parishioners to assist me. When do you plan to leave?"

When will my house be vacant? Oh, and you'll want a key, of course, so your helpers can use the bathroom.

"Why don't I call you in the morning and let you know?" Sean said.

Mahan stood up. "Very well. I'm usually up by six."

"I can promise you it won't be that early."

The priest stood gazing down at the cut roses. Sean realized he'd forgotten to put water in the buckets. Not that it really mattered.

"Amazing," Mahan said softly. "Simply amazing. You are a privileged man."

Sean couldn't think of an answer that didn't sound snide, so he kept his mouth shut. Mahan offered a hand, and Sean shook it.

"And I am privileged to know you," Mahan added. "Thank you for allowing me to be here this evening."

"I'm glad you came. Oh, don't forget the prayers."

Sean fetched the cardboard box and handed it over. Mahan started toward the front door. On impulse Sean grabbed a handful of roses from one of the buckets and caught up with him in the entryway.

"Take these, too. Don't you want some?"

Mahan broke into a smile like a kid offered ice cream. He shifted the box onto his hip and accepted the roses.

"Thank you. I didn't want to ask."

"Don't know why not."

"Well...I doubted you."

"We all have our doubts."

Mahan nodded. "I'll look forward to your call. Good night, Sean."

"Good night."

Sean let him out, then closed the door and leaned his head against it. This had been a long evening, and it wasn't over yet.

He had to decide whether to trust all his worldly goods to Father Mahan's care. The guy might be a priest, and he might be impressed as hell with the roses, but he was still a stranger.

Sean needed help, though. He didn't want to leave the house unattended, and if people were going to volunteer to direct traffic in his alley, the least he could do was let them use the facilities.

Sighing, he glanced at the clock in the kitchen. Not quite midnight. He should hit the sack, and decide what to do in the morning.

He started toward the bedroom, but saw his computer screen glowing in the office and realized he'd never finished his email.

There were probably a bunch more messages by now. Wincing at the thought, he went in and refreshed the index. Another fifty-odd messages, including ones from Rosa and his mom.

A thought occurred to him. He opened his mother's email. She said she wanted to talk to him. He could call late, she'd be up painting.

Sean smiled as he grabbed the phone and dialed his mom's number. She answered with prompt, caffeinated cheer.

"Hi, Mom. How'd you like to do me a really big favor? That is, if you're not busy tomorrow."

🌹 *19*

"There's a line of people around the block waiting to look in your yard, sweetie!"

Sean pulled his mom into the house and into a hug. "I know. Thanks for coming."

She dropped her sketch pad and handbag in order to hug him back. "Oh, of course! How could I say no to babysitting a miracle? But it's still hard to believe."

She held him at arm's length and peered at his face, smiling but anxious. She was still pretty in a weathered way, her hair a ginger-gold cloud around her face, eyes bright blue and eager to take in the world. She was wearing a denim skirt, peach-colored cotton t-shirt and a tangle of amber beads.

"You look like you haven't slept," she said.

"I slept a little. Want some coffee?"

"Maybe later. Can I see the roses?"

"Sure, come on out. You can meet Father Mahan, too."

"Must I?"

"Come on, that's why you're here. He's OK, he doesn't bite and he's not pushy, though he does have a smooth tongue."

Sean led her to the back door and pulled the blinds. Father Mahan and two of his parishioners were by the back wall, shepherding the crowd through the alley. The stream of visitors had been steady since sunrise, maybe earlier. Sean had printed more signs and posted them on the outside of the wall, the gate, wherever he could find a place. The pilgrims were behaving themselves, mostly kept moving, and only occasionally had to be reminded not to leave candles or prayers.

Sean opened the sliding door and invited his mother to step out in the yard. "You'll probably get TV crews, and the cops might come around. You can let Father Mahan do the talking if you want."

"Good. I hate cameras."

"Here they are."

They stopped by the rosebushes. Father Mahan's two helpers

were both cutting roses, handing them to the pilgrims. The bushes were definitely bigger this morning. They seemed to be spreading sideways, becoming hedge-like.

One of the helpers, a pretty *mamacita* wearing a flowered dress and a gold wedding band, glanced at Sean's mother and handed her a white rose. Sean noticed that it had the palest flush of pink along the edges of its petals. That was new.

"Oh, thank you, dear!" His mom smiled and held the rose to her nose. "Lovely."

Father Mahan turned toward them. Sean cleared his throat.

"Mom, I'd like you to meet Father Robert Mahan. Robert, this is my mother, Donna Carpenter."

Mahan smiled. "The artist. I've admired your work."

Sean's mother looked pleased as she shook hands. "Thank you."

"Your son has inherited your artistic inclinations. His music, I mean."

"Oh. Yes, there's hope for him after all. He never could draw to save his life."

"But it's the spirit that makes a great artist," Mahan added. "Or so I've always thought."

"Yes," she said slowly. "It is."

They went back in the house, leaving Father Mahan to return to greeting the column of pilgrims shuffling up the alley. Sean picked up the knapsack in which he'd stowed a sandwich and two bottles of water and his cell phone, and slung it over his shoulder. He'd already put the two buckets of roses in his car.

"Thanks for being willing to keep an eye on the place. I should be back before five."

She went to the front door with him and retrieved her sketch pad. "Take as long as you like, sweetie. I'll be fine."

"I've got my cell, so call if something blows up."

"Great Ghu forbid." She smooched his cheek. "Have fun. I'll keep the Catholics in line."

"They're not all Catholics. We're getting a lot of curiosity seekers, too, now."

"And some entrepreneurial spirits. I heard someone's selling your roses in the plaza."

"What?!"

She shrugged. "Or at least they're claiming they're miracle roses. Twenty bucks a pop."

"Crap!" Sean glanced at his watch. "Crap, I don't have time to deal with it right now."

"I wouldn't worry about it, sweetie. What goes around comes around. Some cop'll probably bust them for selling without a license."

"Yeah. Heh. OK, I'd better go. See you later, and thanks again."

She leaned forward, presenting her cheek to be kissed. "Any time, miracle boy."

Sean took the Cochiti turnoff at La Bajada Hill and drove slowly along the state highway, looking at the area with a new awareness. This road formed one side of the elongated triangle that was slated to become Valle del Sol. There wasn't much to the property at the moment, just scrub desert: sage, saltbush, cactus, and a few junipers, maybe now and then a piñon. He crossed some railroad tracks and slowed down. The development was on his left, now. He saw a few bits of orange spray paint here and there. Survey markings.

The road t-boned into another highway and Sean turned left, almost due south, toward Pena Blanca. He could see cottonwood trees off to the west on his right—river *bosque*—the Rio Grande. After a few minutes he passed through the village, then started to see cars parked along the side of the road.

He kept driving, not wanting to lug the buckets of roses farther than he had to. When cars started showing up on both sides of the road, he turned around and parked facing outbound, then got his pack and the roses and continued on foot. A warm breeze was blowing, and the sun beat down on his head. He'd forgotten to bring a hat.

In a few minutes the cars got thicker, parked haphazardly two or three deep on the shoulder. He passed a news van, walking fast and keeping his face turned away. Finally he reached a cluster of forty or fifty people, mostly Indians, milling around on the west side of the road.

Sean looked for Tom but didn't see him. Rosa wasn't there either as far as he could tell, and he hadn't noticed her car parked along the road. He spotted Pam wrestling with a familiar looking display board and went to join her.

She glanced up from the easel she was trying to keep from blowing over, and smiled. "Hi, Sean! Glad you're here!"

"Do you need a hand?"

"Yeah, sure."

Sean put down the roses and helped her anchor the easel with a couple of rocks. The display was one of the ones that had been at the town hall meeting. Pam retrieved another one from the back of a small station wagon.

"Where's Tom?" Sean asked.

"I don't know," Pam said. "He should be here. It's still a little early, though."

Sean helped her put up three more display boards. Some people wandered over to look at them. Pam got out a box of yellow flyers and gave some to Sean. It was like all the other PRD flyers, talked about quality of life and listed the date of the next meeting. Another plaza rally a week away. Same old.

"Are those the miracle roses?" someone asked.

Sean looked up. Several Pueblo women were gathered around his buckets of flowers, which were sitting in the sand at the foot of one of the displays. He hurried over to them.

"Yes, they are. Just one each, please."

"How much do they cost?"

Sean picked up a bucket, pulled a rose from it, and held it out. "Nothing. Say a prayer for the Rio Grande, if you feel like it."

"Roses for the Rio," Pam said, joining them. "Here, take a flyer, too."

The Pueblo woman glanced at the flyer, then folded it and stuffed it in the pocket of her jeans. Sean watched her walk away, holding her rose and dialing a cell phone. More people came over to get roses, and Sean was kept busy for a while handing them out. When the line slowed down a bit, he glanced at Pam.

"Still no Tom."

She shrugged. "Maybe he had trouble parking."

"This isn't very well organized."

Pam sighed. "No, well. You do the best you can, I guess."

"Hey, Sean!"

He looked up to see Ruby and Angel coming toward him. Seeing them lifted his spirits, and he broke into a huge smile.

"Glad you guys could make it. Did you meet Pam?"

Ruby nodded to her. "Yeah, I remember you. Hi."

"Pam, you might not have met Angel."

Pam smiled. "Hi, Angel. I loved your music last week."

"Thanks."

Angel glanced at Sean, looking slightly puzzled. Ruby stepped past him to poke through the roses in Sean's bucket.

"I saw your roses on TV last night."

Sean shifted the bucket so she could reach it better. "I thought you didn't have a TV."

"I went over to my friend Carla's house. Guess the roses are turning into a big deal."

"Yeah, too big. It's getting to be more than I can handle."

"There ought to be a way to use that."

She was right. All that energy. All that excitement. They ought to be able to direct it to something more active than prayer.

Ruby pulled out a yellow-and-red rose. "Can I have this one?"

"You can have any one you want."

"Could I take one for my mother, too?"

Sean glanced at the others nearby. "I'm only letting people have one each. I probably should stick to that."

"I'll take one for her," Angel said, stepping forward.

Ruby picked out a rose and handed it to him, one of the new white ones with pink edges. Sean didn't remember cutting any of those, but it had been dark. Anyway, nothing about the roses surprised him any more. Angel looked at the one in his hand as if he'd never seen a rose before, then glanced at Sean.

"Still want a lesson tomorrow?"

"Oh, man. Yeah, I could really use it, but my house is a circus right now."

Angel shrugged. "Maybe we could find another place."

"There they are!" cried a woman's voice.

Several women hurried up to Sean reaching for roses, asking

excited questions. Angel caught Sean's eye and gave him a nod that meant they'd talk later, then faded back into the crowd.

More people were walking down the road to join the group milling around the displays and talking. Most of them made a beeline for Sean. Word must have gotten around Cochiti Pueblo that he'd brought some miracle roses.

Ruby took a handful of Pam's flyers and started handing them out. Sean finally spotted Tom hustling along, an electric megaphone in one hand. He came up to Sean and Pam with an apologetic smile.

"Sorry I'm late. Had a little trouble getting here."

"Did you get my email?"

"No, I haven't checked it today."

"Robbins moved the groundbreaking up to Friday."

"Friday?"

"Yeah. So we need to go into high gear."

"Well, let's talk about that after today. Let's see—where should I stand?"

Tom looked around indecisively. Sean gritted his teeth. He was rapidly losing respect for Tom. He was about to make a snide comment when he saw Rosa coming down the road, and forgot about everything else.

She was wearing a cream-colored cotton dress and a silky pink scarf, sandals, and sunglasses. She looked gorgeous. As she came closer Sean saw the scarf was printed, pink roses all over. He automatically handed her a rose.

She laughed. "Thanks. You know the ones I have at home are still fresh."

"Really? What a surprise."

She shot him a skeptical look. "I saw the news."

"Some fun, huh?"

"Actually, I think it's wonderful. Don't you?"

"Try running crowd control for a day or two, then see what you think."

"I guess that must not be fun. Sorry, I wasn't thinking of that."

A Pueblo girl of around nine or ten tugged at Sean's sleeve. He gave her a rose. She giggled shyly and ran away.

More people were crowding around now, standing three

deep, waiting for roses. With an apologetic glance at Rosa, Sean went back to handing out flowers. She watched for a minute, then reached for the bucket.

"Let me help."

Sean gave her the bucket and went back for the second one, which he hadn't yet touched. The first bucket was almost as full. He shook his head. Don't think about it, just give them away.

A loud electronic whine nearby made Sean jump. Tom had gotten up on the tailgate of a pickup truck parked nearby with his megaphone, and launched into his usual spiel.

Sean looked at Rosa. "Weren't you going to bring a friend?"

"Oh, Joe Pino? I asked him and he's interested, but he's helping his granddaughter this weekend. She has a booth at Indian Market."

"I see."

Granddaughter. That was good.

"Did you get my email about Father Mahan?"

Rosa nodded but didn't say anything. Just kept handing out roses, smiling at the people crowding around.

"Maybe after this...?"

"We'll see," Rosa said.

Sean fell silent. She seemed distant, out of reach. He wanted to talk about her lunch with Robbins, about the insanity going on in his back yard. He wanted to be alone with her.

Pam came up to them, grinning and breathless. "I'm out of flyers. Channel thirteen wants to interview you guys."

Rosa looked alarmed, then glanced at Sean. Sure enough, a news crew was working its way through the crowd toward them.

"You should go," Sean said to Rosa. He spotted Angel not far away, looking at the displays. He called to him and waved, and Angel hurried over.

"The press are here. Would you get Rosa away, please?"

Angel looked at Rosa. "Sure."

"Let me take those," Pam said to Rosa, reaching for the flowers. "I'm sorry, I should have realized you wouldn't want to talk to the press. I wasn't thinking."

"It's OK," Rosa said.

"Better go," said Sean, keeping an eye on the advancing

news crew.

He watched Angel guide her off to one side, to the edge of the crowd, past the displays. They kept walking west, toward the river. Angel was still carrying the rose for his mom.

"Mr. Carpenter! You're Sean Carpenter, right?"

Sean turned his head. He didn't recognize the reporter, who wore a suit and tie despite the warm weather. Some new, fresh-faced kid on the weekend beat, eyes gleaming with the realization that he'd just scored a scoop.

"That's right," Sean said, resigning himself.

"And these are the miracle roses?"

"The very same."

"Mind if I ask you a few questions?"

Sean glanced after Rosa and Angel, glad they'd escaped the reporter's attention. He turned to face the camera and forced a smile.

"Sure, go ahead."

20

Rosa walked without looking back, afraid that if she did the news crew would recognize her and come after her. Angel didn't offer any reassurances, just was there. Silent company. Safe. She felt safe, and in realizing it, finally relaxed.

"Thanks," she said. "I didn't mean to take you away from the rally."

"I've heard it before."

"Yeah. It doesn't seem to change much." She glanced at the rose he was carrying. "That's a pretty one."

"Would you like to have it?"

"No, it's yours. I have some already."

They walked a few paces in silence, then Angel said, "It's Ruby's, actually. She wanted one for our mother."

"Oh. Is Ruby here? I didn't see her."

Rosa caught herself about to look back, and looked straight ahead instead. A green swath in front of them, speckled with gold, marked where the river ran.

"She's here somewhere," Angel said. "It's getting to be a big crowd back there."

"I'm not crazy about crowds," Rosa said.

"Me neither."

They walked on toward the river, comfortable together, not needing to talk. Rosa listened to the birds, the whisper of the breeze in the sage, the distant, unintelligible sound of Tom's megaphone. After a while they came to the *bosque*. Rosa took a deep breath as they stepped into the dappled shade beneath the cottonwoods, inhaling the rich scent of the woodlands.

"This is pueblo land, isn't it? Cochiti land?"

"Yes," Angel said.

"It's beautiful."

She stepped over a downed log tangled in weeds. No path here, but the undergrowth wasn't as bad as in Albuquerque.

"I went down to the *bosque* in my neighborhood a week ago," she said. "The water's very low."

They walked to the edge of the river and stood together gazing at it. Up here, above the thirsty irrigation ditches in Bernalillo and Corrales and Albuquerque, there was much more water in the river. It still looked low, though. The Rio really did need help.

"I saw you in the river," Rosa said softly.

Angel didn't answer. She turned to look at him. He was frowning slightly

"I walked out across the river," she said. "It's mostly sandbars down in Albuquerque. And I saw you standing in the water, with a circle of men. It looked like a ceremony."

Angel's eyes widened. Soft, dark eyes. He glanced away at the river.

"I saw you, too," he said after a moment, his voice a rough whisper. "You were walking in a garden, and you had an eagle feather in your hand."

Rosa caught her breath. The feather had been a gift from Cruz. Technically it was illegal to have one—eagles were protected and couldn't be hunted. Only Indians were allowed to have their feathers, for religious purposes. Was Angel angry that she had one?

"And I dreamed about you," Angel added, still gazing at the river. "Two nights ago. You were holding a rose, rubbing it on your face, your arms. All over yourself."

Rosa's heart fluttered. He'd seen her giving herself a *limpia*. How? Why?

Angel turned to look at her again, and lifted the rose he was holding. He cupped the bloom in one hand and brushed it gently across her cheek.

"Like this."

The velvet petals caressed her, sending her heart racing. She gave a small gasp, tasted a whisper of the rose's scent. Angel gazed into her eyes and a tingle ran through her. He leaned closer and kissed her cheek—gently, like the brush of the rose.

Rosa felt her heart opening like a flower. She looked into Angel's quiet, dark eyes.

He kissed her again, on the forehead. Her heart was racing, but she wasn't afraid.

Very slowly, he brushed kisses on the point between her

eyes, then the tip of her nose, then very lightly on her lips. Rosa's heart soared. She was trembling.

She had never been kissed quite like this, with such— concentration. As if Angel was giving it his whole attention.

He drew back and looked at her, eyes troubled. "Sean likes you."

"I know."

"I don't want to hurt him."

"Neither do I." Rosa touched the rose's petals with her fingertips. "But I don't feel that way about him."

Angel gazed at her, then touched her hair. He kissed her again, seriously this time, long and deeply, pulling her against him. Rosa slid her arms around him. He smelled of sage and wood smoke, clean, earthy scents.

After a moment they parted, keeping arms around each other. Angel found an old log they could sit on, and curled his arms around her. Rosa leaned her head against his shoulder. She felt safe in his embrace. Happy.

She hadn't expected this, but strangely she wasn't surprised. It felt right being with Angel. It felt wonderful. She turned her face up toward him to be kissed again, and Angel obliged her.

After a while he raised his head and looked east, toward the rally. "Maybe we should go back."

"Not yet."

They held each other, content in silence, not needing to talk. Rosa watched the river slide by, feeling at peace. A dragonfly hovered over a clump of yellow flowers, then sped off toward the water. Rosa smiled.

Eventually they would have to go back. Eventually they would talk, and decide what path they were going to walk together. They came from different cultures, but she was sure they could find common ground. Eagle feathers, roses, the river. For now she just wanted to stay here. She wanted this moment to last forever.

At last Angel kissed her forehead and loosened his clasp. Rosa pulled his head down and kissed him, greedily, then let him help her stand up. He'd kept track of the rose, somehow, and it was still perfect. They walked slowly back toward the rally, holding hands.

"I guess I should tell Sean," Rosa said.

"No, I'll tell him."

She looked at Angel beside her, the strong lines of his face lighting a thrill within her. He knew Sean better than she did. Maybe he would know how to make it hurt the least.

Sean glanced toward the river, wondering where Angel and Rosa had gone. The TV crew had finally left, after grilling Sean for twenty minutes and then taking a few hasty shots of Tom and the people at the rally. Sean had pushed the "Roses for the Rio" concept and stressed the water issue. Too bad if Tom didn't like it. He'd even mentioned his analysis, saying the Valle del Sol development "might have the potential to consume as much as two percent of the river's volume." If that wasn't qualified enough, oh well.

He glanced at his bucket of roses. He was almost out, finally. Must mean everybody had one who needed one. A lot of people had left already. The wind was picking up.

Pam's roses had run out a little while ago, and she was over by the displays now, answering questions. Tom had finished speaking and climbed down from the pickup.

A burst of wind whipped up dust from the road. Sean squinted his eyes shut against it, then walked over to where Pam stood and slid his bucket into her empty one. He'd never put water in the buckets, he realized. Guess it hadn't mattered.

The people Pam was talking to, a Pueblo couple, thanked her and left. She turned to Sean and smiled.

"This went pretty well, I think."

Sean nodded. "Better than I expected, considering how disorganized it was."

"I'm glad you brought the roses. They really make a difference."

"Thanks."

She looked at the bucket near their feet, smiling softly. "They *are* a miracle, aren't they?"

Sean shrugged. "I don't know. I guess so."

"Where did they come from?"

"My yard. Didn't you see it on the news?"

"I don't have a TV."

"Oh."

He found it refreshing, actually, that she didn't know the craziness that was going on or seem to care. She enjoyed the roses, plainly. She understood there was something strange about them. She had to be aware that she'd given out more roses than that bucket should have been able to hold, but she wasn't bugging him to explain why, and he was grateful for that.

Was that what faith was about? The ability to accept the impossible and keep on going through your day? He didn't know if Pam was religious. She hadn't mentioned anything that would give him a clue.

A gust of wind blew over one of the displays. Sean and Pam hastened to pick it up.

"Guess it's time to put these away," Pam said.

"Let me help you."

They broke down the displays and the easels, and started carrying them to Pam's station wagon. Sean brought two easels while she carried all the foam display boards, then they went back for the rest of the easels.

Three Pueblo ladies were standing around the bucket of roses. Sean picked it up and let them choose the ones they wanted while Pam took another easel to her car. When the ladies had gone, Tom came over to Sean.

"I've found out about something that might help us," Tom said in a lowered voice. "Something we can use against Robbins Corp."

"What?"

"An illegal gravel pit, not far from here. Looks like they're going to use it during the construction."

Sean felt a burst of excitement. This could be the break they needed.

"You're sure it's illegal?"

"Pretty sure. The guy who told me about it is going to take me over there now to a look at it. Want to come?"

"Yeah! Just let me get rid of these buckets."

Sean picked up the last easel and carried it to Pam's car with Tom tagging along behind him. The displays and all had pretty much filled the station wagon to the roof. Pam accepted the last easel and crammed it into the back seat.

"Do you have room for these?" Sean asked, holding out the buckets. "I'm going to take a look at something with Tom, and I don't want to take them all the way back to my car."

"Sure. What are you looking at?"

"A gravel pit Robbins Corp. is using. It might be illegal, so we might be able to get them busted."

Pam looked interested. "Can I come?"

"I don't think there's room in the Jeep," Tom said, frowning.

"I don't mind squishing," Pam said, taking the buckets from Sean and putting them in her shotgun seat. She pulled the last of the roses out. "Two left. One for you, one for me!"

She handed Sean a red rose and kept a yellow-red one for herself. The yellow of this one was deep, almost orange, and the red was all down at the bottom of the petals. The red rose she'd given him was two shades, a lighter red streaked through the dark. The roses were changing. Growing.

Pam turned to Tom with a grin. "Lead on!"

Tom seemed to hesitate, still frowning. He looked at Sean, then back at Pam, and shrugged.

"OK, why not."

He led them up the road to where a rag-top Jeep was parked. In the driver's seat was a big Hispanic guy with a snake tattoo on his neck. He gave Tom a questioning look as they walked up.

"Got an extra passenger. It's OK if they both go, right?"

The guy glanced at Sean, then looked Pam up and down, unsmiling. He scoped her so candidly Sean wondered if she found it offensive.

"Yeah, OK. Might need more gas money."

"We'll work it out. This is Joe," Tom said. "Sean and Pam."

Joe nodded and started the Jeep. Pam and Sean climbed in the back, and Tom got in the shotgun seat. Pam broke the stem off her rose and tucked the bloom behind one ear, a flash of yellow in the coppery frizz. She tossed the stem out of the window and grinned at Sean.

"This is going to be fun!"

Angel let go of Rosa's hand as they came near the road, and she stifled a sigh of disappointment. The rally seemed to be breaking up. The truck where Tom had been speaking was gone. A few people were still walking around with roses and yellow flyers in their hands, but most of them seemed to be heading for their cars. It looked like a lot of folks had gone home already.

Rosa looked for Sean but didn't see him at once. She and Angel started walking up the road, and she spotted Sean and Pam getting into a Jeep she didn't recognize.

"There he is. And there's Tom, too. What are they doing?"

A gust of wind stirred dust up around the Jeep, forming a dust-devil in the road. Rosa saw dancing figures in the dust and let out a gasp.

"What is it?" Angel said.

"Don't you see them?"

"See who? Sean?"

"*Koshare!*"

21

The Jeep pulled away. The *koshare*—half a dozen of them at least —danced after it. Rosa felt a stab of dread and started to run.

"Rosa! Wait!"

She kept running, heard Angel's steps pounding after her. "Something's wrong!" she called. "We have to stop them!"

Angel sped past her, his longer legs carrying him up the road faster than she could run, but not fast enough to catch the Jeep. Rosa reached her car parked on the shoulder and called him back.

"Angel! Come on, we'll drive!"

She pulled her keys from her pocket and fumbled at the lock with trembling hands. Got it open and jumped into the driver's seat. Angel came pounding back and climbed in next to her, and Rosa hit the gas.

"You run fast," she said after a moment.

"We have races on feast days," Angel said, breathing hard.

Rosa saw the dust devil ahead, still roiling with *koshare*, trailing after the Jeep. She pressed on the gas, then hit the breaks as a clown appeared in front of her car, gesturing for her to slow down. Angel slapped a hand against the dashboard to keep from being thrown forward.

"Do you see that one?" Rosa asked.

"No."

Angel looked ahead, frowning. The *koshare* hopped onto Rosa's car and faced forward, striped legs splayed across the hood, gesturing with a hand to Rosa to drive on.

"It doesn't want me to catch them. It just wants me to follow them."

She started driving again, more slowly, keeping back from the Jeep but keeping it in sight. They were still passing cars on the side of the road now and then. Rosa saw one that she thought was Sean's, but the Jeep drove on past it.

"There's Ruby!" Angel said suddenly. "Stop!"

Ruby was walking along the road away from them with two

other Pueblo women. Rosa slowed down and Angel rolled down his window.

"Ruby, get in!"

Ruby turned and gave him a surprised look. Rosa stopped the car.

"What's the matter?"

"Just get in," Angel said.

Ruby said something to her companions and got into the back seat. As soon as she had the door closed Rosa started off again.

"What's going on?" Ruby said.

"Are they still there?" Angel asked Rosa.

She nodded. "Do you see the dust devil?"

"Yeah."

"They're all around the bottom of it."

"What is?" Ruby said, sounding exasperated. "What's going on?"

"*Koshare*," Angel said. "She's seeing *koshare* following that Jeep."

"There's one sitting on the hood of my car now."

Angel looked at her, then looked ahead again. He was frowning, maybe in annoyance.

"Sean and Pam and Tom are in the Jeep," he said.

Ruby didn't say anything. After a minute Rosa heard the click of her fastening her seat belt. Angel fastened his, too, then reached across Rosa and pulled hers around her. His closeness sent tingles through her, his hands brushing against her as he pushed the tab into the buckle.

"Thanks," she said. "I hope we won't need it."

The Jeep was driving fairly fast. Rosa kept pace. The dust devil swayed back and forth across the road, but continued after the Jeep.

"That's weird," Ruby said after a couple of minutes. "It's like the dust devil is following them."

Rosa nodded. She was gripping the steering wheel so hard her fingers were starting to cramp. She tried to relax.

"Sean has a cell phone," Ruby said. "Should I call him?"

Rosa looked at Angel, who gazed back at her, worried. Rosa tried to decide if that was the right thing to do. She wasn't collected enough to ask for guidance.

"No," Angel said. "Text him."

Rosa heard Ruby getting out her phone and the beeps it made as she punched in Sean's number. A long pause followed.

"OK, I sent it," Ruby said. "No answer yet."

Rosa swallowed. She wished the anxious knot in her stomach would go away, but she kept thinking of things Miguel might say. What if the driver had a gun? What if Sean and the others were hostages? She wished Miguel was in reach, or that she had asked him to come with her today.

The Jeep turned onto the road heading back toward the interstate and sped up. Rosa followed at a distance. The dust devil started fading on the wider pavement, but she could still see the *koshare*. The one sitting on her car hopped off and ran to catch up with the others, reminding her of how easily Angel had dusted her.

Silence stretched as they drove on for several miles, then the Jeep slowed and turned left onto a smaller road. Rosa waited before following, knowing she'd be in greater danger of being spotted on the less-used road. It was narrower, though, and the dust-devil came back. The wind was getting stronger, blowing billows of dust across the road, sometimes obscuring the Jeep altogether. Rosa drove slowly, her heart pounding.

"Santa Maria, guide us," she whispered. "Help us do the right thing. Help and protect our friends."

About a mile from the highway the Jeep turned off onto a dirt road, crossing a cattle guard set into a barbed wire fence. Rosa slowed down even more and followed.

"Where are they going?" Ruby said. "There's nothing out here."

"It's National Forest land, I think," Angel said.

The forest consisted of scattered scrub, mostly juniper. The road started to slope upward. Rosa couldn't see the Jeep any more, just the cloud of dust raised by its passing. *Koshare* still danced in the dust, their striped arms and legs flailing, calling her onward.

The Jeep disappeared over a rise, and the dust devil disintegrated. Rosa slowed down, frowning. Maybe they'd reached their destination. Miguel would have told her not to go barreling in there. She tried to think like a cop, and decided to park the car.

She pulled off the road and made for a large clump of juniper, parking behind it so the car wouldn't be visible from the road. She shut off the engine and got out. Angel got out too.

"Rosa?"

She looked at him, then started walking up the slope. She could hear the Jeep's engine. Maybe she shouldn't have stopped. She ran, hoping to catch sight of it from the top of the hill. Suddenly she heard its engine shut off.

She stopped, and Angel stopped beside her. He frowned as he leaned forward, listening. After a moment he started walking up the hill.

Rosa glanced back toward the car. Ruby was waiting there, still in the back seat. Good, because she'd left her keys in the ignition.

She followed Angel up the hill. The thump of a car door closing made both of them freeze for a moment. Angel crouched down and continued forward slowly in a half-lope, half-crawl. Rosa copied him, keeping her head down.

Angel went to hands and knees, then to his belly. With a twinge of regret for her white dress—she should never have worn it to an outdoor event—Rosa did the same, crawling after him. He moved up beside a small bush and stopped. Rosa joined him and found herself looking down into a gravel pit, its steep sides shaped like an inverted cone, with a ramp coiling down into it. A large backhoe sat halfway down the ramp on the far side.

"Land-eater," she whispered.

Angel glanced at her, then looked back at the pit. The Jeep was parked at the top of it, off to their left, almost concealed by the bush. Tom, Sean, and Pam were standing beside it, looking down into the pit. The Jeep's driver got out and strolled toward them. Rosa didn't recognize him.

"They're gone," she whispered.

"Hm?"

"The *koshare*. I don't see them any more."

"Maybe this was what they wanted us to see."

Rosa frowned. It made sense, but it didn't feel right. The

feeling of dread was still there.

Sean looked down at the pit and whistled. The backhoe had no company logo on it, he noticed. That in itself said something, if it really was Robbins Corp. equipment.

He glanced at Tom. "Looks like they've already been using it for a while."

"Yeah."

Sean turned and looked at Joe, who was coming up beside him. "How did you find out about it?"

"What?" Joe said.

He held a hand to his ear and stepped closer to Sean. Maybe the wind had kept him from hearing. Sean started to repeat the question. Joe suddenly turned and punched him in the gut.

Sean went down, gasping. He looked up and saw Joe standing over him. Beyond him, Pam was struggling with Tom. Made no sense.

Joe reached toward him and Sean scrabbled backward, his hands hitting sharp gravel. He winced and rolled. Joe came after him and aimed a kick at his groin. Sean flinched away and took it in the thigh instead, letting out a yelp of pain.

Joe kicked him again, in the back. Sean felt himself sliding, falling, rolling down into the pit. The last thing he saw was Tom flinging Pam after him.

$$\maltese \ 22$$

"Run to Ruby," Angel said hoarsely. "Tell her to call the police."

Rosa could barely breathe, and she feared her terrified gasping would be heard. She backed away from the bush, then turned and scrambled down the hill on hands and knees. Ruby got out of the car and started toward her. Rosa got to her feet and ran the rest of the way, grabbed Ruby by the shoulders.

"Call 911!"

Ruby's eyes went wide, then she took out her cell phone and punched in the number. Rosa looked back toward the hilltop. She couldn't see Angel at first and her heart leapt in panic, then she spotted him curled up beside the bush.

"What do I tell them?" Ruby asked.

"Shh! Tell them to get out here," Rosa said in a low voice. "Sean's been attacked."

An engine started up. Rosa flinched toward the ground, then pulled Ruby with her behind the nearest bush. It wasn't until they were crouched there that she realized the engine was too loud, much too loud to be the Jeep.

"Stay here," she told Ruby. "Tell the police a man and a woman have been attacked and thrown into a gravel pit. The attackers are still here, but maybe not for long."

She left Ruby behind the bush and scrambled up the hill again, dropping to her knees and then crawling up beside Angel. He held out a hand to keep her back. She flattened herself against the ground, then slowly crawled up next to him on her elbows and peeped over the hilltop.

"Are they coming?" Angel whispered.

"She's calling. Oh, God!"

The backhoe was moving. Rosa clutched Angel's arm as the machine picked up a scoopful of gravel in a bucket almost as big as her car. Horrified, she watched it swing its arm out over the pit.

Sean was bruised all over, so dizzy he feared he'd throw up. His hands were cut and bleeding from the gravel. He struggled to his knees.

"Pam?"

She was lying beside him, looked unconscious, the yellow rose tangled in her hair. A growl penetrated his awareness, sounding at first like Zozobra moaning on Fiesta day. His fuddled brain rejected that, and reclassified the sound as mechanical. Coming from behind him.

He turned, lost his balance, and fell onto his elbow as his gaze fixed on the huge shadow overhead. It tipped toward him, and the gravel poured down.

Rosa buried her face in Angel's arm. Too late, they were too late! She gave a gasping sob, then held her breath, struggling to be silent.

Angel's hand covered hers. "Rosa," he said softly. "We have to go."

She looked up at him and coughed. He put a finger to his lips. "We have to get out of here, or we're next."

She heard a rushing sound from the pit again—another bucketful of gravel. Her jaw shivered and she clenched her teeth to stop it. She nodded, then began to crawl backward down the hill.

Her knees and elbows were starting to hurt from scrapes. She turned around and got to her feet, staying crouched low until she was well below the hilltop. When it was safe to stand she scrambled down to the bush where Ruby was waiting, with Angel close behind.

Ruby still had the phone to her ear. "What's happening?"

Rosa's throat closed and she couldn't speak. A shudder went through her. Angel held out his hand for the phone, and quietly told the dispatcher about the backhoe. He gestured toward the car, and they all hurried over to it and climbed in.

Rosa sat with her hands on the steering wheel, shaking. She still couldn't believe what she'd seen. Tom had been a part of it. *Tom.* He'd betrayed them!

She heard the backhoe grunting and chuffing. It seemed to be getting louder. Looking toward the hilltop, she saw it roll up out of the pit. She flinched, though it was moving away from her.

Another engine roared to a stop, then sat rumbling. Rosa could just see the top of a large truck cab. After a minute the backhoe rumbled toward it, then appeared to climb. The truck must be hauling a flatbed trailer. They were taking the backhoe away.

Rosa looked at Angel. "I c-could pull the car onto the road. Block the way."

He shook his head. "Too dangerous. The police are coming. Just sit tight and be ready to drive.

Rosa swallowed and looked back up the hill. The backhoe was perched, unmoving. She saw its driver — the stranger — get out and walk forward, and she flinched again. If he turned around and looked, he'd see the car. She put her hand on the ignition, ready to crank it.

Long minutes passed. Rosa kept seeing the gravel pouring down into the pit on top of Sean and Pam. She stared at the motionless backhoe, watching for the man to appear and look down the hill at her.

Angel spoke quietly into the cell phone now and then, mostly just saying "Yes." The dispatcher was keeping him on the line.

Rosa glanced back down the road, looking for a sign of the police. Were there cops in Pena Blanca? At Cochiti? Or would it be state cops from Santa Fe? That could take a while, it was almost twenty miles away.

The truck engine revved and the cab started to move. Rosa stared at it until the top of the backhoe moved away out of sight. She'd parked to shield her car from view of the hilltop. Once the truck passed the juniper she was parked behind, the car would be visible to anyone who looked back.

They wouldn't look back, she told herself. They had no reason to think they weren't alone. The logic was no comfort to the part of her that was ready to scream in panic. Her hand on the keys was slick with sweat. She wiped it on her skirt.

She could hear the truck's engine getting louder as it came down the hill. She heard it go past, then saw it in her rearview mirror, rumbling away down the road they'd come in on. She turned in her seat, trying to see the license plate, but there was too much dust. The Jeep appeared a moment later, hanging back from the dust raised by the truck. She half expected to see *koshare* dancing behind them, but there was nothing.

She watched until she couldn't see them any more, until the dust raised by their passing drifted away. Angel handed the cell phone back to Ruby and got out of the car. Rosa took her hand off the keys and sobbed. After a minute she got hold of herself and fumbled behind her seat for the box of tissue she kept there. Ruby pushed it into her hand.

"Thanks."

Rosa wiped her face and blew her nose. She looked up in time to see Angel disappearing over the hilltop.

Fear stabbed her and she turned to look down the road. No sign of the truck or the Jeep coming back. She swallowed, trying to calm down. Noticed the rose lying on the seat beside her. She picked it up and got out of the car, then walked up the hill after Angel.

When she reached the bush where they'd hidden on the hilltop, she looked down into the pit. Angel was down there, shoveling gravel aside with his hands. Probably futile, but she understood that he had to try.

A shudder went through her. She knelt beside the bush and said a prayer for Sean and Pam's souls, then stuck the rose into the dirt and stood up again. Tears slid down her cheeks again as she started down into the pit.

23

Sean saw stars, but not real stars. They were five-pointed stars, and they were gold. The sky was unnatural, too—a deep turquoise, deeper even than New Mexico's normal incredible blue. He felt a great sense of peace and contentment. He couldn't move, but the sky kept him safe from harm.

Part of him knew that didn't make any sense. The same part knew something was wrong, but he couldn't remember what. He felt an overwhelming desire just to rest, to lie still.

Pam needed help, though. He clung to that, wondering where she was. He remembered seeing her lying on the gravel, a yellow rose in her hair.

Gravel! Pouring from the sky like rain! The memory sharpened his wits, and he struggled to move now, struggled to climb out of the stupor he'd been in.

A hand covered his, and a woman's voice said his name. He knew the voice. He stopped struggling and opened his eyes.

Rosa was sitting next to him, looking worried. Angel was standing beside her. He smiled, and Sean smiled back.

"Dude."

"Welcome back," Angel said. "We thought we'd lost you."

The words brought memory crashing back, and with it came the pain of a thousand bruises. Sean closed his eyes and tried to swallow, but his throat was dry.

"Water," he said, his voice coming out in a croak.

He opened his eyes again and saw Angel offering a plastic cup with a straw in it. Sean took a couple of sips and coughed a little.

He was in a hospital bed. He didn't remember anything after the gravel, but they must have got him out fast. He shouldn't have been able to breathe for very long under there. In fact, it should have crushed him. He should be dead. He was sure that's what Tom had intended.

"Where's Pam?" he asked.

"In another room," Angel said. "Ruby's sitting with her.

She's doing OK, considering."

"How'd you find us?"

"Rosa saw *koshare* following you."

"Oh." Sean looked at Rosa. "Thanks."

She smiled and squeezed his hand. Nice, but too bad it took nearly getting killed to make her hold his hand.

He felt woozy, and a little nauseated. Drugs, probably. They'd doped him up. He still hurt, though. No fair.

"It was Tom," he said, afraid he'd pass out before being able to explain.

"We know," Angel said. "We saw."

"Oh, good. You can tell the cops, then."

With that worry out of the way, he slipped back toward the darkness. He felt Rosa's hand touch his brow, warm and soft. He smiled, thinking he'd have to tell her that he did have faith, really, so she could give him her medicine with a clear heart.

When he woke it was night. A faint light filled the room, and it was quieter than before, though he still heard hospital noises from out in the hall. He turned his head toward the chair where Rosa had been sitting. His mother was sitting there now.

"Hi, sweetie," she said, reaching to smooth his hair. "How're you feeling?"

"Rotten."

"You want a pain pill?"

"N-no. What time is it?"

She glanced at her watch. "Almost eleven. Don't worry, Father Mahan said he'd stay at the house. You're right, he's a good one. I wasn't so impressed with the bishop."

Sean frowned. "The bishop was at my house?"

"Yes, he brought a whole committee to investigate the miracle roses. They were there for more than an hour and drank three pots of coffee and pontificated all over your living room. I was ready to strangle them."

The image of his mother strangling the Archbishop of Santa Fe made Sean close his eyes again. He couldn't cope with it. He couldn't cope with the miracle roses, either, right now. Too much.

"There's a police detective waiting to talk to you," she said. "You feel up to it?"

"Um."

"Maybe not just yet. He just wants to hear your side of it. They've already interviewed Rosa and the Madalenas."

He looked at her. "Rosa still here?"

"No, they left. I think she was going to spend the night at their place in Cochiti. They said they'd be back tomorrow."

Sean sighed. He was really tired, and he ached all over.

"Guess I'll take that pill now."

"Sure, sweetie. I'll get the nurse."

He lay staring at the ceiling, remembering the gravel pit. Everything he thought he knew about Tom was a lie, apparently. So PRD was a lie, the rallies were a lie. No wonder Tom had been unenthusiastic about Sean's suggestions. He was a toady, a plant. He must have been working for Robbins all along.

A shadow darkened the light coming in the doorway. Sean looked that way and saw an unfamiliar man standing there, Hispanic, on the tall side, wearing jeans and a western shirt. Sean's heart jumped in fear as the man came into the room.

"Mr. Carpenter? I'm Detective Montano."

The man showed him a badge in a leather case. Sean sighed with relief.

"Oh. Hi."

"Sorry to bother you. I won't stay long, but I need to know if you recognized the man who attacked you."

Sean tried to shake his head. Mistake. He swallowed, then said, "No. Never met him before. Tom said his name was Joe."

"OK. Thanks."

"Did you catch them?"

"Yeah, they're being held. They're not talking."

"Kyle Robbins sent them."

"Why do you say that?"

"Only thing that makes sense. I was trying to stop his development. Tom must be working for him. He probably hired the other guy. Can't you check his phone records?"

"Nowadays people use disposable cell phones for that kind of planning. Harder to track down. But I'll give it a try."

"What about the gravel pit? Is it really illegal?"

Montano shook his head. "It's been abandoned for decades. The land's part of the National Forest now. They trucked in the backhoe. They were hauling it back out to the freeway when we caught up with them."

Sean frowned. "So you can't tie them to Robbins Corp."

"We're checking who owns the backhoe, but unless that pans out, no. There's no connection."

Sean's mother came back, accompanied by a skinny brunette nurse with her hair in an untidy knot and a paper pill cup in one hand. The nurse glared at Montano.

"I'm sorry, you'll have to leave."

"OK." Montano nodded to Sean. "We'll talk some more when you're up to it."

Sean flapped a hand in farewell. He was losing it, he could tell. Probably didn't need the pain pill, but he swallowed it anyway and thanked the nurse, who gave him a perfunctory smile.

"Go back to sleep, sweetie," his mom said, smiling fondly at him as she settled back into the chair.

"You don't have to stay," he told her.

"I don't mind, sweetie pie. You just rest."

Sean's eyes were trying to close. He fought it for a moment, long enough to notice a vase of roses on the nightstand.

"You bring those?"

She glanced at the flowers. "Yes, it was Father Mahan's idea. He said you could probably use some extra blessings."

That's OK, Sean thought as the drowsiness took him down. I've got gold stars and a turquoise sky.

Rosa woke early, smelling unfamiliar dust and hot coffee. She sat up and blinked at the sunlight leaking through Venetian blinds. The room was a guest room, and also a sewing room by the evidence of a work table and shelves full of fabric in plastic storage boxes. The quilt on the bed looked homemade. The designs on it were like the cloud symbols on Pueblo pottery.

Rosa got up and looked for her clothes. She was wearing a t-shirt borrowed from Ruby, oversized for her. Her dress had been in bad shape after crawling around in the dirt, and Ruby had offered to wash it. She didn't find it in the room, but a pair of shorts with a drawstring waist was lying on the dresser beside her purse.

Rosa put them on, cinched the drawstring as tight as it would go, and ran her fingers through her hair to make sure it wasn't sticking up all over the place. She found her sandals and got into them, then wandered out into Ruby's living room, yawning. Nobody was there, so she went to the kitchen, where she found Ruby making breakfast and Mrs. Madalena sitting at the kitchen table, patiently picking weeds and goatheads out of the fringe of Rosa's pink scarf.

"Morning," Ruby said, handing Rosa a mug of coffee. "Sleep OK?"

"Yeah. Thanks." She took a swallow of coffee and sat down at the table. "You don't have to do that, Mrs. Madalena."

"I don't mind. I like touching it."

Mrs. Madalena was small and thin, the physical opposite of her daughter except that they were both short. Her hair was braided and tied in a bun, and her dark brown eyes were bright with curiosity. Something in the lines of her face reminded Rosa of Angel.

"Where's Angel?"

"Out," Ruby said. "He'll be back for breakfast."

Doing something they weren't going to talk about. Rosa resigned herself to not knowing. There were probably some things she would never know about Angel.

She liked his family, though. Mrs. Madalena might be quiet, but she was sharp as a whip. She'd figured out within an hour of meeting Rosa that she and Angel were...were what? In love? They hadn't talked that far. They hadn't talked much at all about themselves yet.

It didn't matter. Mrs. Madalena had spent the first part of the evening watching Rosa, occasionally asking a subtle question. By the time she'd gone to bed—earlier than the younger generation—she had apparently made up her mind, because she'd kissed Rosa's cheek exactly as she'd kissed Ruby's and Angel's. The glance Rosa had seen the siblings exchange had told her this was unusual.

"Mass is at nine," Ruby said. "We can go into town to see Sean after."

"Sounds perfect," Rosa said.

Angel came back just as Rosa was helping butter the toast. He shot her a smile, then brushed past her as he went to kiss his mother. Rosa caught a whiff of wood smoke. Had he been in a kiva? Did they even have a kiva at Cochiti? All she had seen of the pueblo was houses. There wasn't a historic structure like at Taos or Acoma.

She might as well not worry about it, because she probably wouldn't find out. She finished buttering the toast and set the plate in the middle of the table. Breakfast was ready, and Rosa did justice to her share of eggs, ham, and a hot red chile sauce that her mother would have approved. She'd been too tired and upset to eat much the night before, and now she was starving.

"Your dress got torn," Ruby told her. "Mama fixed it."

"Thank you!"

Mrs. Madalena gave her a pixie smile, the corners of her eyes crinkling. "It isn't perfect, but I don't think it will show."

"I'm surprised it wasn't completely ruined," Rosa said, sipping her coffee.

She noticed Angel watching her across the table, and paused, returning his gaze over her mug. She knew he was thinking of the day before, the horrible time at the gravel pit. A small smile curved his lips. He was proud of her. Rosa felt herself blushing, not with embarrassment, but with pleasure.

Sean was sitting up in bed talking on the phone when he saw Angel, Rosa, and Ruby come in. He nodded to them, and accepted the keychain Angel dropped into his hand.

"Hold on a second, Forrest." He lowered the phone. "How did you get these?"

"Your mom asked me to drive your car back into town," Angel said. "You weren't awake."

"Oh. Thanks! OK, Forrest, where were we? Right. Just add a box to the front page, and inside put 'To everyone who received a miracle rose, please bring your rose to the Valle del Sol construction site on Friday, August 24th. To save the Rio Grande we must stop this water-hogging development.' And then put the map underneath. That's it. Yeah. Thanks, Forrest! I owe you. Bye."

He hung up and looked at Rosa, and couldn't help breaking into a silly grin. She was wearing the same dress she'd had on the day before, with the pink rose scarf. Still gorgeous, though her eyes looked a bit strained.

"What's going on Friday?" she asked.

"Valle del Sol's groundbreaking."

"Oh, yeah. Fighting back, eh?"

"You got it. Since we're on our own I figured it was time to take the initiative. We have a website that's getting a zillion hits, so we might as well use it. Maybe we'll get enough people to stand in front of the bulldozers, or at least enough to make a show of it. I'm calling the media next."

"I take it you're feeling better."

"Much. Still sore all over. I hear my face is a mess, too. Haven't looked at it."

"It's...colorful."

"Mom says it's a face only a mother could love."

Rosa gave an anxious little smile and glanced at Angel. He looked back at her, his expression unreadable, then faced Sean.

"Is there anything else we can help you with?" Angel asked.

"Don't think so. You might check with Pam — her car was out there too."

"Pam's car is at home, thanks," said a voice from the doorway.

It was Pam, on the arm of an older man who clearly shared a lot of her DNA. He had the same freckles and red hair, though his beard was flecked with white.

Pam was wearing a pale green velour robe and walking slowly, with a slight limp. Her face was bruised, notably along one side of her jaw. Bastard Tom must have clocked her one. She smiled, though, looking determinedly cheerful.

"I was just out for my constitutional and decided to see how you were doing. This is my dad, by the way — James Weston. Dad, this is Angel, and Rosa, and Ruby."

"You're the ones who saved my daughter. I can't thank you enough."

They murmured appropriate comments, and Angel shook Mr. Weston's hand. Pam reclaimed his attention.

"And this is Sean."

Mr. Weston nodded gravely. "How do you do. You're a lucky young man."

"Don't I know it!"

"They're saying it's a miracle you survived. That gravel should have crushed you instantly."

"Let's not talk about it, Dad."

A shadow of pain crossed Pam's face. Sean searched for a way to distract her from the bad memories.

"Hey, how come you rate a robe? I'm stuck in this backless thing!"

Pam flashed a grin. "I have loving parents."

"It's missing something, though." Sean tilted his head to one side, pretending to study her. "I know!"

He reached over to the vase of roses and picked out a yellow one, broke the stem off short, and leaned forward to tuck it behind Pam's ear. At once her eyes misted up with tears.

"Thank you," she said unsteadily.

He hadn't meant to make her cry. "Makes you look like springtime," he said, trying to get her to smile.

She did smile, bravely if crookedly. "You're just saying that 'cause it's true."

Sean laughed, and she laughed too, and swiped surreptitiously at her eyes. She stayed a few minutes, chatting cheerfully about unimportant things, then went back to her room with her father. Sean watched her limp around the corner and out into the hall.

"I hope she'll be OK."

"She will," Ruby said. "She's strong-willed."

He looked at Rosa, who was looking at Angel as if she wanted to ask him a question. Angel turned to Sean.

"If you think of anything you need, let us know."

"Yeah, a newspaper. I want to find out if they got Guzman to talk."

Rosa glanced up. "Guzman?"

"Yeah. Emilio Guzman, also known as Joe. That's Tom's little helper. Apparently Tom's got himself a fancy lawyer, but Guzman got assigned one from the Public Defender's office. I'm hoping he'll rat on Tom. No honor among thieves, you know."

"Guzman." Rosa frowned. "Sounds familiar."

"He wasn't the guy in your yard, was he?"

She gave him a frightened glance, then shook her head. "I don't think that guy was as big. But it's hard to tell. I only got a glimpse of him, and it was dark."

"I'll tell Detective Montano to ask Guzman about you. Maybe we'll get lucky."

Rosa shivered and took a step sideways, closer to Angel. Sean couldn't blame her. He could personally testify, and intended to do so, that Guzman was one badass dude.

"I'll get you a paper," Ruby said, starting for the door. "Be right back."

Sean watched her go, thinking her departure a bit abrupt, but then that's how she was. Rosa cleared her throat.

"I've got to get home. Poor Bruja's probably starving. I'll call you, OK?"

"Or text me. I saw Ruby's text, by the way, but not 'til this morning." He looked at Angel. "Thanks for trying to warn me."

Angel gave a sober nod. There was a tiny crease of concern in his forehead.

"They might let me go home today," Sean said.

Rosa stepped closer and gave him a chaste kiss on the cheek. "I'm glad you're all right."

"Thanks to you. You too, Angel."

Angel smiled. "You've got other protectors, too, I think."

"I need every one I can get."

They both said goodbye and walked out together. Angel was probably walking Rosa to her car. Guardian Angel. Sean chuckled to himself, then sat back to wait for the paper Ruby'd promised.

"Should we have told him?" Rosa asked as she opened her car. It was still covered with dust from the day before.

"I think I should wait until he's back on his feet."

"That won't be long."

"No."

She got in the driver's seat, and Angel climbed into the shotgun seat. She'd already told her mother she was bringing a guest to dinner. They hadn't discussed what would happen after that. Either she'd drive Angel back home and get a short night's sleep before Monday morning, or ...

"Did you want to spend the night at my place?" Her heart raced even as she said it.

Angel was silent for a moment. "Should I?"

"Well, you're welcome to, only...." Rosa cleared her throat. "I don't want to get too intimate yet."

"OK."

She looked at him, afraid he'd be angry. Instead he was smiling. The tension in her chest eased a little.

"We've got plenty of time," he said. "If you've got a couch I can sleep on, I'm happy."

"It's a futon couch. It's a little firm, but it's comfortable."

"OK, then." He leaned toward her and kissed her. "Let's go rescue Bruja."

Rosa smiled and started the car, relieved that her biggest concern wasn't going to be a problem, at least for now. She and Angel talked all the way to Albuquerque. She'd never heard him talk so much before, or with such animation. He told her how he'd become a musician, how his uncle had taught him to make flutes and play them, how the music he played in kiva ceremonies filled him with feelings of ecstasy.

So there was a kiva of some kind at Cochiti, or at least a kiva society. She smiled as she listened, feeling privileged to hear the things Angel was telling her. She suspected he didn't tell them to many people. Sean, maybe. Ruby, maybe. The people who were closest to him.

Bruja greeted them with anxious yowls. Rosa picked her up and cuddled her, murmuring apologies, then introduced her to Angel. Angel stroked the top of Bruja's head, and she instantly started purring. Rosa carried her to the kitchen and gave her a can of wet food and a scoop of kibble.

Returning to the living room, Rosa found Angel gazing out

the back door. He glanced at her, eyes marveling.

"That's the garden where I saw you walking."

Rosa took his hand. "Come and walk there with me."

They went out into the mid-afternoon heat that was cut only slightly by the dappled shade of the elms. Rosa showed Angel her plants, telling him a little about their uses in *curanderismo*. He listened with interest, nodding, adding comments about how his people used some of the same plants.

"And over here's my statue of Our Lady. Oh!"

A bush covered in pink roses had grown up around the pedestal. At first glance it looked like the statue was floating on top of the flowers.

"That wasn't there before!"

Angel looked at it. "What, the statue?"

"The roses!"

Rosa reached out and touched the flowers. Pink, like the rose she had used for a *limpia*.

"Santa Maria," she whispered. "I stuck one of Sean's roses in the ground here."

"When?"

"Thursday night."

She looked at Angel. A smiled grew slowly on his face, and he took her in his arms.

"Three days for a miracle. Not bad."

$$\clubsuit\ 24$$

During the next few days Sean felt like he was getting his life back together. He'd taken the week off, on Nick's orders and under protest that he really was OK to work.

"I don't care how you feel," Nick had said Monday morning when Sean had dragged his achy ass into the office. "How you look will frighten the clients. Go home and get well, miracle man. I'll see you next week."

By Friday the bruises were pretty much gone. The miracle roses were booming in Sean's back yard, managed by a 24-hour crew of volunteers including a fleet of church vans that were shuttling people back and forth from the nearest big parking lot. No more lines in the alley, no more unhappy neighbors and cops. Donations were more than covering the gas money, according to Father Mahan. Sean suspected the church was making a tidy profit, but he didn't comment. It was *Guadalupana's* church, after all.

The Valle del Sol groundbreaking was scheduled for 1:00 p.m. on Friday. Sean left the house at eleven, accompanied by his mom, who said she wouldn't miss it for the world. Rosa was coming up from Albuquerque, and Ruby and Angel would be there of course. Father Mahan was driving the bishop's miracle committee, who all wanted to be present. Even Pam was coming, which Sean thought was brave of her. He himself felt a twinge of nervous fear as he passed the turnoff to the gravel pit.

Before he got to Pena Blanca, he saw the flashing lights of police cars at a roadblock up ahead. At first he thought Robbins had pulled strings to keep people out, then he realized one of the cops was flagging him to turn left into an empty field on the side of the road. A line of cars was parked along the far fence. Sean stopped and rolled down his window.

"What's happening, Officer?"

"You're here for the groundbreaking, right?"

"Yeah."

"Go ahead and park. The shuttle bus'll be back in about ten

minutes."

"Shuttle bus?"

The cop glanced south down the road. "There's too many cars down there already. The village is overflowing. If you want to go, you'll have to ride the bus."

Sean gaped in astonishment. "When did people start arriving?"

"There were a few yesterday afternoon, but it didn't get really hairy until around ten last night."

"Wow. OK, thanks."

"Have a rose," Sean's mom said to the cop.

She pulled a red bloom out of the bouquet she was holding and passed it to Sean to give to him. The cop grinned and tipped his hat.

"Thanks, ma'am. I've been wanting one of these, if it's what I think it is."

"It most certainly is," she said, smiling.

Sean drove into the parking lot, getting out of the way of the three cars that had already stacked up behind him. He parked the car, shut off the engine, and looked at his mother. She smiled.

"Wonder of wonders."

"Miracle of miracles," Sean answered numbly. "Holy cats!"

A few minutes later a yellow school bus drove past, did a turnaround in another empty lot across the road, and pulled up facing south. Sean and his mom got in along with about forty other people, almost enough to fill all the seats. The bus rumbled past several full parking lots, then through Pena Blanca, which was indeed overflowing with cars parked in every possible space and some impossible ones as well. Cars were parked all along both sides of the road south of town, too. Double and triple parked, as they got closer to the Valle del Sol site.

The bus pulled up in the same place where they'd had the rally. A large billboard for Valle del Sol had been erected since then, right beside where the road entered the development. It looked expensive, and was riddled with shotgun holes.

Sean stepped off the bus and stood staring in amazement. The site was covered with people. Hundreds of people — thousands, even — all holding roses. They were milling around, talking, a few dozen taking shelter from the sun beneath a large tented awning that had been erected off to the right a short distance from the entrance. Probably the tent was meant to shade dignitaries who were invited to the groundbreaking. It belonged to the people now.

"Did you give this many roses away?" Sean's mother asked.

"Um...yeah, probably. I didn't expect this many to show up. I thought we'd be doing good to get a couple hundred."

Near the tent Sean spied some familiar-looking display boards on easels. He and his mom strolled that way, exchanging hellos with the people they passed. The mood in the gathering was upbeat, excited. Sean caught snatches of conversation about the Rio Grande, about the roses, and about water. Many of the people seemed to be exchanging stories of how they'd acquired miracle roses.

A familiar mass of curly red hair drew Sean's attention. Pam was standing near the displays talking with a Pueblo woman. She wore a tie-dyed t-shirt and jeans, and had the yellow rose behind her ear again. She noticed Sean and waved, smiling. Sean worked his way toward her.

"Hi, Sean!" Pam said. "Isn't this something?"

"Yeah, it's incredible. Mom, this is Pam Weston. My mom, Donna Carpenter."

Pam smiled. "We met at the hospital."

"Yes. Nice to see you back on your feet!"

"Thanks. I've admired your work.."

"Pam's an artist," Sean said.

"I'm just getting started," Pam said hastily.

"My sympathies," Sean's mom said. "That's the hardest part. We should have lunch some time, if you'd like to talk shop."

"Thanks, I'd love that!"

Sean looked over the displays. They'd evolved into collages, with photos and drawings of roses, hand-lettered pro-Rio signs, and testimonials pasted over the Valle del Sol information. Someone had taken colored markers to the map of the golf course and turned it into a giant, crazy rainbow serpent. One display had become a message board, covered with multicolored sticky-notes from people wanting to make contact, meet friends, or form carpools.

"I like the redecorating," Sean said.

"Oh, yeah. That just sort of happened. Cool, isn't it?"

"Very cool."

"I'm really jazzed that so many people showed up! Kyle Robbins will *have* to pay attention to this!"

Sean had to agree, though he wondered what Robbins would do. Possibly try to get everyone arrested, though that wouldn't look too good for Robbins. And the cops, at least the local ones, seemed to be in sympathy with the pro-Rio movement.

The buses kept coming, dumping more and more people at the site entrance. Sean kept an eye on the time and a lookout for more of his friends. Forrest arrived, a rose tucked jauntily in his hat. He said hello to Pam and Sean's mom, then led fifty-odd people who happened to be standing around the displays on an impromptu hike down to the river. Nick showed up, too, with his wife and baby daughter wearing roses pinned to their shirts.

At half past noon the first news van trundled onto the development site and parked beside the fence. Three others appeared shortly afterward. Sean was pleased to see all the local channels represented, then a van marked CNN arrived, and he felt a cold rush of adrenaline. National coverage!

"You're the miracle rose man, aren't you?" said a girl in a pink tube top and shorts next to Sean. "Can I have your autograph?"

"Uh—sure, I guess."

She scrounged up a pen and a pink sticky note, and Sean scrawled his name for her. The girl thanked him and went away, grinning.

"I'd like an autograph, too," said a Pueblo woman shyly.

Before long Sean was surrounded by a clot of autograph-seekers. He thought it was nuts, but he signed their bits of paper. He was starting to get writer's cramp when Rosa came up.

She had on a yellow sun dress with white embroidery on all its edges, and was carrying a pink rose. A flash of gold around her neck drew his notice. Not the Kokopelli he'd given her—that was silver. It was a *Guadalupana* medallion, he saw as she came closer.

"Hi, Sean. I'd like you to meet a couple of friends of mine. This is my teacher, Cruz Cordova."

"Nice to meet you," Sean said, shaking hands with the

Hispanic woman, who was petite but looked formidable nonetheless. She had a white rose braided into her hair, and the Pueblo man with her held a pink one.

"And this is Joe Pino, from Sandia Pueblo," Rosa said.

"Hi."

They shook hands, and Pino glanced around. "Some party you got going here."

Sean laughed. "Yeah." He saw Angel standing behind Rosa, and traded nods. "Where's Ruby?"

"She'll be here. She's bringing our mother."

"Wow, OK."

"Mr. Carpenter?" called a man's voice nearby. It was one of the newscasters.

"Here we go," Sean said to Rosa, then turned to the people waiting for autographs. "I'm sorry, I'll have to get to you later."

They looked disappointed, and a few grumbled, but they dispersed. Rosa and Angel had already disappeared, leaving Sean to the mercy of the reporter. The guy was dressed casually but well, and had a slick look to him. He offered a hand.

"Rex North, CNN. We'd like to get an interview, if we could. You, too, ma'am," he added to Sean's mother who'd begun to sidle away.

"Me?"

"Yes, with those roses. They're beautiful."

She looked at Sean. "Well, what the heck! Why not?"

North's crew set up cameras, then Sean answered his questions, which were only half about the roses, much to Sean's relief. The other half were about the Rio campaign, and were intelligent, well-informed questions. North occasionally directed one to Sean's mom, and she got to mention her artwork. Just for that Sean was grateful to the reporter. You couldn't buy that kind of publicity, at least, most people couldn't.

North was still grilling them when Sean saw a limousine pull into the site, crawling through the crowd toward the tent. It came to a stop and sat still for a long time, then finally the doors opened and Kyle Robbins and three other men got out. One, a large guy in a suit that had interesting bulges beneath the armpits, stuck close to Robbins.

One of the news crew caught North's eye and signaled

urgently to him, and North wrapped up the interview. He shook Sean's hand again, thanked him, and after consulting with the crew member, hustled off toward the limo, trailed by a guy with a camera on one shoulder. They returned a few minutes later, looking annoyed, and went back to their van.

"Guess Robbins isn't giving interviews," Sean said to his mom.

Sean gave them, one to each of the local news crews demanding his attention. He glanced at his watch after the last one and saw that it was past one o'clock. No groundbreaking had happened yet. The limo was still there, but he didn't see Robbins. Curiosity got the better of him, and he wandered over toward the tent, pausing now and then to sign an autograph.

Robbins and the other men from the limo stood in a small clot under the tent, looking defensive. Robbins was talking on a cell phone. A man in the crowd, a tall, farmer-looking guy with dark hair and a beard, was calling out questions to him, trying to engage him in a debate. Robbins ignored him, but when he caught sight of Sean he put the cell phone away and walked toward him, followed closely by the body guard.

"Mr. Carpenter. Congratulations on the response to your little protest."

Sean raised an eyebrow. "Little?"

"Oh, I assure you, it's little in the greater scheme of things. You've made a splash—even given people a chance to vent, which is good. But you haven't changed anything."

The people under the tent had fallen quiet, listening. Sean noticed a news camera at the back of the crowd.

"Hm," he said, glancing around. "I don't see any broken ground."

Robbins smiled, flashing white teeth in a gesture of aggression. "There's always tomorrow. This was a good show, but all good things come to an end."

"Screw that!" called the farmer-dude. "We'll camp out here as long as it takes!"

A chorus of agreement followed. Robbins stared the farmer down, waiting.

"You'll be arrested, then," he said when it was quiet enough. "You're all trespassing, did you know that?"

Angry shouts rose from the crowd. The bodyguard said something in Robbins's ear. Robbins shook his head.

"Go ahead and camp," he shouted, turning back to Sean. "I can wait a week or two. Eventually you'll have to get on with your lives."

"Can you wait out a General Stream Adjudication?" Sean said.

Robbins didn't answer, but the smile vanished. Sean felt a rush of success.

"We'll do it if we have to," he said.

"I don't think that would be too popular with the land-owners in your group," Robbins said.

"Try us."

Robbins stared at him, then smiled. "You're bluffing."

"Nope. I've already consulted a group of lawyers. Not those PRD toadies you hired, real water rights specialists. Oh, and just so you know, if anything happens to me or any of my friends or family, the GSA gets launched automatically."

Robbins's eyes narrowed. "Paranoid, Mr. Carpenter?"

"Just cautious. Once burned twice shy, you might say."

Robbins's stare went cold. "I don't know what you're talking about."

"Don't you? Gee, it was all over the news."

The people watching murmured. They'd all seen the coverage of the attack on Sean and Pam. The press hadn't speculated about a connection to Robbins Corp., and Sean had been careful not to say anything that could get him slapped with a lawsuit, but people weren't stupid. They could add two and two.

The bodyguard was whispering to Robbins again. Robbins grimaced, glanced toward the news camera, and turned away without another word to Sean. He and the dignitaries pushed their way through the crowd back to the limo, ignoring the catcalls and shaking fists of the crowd.

"That was awesome, Sean," said Forrest, who'd come up beside him. "Way to stand 'em down!"

"Thanks. Hope it works."

"It's a start."

Sean nodded, though he had doubts. He kept them to

himself, and instead accepted the congratulations and handshakes and back-slappings that woke his bruises. He stayed under the tent, signing autographs and answering questions. Pam came and joined him, and wound up signing autographs, too. Sean's mom stood nearby, handing out roses from her bouquet, which never got any smaller, much to her evident delight and amusement.

Father Mahan brought the bishop's committee to meet Sean, and they talked for a while about the roses. They were still considering whether to verify it as a genuine miracle. Sean listened, not really caring one way or the other. The roses had done their job.

Eventually Rosa and Angel returned, along with Rosa's friends and Angel's mother and sister. Ruby caught Sean in a surprise hug.

"You did great! This is fantastic!"

"Thanks. Overwhelming."

"Yeah, uh-huh. When you get tired of it, come on over to my house. We're going there now to get some lunch."

Lunch. Suddenly Sean's stomach grumbled.

"That sounds great. Would you mind if I brought my mom?"

"Bring her," Ruby said, nodding. "You aren't going to get any lunch in Pena Blanca, that's for sure!"

It was true. Sean had been thinking about that. There were no services set up for all these people. They *couldn't* camp here, not without some fast work and a lot of expense. In that sense he had been bluffing, and Robbins probably knew it.

Rosa touched Sean's arm. "I want to show you something."

"OK."

She led him out of the tent, toward the river. Angel and the others followed, and some of the crowd tagged along. Rosa walked past the edge of the milling crowd and over to a small rise beside the fence. She pointed to a pink rose stuck in the dirt. At first Sean thought it was just another rose, then he realized it had two blooms. It was a baby rose bush.

"Where did that come from?"

"I planted it. It's the rose I brought with me."

She stepped over to it and gave it a gentle tug. The rose stayed put. Sean joined her and pulled gently on the stem, then more firmly. It was rooted.

"Whoa, man," Sean said, looking at Rosa.

"That is awesome," said Pam. She stepped forward, took the yellow rose from behind her ear, and stuck it in the ground a few feet away.

"I want to plant one!" cried someone in the crowd.

A girl, a pre-teen, dashed over to them with a yellow-and-pink rose in her hand. She started to plant it next to Rosa's, but Sean stopped her.

"Give it some room to grow," he said. "Over here would be better."

He patted the ground about five feet away from the pink rose. The girl ceremoniously pressed the stem of her rose into the dirt. The flower bobbled a little, but stayed erect.

"There!" She grinned at Sean and darted off.

Sean stood up and saw more people planting their roses. All around them people were sticking roses into the ground. The wave swept through the crowd as word spread. Sean looked at Rosa, who smiled.

"Let's see if Robbins can bulldoze that."

Sean laughed and shook his head, thinking of the regenerating rosebushes in his yard. Robbins had no clue what he was up against.

An hour later Sean was sitting in Ruby's living room, along with his mom, Rosa, Cruz, Joe Pino, and the Madalenas. Pam and Forrest had come along, too, after Ruby assured them they were welcome. Mrs. Madalena puttered around the room making sure everyone had a soda, a tortilla, and a bowl of sinus-clearing chile stew.

"I've been thinking," Sean said. "You know the rescue guys who dug us out of the gravel said we shouldn't have survived." He looked at Pam, who gazed back, a shadow of remembered fear in her eyes. "I think that must have been another miracle."

"Someone was protecting you," Angel said.

"Yeah. I think so."

It was strange to admit that, being a non-religious person.

However, there were some things he couldn't deny, like the roses that were now busily growing on the Valle del Sol site.

"Did you see—anyone?" Rosa asked.

Sean shook his head. "Just stars. Gold stars in a turquoise sky."

"I saw that, too!" Pam said.

"It was *La Guadalupana*," Rosa said quietly. "That's what her mantle looks like."

Sean frowned, trying to remember his brief frenzy of *Guadalupana* research. Mrs. Madalena picked up a photo frame from a shelf and shuffled toward him.

"I have a picture. See?"

Sean gazed at the image of *Guadalupana*. It was a copy of the original image—he recognized it—the miracle image. The Virgin's cloak was the exact shade of blue he'd seen before he woke at the hospital, evenly scattered with gold stars.

"Son of a gun," Sean said. "It was her."

He showed the picture to Pam, who exclaimed and agreed. A discussion of miracles ensued. Sean just listened, mostly. He still wasn't sure what to think of all the miracle stuff. Maybe he'd talk to Father Mahan about it.

Forrest had brought a newspaper along, and pointed out a story about the arraignment of Tom Evans and Emilio Guzman. He read bits of it aloud.

"Looks like Guzman's going to enter a plea."

"Maybe he'll cut a deal and give evidence against Tom," Sean said.

"If he has any evidence to give," Forrest said. "Probably Tom was the middle man, and Tom isn't talking."

Sean shook his head. "So Tom takes the fall, Guzman gets a slap on the wrist, and Robbins goes scot free."

"You don't know for certain that Robbins was behind it," Angel said.

Sean looked at him. "I'm sure."

Pam stood up and put her bowl on her chair. "I'm just hoping Tom and that Joe guy go to jail for a few years at least." She drained her soda can and took it out to the kitchen.

"Who's Joe?" Forrest asked.

"Guzman," Sean said. "Emilio Guzman, the hit man. Tom

called him Joe."

"Guzman!" Rosa said, jumping up and almost spilling her stew. "I *have* heard it before!" She pulled out her cell phone and punched in a number, looking agitated while she waited for an answer.

"Miguel, it's Rosa. Do you still have that recording? Tell me you didn't erase it!"

25

"Get Guzman. Yeah, Emilio. OK."

The recording was distorted, but clear enough, even over the television. Sean reached for his phone and dialed Rosa's number. The news anchor came on, reporting that Kyle Robbins had been indicted for conspiracy to commit murder on the strength of Rosa's recording from her lunch with Robbins.

"Hi, Rosa, it's Sean! You watching the news?"

"Yeah."

"Congratulations, he's going to trial."

"Thank God! Maybe it'll all be over soon."

"Hold on—shh."

The TV was showing the Valle del Sol site, now covered in blooming rosebushes. People wandered through the garden, though not nearly as many people as had been there on groundbreaking day. The reporter was talking over the video.

"—Board of Directors of Robbins Corporation announced today that the Valle del Sol development has been canceled. The land will be donated to the National Forest and combined with an adjoining piece of Forest land."

Sean whooped, jumping up from his chair. He heard Rosa laughing over the phone.

"This calls for a celebration!" he said. "Dinner at Pranzo, my treat! Can you come up tomorrow night?"

"Yeah, I'm free. Can Angel come, too?"

"Sure. Angel and Ruby should definitely be there. I couldn't have got through this without them!"

"Me neither," Rosa said, a shy note in her voice.

They hung up, and Sean went out to the back yard. The evening was cooling off. Father Mahan's volunteers were wrapping up for the night. The yard looked rather different now, with a high fence across the back and the roses growing all around the inside of the wall. The fence had large warning signs on the alley side and a security guard posted outside, all of it paid for by the church from donations given by pilgrims. It had enabled them to limit the visiting hours for the roses, giving Sean his yard back at least during the night.

Sean said goodnight to the volunteers and waited for them to clear out, then brought his flute into the back yard and played. Not the rain chant, but a new happy song that had been growing inside him. A song for the miracle roses. He played because that was his way of praying, his way of giving thanks, as he walked among the roses beneath the stars.

Rosa and Angel lay on their backs on the little patch of lawn in Rosa's garden, gazing up at the night sky and enjoying the whisper of a cool breeze. They always spent evenings out here when Angel was visiting. Since the day of the Valle del Sol groundbreaking, he'd spent about half his time here, and Rosa had gone up to Cochiti every weekend.

"The sky is terrible here compared to your house," Rosa said.

"Not terrible. Just different."

Rosa searched the sky and found only three stars that she could see. The darkness had a glowing orange-red hue that she never used to notice before. She was conscious, too, of the city noise. At Cochiti it was so dark, so quiet, and the sky was dusted with so many stars.

She closed her eyes, thinking of walks she and Angel had taken together under the stars, by the river. A quiet joy had been building inside her for days. From the first, being with Angel had felt right, and that feeling had only increased.

She reached for his hand, grass tickling the back of her arm. Angel threaded his fingers through hers. She loved his fingers, strong but gentle, able to thrill her with the lightest, fluttering touch. He had been so patient.

"I have something to tell you," Rosa whispered.

Angel didn't answer. He was listening, she knew. He seldom prompted, but she'd learned it didn't mean he was uninterested.

A flicker of doubt went through her. She swallowed.

"I'm a virgin."

Angel didn't move, didn't speak. Rosa turned her head to look at him, and found his dark eyes gleaming back at her.

"I've been waiting for marriage," she whispered.

"Oh," he said softly. "Would you like to marry me?"

She almost laughed. It was so like him. No elaborate preparations, no ceremony, no presentation. She wondered if he'd even thought about it before.

"Yes, please," she answered, and then the laughter escaped, burbling up in her throat.

She raised herself onto her elbow and touched Angel's face with her free hand, then bent her head to kiss him. He pulled her down on top of him and wrapped his arms around her, holding her closer than he ever had before, leaving her no doubt about his feelings, his desires.

She didn't resist, but let herself melt against him. She'd been giving herself to him little by little ever since that day at Valle del Sol. Now she would be his completely. Her heart filled with happiness, and the only flutter of hesitation that was left drifted away on the cool evening breeze.

The doorbell woke Sean when it was still half-dark. He dragged himself out of bed, grumbling that it was Saturday, and hauled on a t-shirt and jeans. Shuffled his way to the front door and looked out the peephole. Four people on the doorstep, one of whom looked familiar, all of whom looked anxious. He was pretty sure they were some of Father Mahan's volunteers. He opened the door.

"What's the matter?"

"We thought maybe you could tell us what happened."

"What happened?"

"To the roses."

Sean frowned, then glanced toward the back of the house. He went to the back door, pushed aside the blinds, and looked out.

The roses were gone. A hedge of pale green stuff stood in their place. Sean opened the door and went outside, noticing that the air smelled damp. The sky was overcast with clouds. That was why it had seemed dark.

He walked up to the bushes. Not a rose in sight. He rubbed a couple of the small, pale leaves between his fingers and smelled them.

"Sage."

The volunteers had followed him and stood waiting hopefully, as if Sean could make the roses come back. He turned to face them and shrugged.

"I don't know. They were roses when I went to bed."

The volunteers exchanged disappointed looks. One of them took out a cell phone. Sean went back in the house and started a pot of coffee.

By seven his phone was ringing non-stop. Miracle roses had faded overnight, shriveling and losing their petals. Friends and the media wanted to know why. Sean couldn't help them, and when he told them the bushes were gone too they just got upset.

Finally he unplugged the phone. He recorded an answering message saying the roses were gone, he didn't know why, please don't ask about them. Then he plugged the phone back in and switched off the ringer.

He sent a text to Rosa, then locked up the house and drove out to Pena Blanca. A few cars were parked outside the Valle del Sol site. Sean parked by the fence and got out.

A moist breeze stirred the branches of the vast field of sagebrush that covered the site. All the roses were gone. A handful of people were wandering through the bushes, or standing and staring. Sean stared too, remembering the blanket of color that had sprung up after groundbreaking day. Beautiful color, but unnatural. The sagebrush was more appropriate to the landscape.

"Easy come, easy go," he said softly. "Thank you, Lady. We enjoyed them while we had them."

By evening the clouds had massed into a storm, the first in months. Sean drove to Pranzo with his window down, reveling in the ozone smell of rain.

Angel and Rosa were waiting outside the restaurant, standing under an awning while spits of rain fell and the wind whipped at their long, dark hair. Rosa was wearing a pale purple blouse, paisley skirt, and a pink rose behind her ear. Sean looked at the flower, startled.

"Hey, is that—"

Rosa glanced at a family walking past. "It's from my garden."

"Oh. Did you hear about the rose bushes?"

Rosa nodded. "On the radio on the way up, but I knew anyway. The roses you gave me faded, the cut ones."

Sean looked at Angel. "Where's Ruby?"

"At home, working. She can't make enough of those new pots with the roses. She sells them all out right away."

"Bet you she takes them to Indian Market next year."

Angel smiled. "No bet."

They went inside and were shown to a table. Sean felt a slight tension among them, and wondered if something was wrong. He tried to think of an innocuous subject.

"So, I've got my house back. Want to come give me a lesson tomorrow, Angel?"

"If you still want one."

Before Sean could ask what he meant, Angel put his hands on the table, clasped in front of him. "We have something to tell you," he said, looking at Rosa.

She smiled back at him, then glanced at Sean. Angel took her hand.

"We're engaged," he said

Sean stared. "As in, to be married?"

Rosa nodded. "Don't be angry, please."

"Angry? I'm not angry." He wasn't, but his brain still hadn't quite wrapped around the idea.

"Good," Rosa said. She reached in her purse and laid the Kokopelli pendant on the table in front of Sean. "I should give this back to you. Not because I don't like it, I do. But—"

"Keep it, then," Sean said, proud that his voice didn't quaver. "He's your totem."

Rosa gazed at him. Beautiful Rosa. She'd always been out of reach, he realized. He brushed aside a twinge of hurt. He was happy for Angel and Rosa, and there were other possibilities. Pam, for one.

"Then you should have this one," Rosa said, reaching up to unfasten her necklace. She held it out to him, glinting gold against her hand. *La Guadalupana.*

"She'll watch over you," Rosa added.

Sean took the little pendant from her hand, gazing at the familiar figure surrounded by radiant light. He looked up at Rosa and smiled.

"Thanks. She already does."

Glossary

Most of these words are Spanish; some of the definitions are colloquial and specific to New Mexico.

Abuelo	Grandfather
acequia	a community-owned and maintained irrigation ditch
bosque	a forest, specifically growing along a river
bueno	good
carne adovada	meat (usually pork) marinated in red chile
chiles rellenos	whole green chiles stuffed with cheese, battered, and fried
cocinas	cuisine
cojones	balls (literally, "testicles")
Conquistadora, La	popular name for a small, wooden statue of Our Lady of the Assumption, first brought to Santa Fe by Spanish settlers in 1625
curandera	healer, practitioner of traditional medicine (feminine)
curanderismo	traditional or folk medicine involving herbalism and sometimes elements of magic, mysticism, and/or Catholicism; found in the Americas especially among native and/or Latino cultures
empanada	a small, stuffed pastry made of pie crust, often filled with fruit, shaped into a half moon and baked or fried
envidiar	envy

Guadalupana, La	the Virgin of Guadalupe, who is believed to have appeared to a shepherd near Mexico City in 1531, and to whom a number of miracles have been attributed
hija	child (literally "daughter") (feminine)
katsina	a deity or "spirit messenger," specifically in the Hopi tradition but also found in other Pueblo tribes (anglicized to "kachina"); also, a small statue carved from cottonwood root and painted to represent a deity
katsinam	plural of katsina
kiva	a ceremonial room at a Pueblo
kiva fireplace	a traditional, beehive-shaped fireplace often found in New Mexico architecture
Kokopelli	a modern symbol, depicted as a curved or humpbacked flute player, possibly a derivation of Kookopölö, the Hopi katsina of fertility
koshare	a "clown," often a trickster figure, traditional at many Pueblo dances
La Conquistadora	see Conquistadora, La
La Guadalupana	see Guadalupana, La
Lahlanhoya	the Hopi flute player katsina
limpia	cleansing
loco	crazy
maestra	master; teacher (feminine)
natillas	a custard made with milk, eggs, vanilla, and cinnamon
nicho	a small niche in a wall

paella	a Spanish dish of rice, saffron, and a variety of vegetables, seafood, and poultry
plática	conversation
pobrecita	poor thing (feminine)
portal	a covered porch, usually along the front of a building
primo	prime, excellent
quesadilla	a flour tortilla stuffed with cheese and sometimes meat, onions, or other vegetables, folded in half and grilled
ramada	an open shelter designed for shade, often roofed with brush or branches
rellenos	see chiles rellenos
Rio Abajo	downstream
Rio Arriba	upstream; also, a county in northern New Mexico
sopaipilla	a leavened bread of thin dough cut into shapes and deep fried to puff up hollow, an accompaniment to New Mexican meals
Susto	psychological trauma (literally "fear" or "fright")
yerba buena	mint (literally "good herb")
zaguan	entryway, especially a passage into a hacienda, often with a gate that incorporates a smaller door
Zozobra	a giant puppet, also called "Old Man Gloom" that is burned every year during the Santa Fe Fiesta

About the Author

Pati Nagle was born and raised in the mountains of northern New Mexico. An avid student of music, history, and humans in general, she loves the outdoors but hides from the sun.

She writes in a variety of genres, but is most often drawn to fantasy, historical fiction (as P.G. Nagle), and mystery (as Patrice Greenwood). Her stories have appeared in *Asimov's Science Fiction*, the *Magazine of Fantasy & Science Fiction*, and in various other magazines and anthologies.

Nagle still lives in the mountains in New Mexico, with her husband, two feline muses, and lots of wildlife. She loves to walk in the woods and look up at the stars.

Books by Pati Nagle

Immortal Series

Immortal
Eternal
Forever

Blood of the Kindred Series

The Betrayal
Heart of the Exiled
Swords Over Fireshore

Other Novels

Dead Man's Hand
Kokopelli and the Virgin
Pet Noir

Collections

Coyote Ugly and Other Tales
Many Paths: Stories of the Ælven

About Book View Café

Book View Café Publishing Cooperative (BVC) is a an author-owned cooperative of over fifty professional writers, publishing in a variety of genres including fantasy, romance, mystery, and science fiction.

In 2008, BVC launched a website, bookviewcafe.com, initially offering free fiction and gradually moving to selling ebooks of members' backlist titles, then original titles. BVC's ebooks are DRM-free and are distributed around the world. BVC returns 95% of the profit on each book directly to the author. The cooperative has gained a reputation for producing high-quality ebooks, and is now moving into print editions.

BVC authors include New York Times and USA Today bestsellers; Nebula, Hugo, and Philip K. Dick Award winners; World Fantasy and Rita Award nominees; and winners and nominees of many other publishing awards.

bookviewcafe.com